Published by Zendow Press; KamalaDevi.com

Library of Congress Cataloging-in-Publication Data
Devi, Kamala
Don't drink the punch : an adventure in tantra / Kamala Devi.

ISBN: 978-0-9896485-4-7

First edition copyright © 2005 Kamala Devi
Second edition copyright © 2014 Kamala Devi

All rights reserved. No part of this publication may be reproduced without prior written permission from the author. This book is available at special quantity discount for bulk purchases for sales premiums, fundraising, and educational needs. For details, inquire by sending an e-mail to KaliDas@KamalaDevi.com.

- **My Gurus:** Rosa Espinoza de Knapp, Spencer & Laurie Kagan, Cain Carroll, Swami Sivananda, Amma, Osho, Kali, Robert Frey, Greg Clowminzer, Sri Param Eswaran, Dawn Cartwright, and Yogi zYoah aka Jack Wexler.

- **Tantra Puja/Visioning Council:** Adam, Andy, Damien, Francoise, Greg, Ivy, Jerome, Kirin, Lourdes, MaryKay, Michael, Nirvir, Paul, Rachila, and Satyam.

- **Content Reading:** Dean Clark, Jack Forem, Rayna McInturf, Lynn Pollock & Todd Whitaker.

- **Copy Editing:** Michelle Devon at www.accentuateservices.com, Linda McClure & Ford Peck.

- **Graphic Design:** Miguel Kagan

- **Back Cover Photo:** Spencer Kagan

- **Creative Muses:** Carlos Kagan, Viraja Ma, Cheri Reeder, and Saraswati Lee Ting.

Dedicated to Michael for being you.

Don't Drink the Punch
An Adventure in Tantra

Kamala Devi

Table of Consciousness

Act I

1 Redhead on the Rise 11
2 The Royal Treatment 17
3 Lava Lunch 23
4 The Natives Are Restless 29
5 Sex Circus 35
6 Elephant and the Bearded Lady 45
7 Crash Course in Chakras 53
8 Thai Jellyfish Massage 65
9 A Lesson in Non-Attachment 75

Act II

10 Blind Love Follows Blind Faith 81
11 1st Impressions, 2nd Thoughts 89
12 Not in Kansas Anymore 97
13 Ejaculation Control or Mind Control? 103
14 Sign on the Dotted Line 109
15 Ashram Life 115
16 Initiation by Fire 121
17 Magic Bus 127

Act III

18 Ganesha Governs the Root 135
19 Nazi Health Clinic 143
20 Snake Charming 153
21 Grad School in Goa 161
22 Sensual Scavenger Hunt 167
23 Hot Monkey Love 173
24 Chakra Puja 179
25 Pushing Buttons 187
26 Looking for a Lost Guru 197
27 Who am I? 203
28 Contemplation Camp 211
29 Heart Broken Open 219
30 Goddess Worship 229
31 Sound of Spirit 239
32 Kirtan in Kerala 247
33 Back Water Boat Ride 255
34 Close Encounters of the Third Eye 259
35 Naked in the Cemetery 269

ACT IV

36 The Wrath of Kali-Durga 281
37 Cosmic Car Alarm 289
38 Tea with Divine Mother 293
39 There's No Place Like Home 297

Recommended Reading 305

"You probably remember him as the one who enrolled in USC's prestigious film program, then mysteriously disappeared. Nobody would've pegged him as the type of fellow to join a cult. To film an independent documentary about cult survivors, perhaps, but not to be swept away to another country, indoctrinated into dangerous sex rituals, then come back a totally different person, but I'll let him tell us all about it. It's my honor to introduce our guest speaker this evening..."

— The Widow Mrs. Kriesberg, Hollywood, CA, USA

Act I
Shiva Meets Shakti

1 Redhead on the Rise

Riding down the escalator at the Bangkok International Airport, I spot an unkempt tangle of red hair coming up the other direction. Green eyes beam out from a soft, clear face and penetrate my soul. For a breath of a moment, we're at the same level. Then, she floats above me. I stumble back, up a few steps. This makes her laugh, but she continues to rise out of my field of vision. I race to the bottom and, without a second thought, take the escalator back up, following her into an empty airport coffee shop.

She's reclining in a chair with a pencil perched over a sketchbook on her lap.

"Do you speak English?" I ask.

"Yes, of course," she says.

"Would you like my company, or do you prefer privacy?"

She kicks the opposite chair out from under the table in a 'suit yourself' gesture. I arrange my luggage so that it's out of the way but clearly in view. She takes off her brown button-down sweater and exposes a faded orange t-shirt with loose threads around the collar.

"Are you traveling alone?" I ask.

In a sweet Brazilian accent, she says, "Single women don't travel alone. Someone always shows up to buy us a drink, carry our bags, or chase us up escalators."

"I'm Sal."

"Pleasure to meet you," she says, ignoring my offer for a handshake and placing her hands at her heart like the airline

11

stewardesses do when they say Sawadee on Thai Airlines.

"And your name?" I ask.

"Saraswati. You can call me Sara if it's easier."

"Is that Brazilian?"

"I am from Brazil, but my name is Sanskrit."

"How did you get a Sanskrit name?" I ask.

"How did you get a name like Salvador?"

"Sal is short for Solomon," I explain, "it's Hebrew."

"You're Jewish?" she asks.

"By culture, yes, but I'm not practicing," I say.

"Then you won't mind if I call you Salvador," she flirts. "I was given my name by my guru. I've been living at an ashram and practicing yoga in Spain for the last year."

"And, what does your name mean?" I ask.

"Saraswati is the Hindu Goddess of wisdom and creativity. Here's a picture." She flips to a page in her sketchbook, revealing a beautiful sketch of an Indian woman in a white sari who is playing a sitar.

"So, what brings you to Thailand?" I ask.

"Yoga." She smiles. "You? What brings you here?"

"Well, I work for a travel show out of LA. I mean, worked. I used to work, past tense. I quit this weekend, on a job in Chang Mai, or I got canned. I'm not sure which."

I run my hand through my brown shaggy hair. I try to stop talking, but can't resist the way her eyes seem to plead for more detail.

"I had a secure job in the television industry for the last six years. There were all kinds of travel benefits. In fact, you may have even heard of the rich director and his sleazy mistress, but I won't mention any names. From the outside, it looked glamorous, but the truth is it sucked.

"The only foreign language I learned was, 'Where's the shopping district?' I guess I shouldn't complain. I got an all expenses paid vacation out of the deal. I'm thinking about going to Phuket and maybe Koh Samui over the next two weeks."

"Just two weeks?" she asks.

"Yeah, I'll be starting film school at the University of Southern California soon," I say. "Ever heard of USC?"

The waiter in a green apron interrupts us and takes Sara's order.

"I'll have what she's having." I continue, "It's a pretty big deal, getting accepted. I've wanted to go for ten years, since I completed my undergraduate work."

"Should I be impressed or something?" she asks.

"Actually, I'm sort of relieved that you aren't. Everyone makes such a big deal out of it. I haven't even started, and I'm already stressed, which is another reason I need this vacation."

"That's the problem with most Americans," she declares. "They travel to run away from their lives."

"And you? What are you running from?"

"Not from, toward." She says, "I'm on a pilgrimage, so I guess you could say I'm running toward the Truth."

"In Bangkok?" I ask.

"This is a stopover. I'm on my way to India. The best deal I could find was a round-the-world ticket, and this was the direction it happened to be going. I'm here for another 48 hours."

"India? Wow. I've never been, but people on my crew say it's dirty, overcrowded, impoverished, and there's no way to avoid getting sick there. The lady who does our makeup says she would only recommend it to the very brave or the very naïve."

"That pretty much sums up what I've heard as well," Sara admits. Retrieving her drink from the waiter's tray, she sweetens it before tasting it.

I take a sip of mine and nearly spit, "What is this?!"

"It's a half-tea, half-coffee special. This is one of the

few places in the world that serves it, but I bet it'll spread to the rest of the world soon," she predicts.

"It's a bold but decidedly bad idea," I say, ripping into sugar packets. "Like India. What draws you there?"

"I'll give you one guess," she invites.

"The Taj Mahal."

She laughs. "I won't count that as a real guess."

"Okay," I say, putting my fingers on my temples and pretending to tell her fortune. "Something tells me you're going there to study with some enlightened guru."

"Not bad, Salvador. I would've settled for 'yoga,' but your guess is more specific. My guru wants me to study with his master," she says.

"And he's enlightened?"

"I'll find out. When my grandmother died, I had no more family left in Brazil, so I rented out her house and came to Spain to meet my yoga teacher's guru. Now, to make a long story short, if I want to continue my training, I have to meet his guru."

"Ah, but I prefer the long story," I say, in my most charming voice.

Sara continues, "Nana's death taught me a few things about life. When her cancer started, I saw that it was her body that got sick, not her, because my hatha yoga practice taught me that I am not my body. Then, her mind deteriorated until her memory was rotten. Through meditation, I learned that I am not my mind. Over time, she became incapacitated. I'd never fed an elder person before, so it was hard to be a mother for my mother's mother. She became angry, always yelling at me that she wasn't hungry. That's when I recommitted to my spiritual practice and realized there is difference between the true Self and the personality."

Even though I don't get everything she's saying, I'm hypnotized by the way her delicate hands dance to her direct speech, which seems to flow without hesitation or awkward pauses.

"My yoga teacher suggested I read *The Tibetan Book of the Dead* to her as she passed over to the other side, but Nana wouldn't allow it. She said it was boring and brainwashing. So I read it to myself while she coughed herself to sleep in the other room.

"After she passed, I wanted to know the real meaning of yoga, not just the rituals or practices that I read about. I want to experience the real thing."

"There's a lot of Buddhism right here in Bangkok," I offer.

"Yes, I plan to visit a few temples, but my main purpose is to rest my body and get some Thai massage before entering India."

"What's Thai massage?" I ask.
"You've never had one? It's like having yoga done to you. You lay down in total surrender, and they move you around, using their whole body to massage your muscles and open all your energy channels."

"Does it hurt like yoga?" I ask.

"I guess it could, if you're really tight, but a little pain can be good to keep the ego in check. I want to go to Wat Po; it's supposedly where Buddha's physician studied."

I pull out my dog-eared *Lonely Planet* and say, "I know Wat means temple, but what the hell is Po?"

She laughs with me, and then I ask, "Have you ever been to the red light district?"

"What are you, some kind of pervert?" she quips.

"No, it's just this area is notorious for its nightlife and its brothels and discos. Haven't you ever heard that?"

"Of course, I'm teasing. The guy sitting next to me on the plane says Bangkok is the sex-change capital of the world. He told me all about the exotic lady-boys who dance and turn tricks throughout the city."

Here's my big chance, I take a blurt, "How about if you come with me to experience a Thai massage, and I'll go with you to see what there is to experience in the red light district."

"That's a deal," she says, sealing it with a smile.

I spread the *Lonely Planet's* map across the table to discover the Wat Po is walking distance from the Royal Hotel, which is where my company prearranged for me to stay.

"We can drop our bags off at my hotel and walk over to get a massage. Afterward, I can help you find a hostel if you want," I proposition.

"Or I could stay with you," she offers.

"That was easy," I say. "I usually have to buy a woman a few beers before she decides to come back to my room."

Smiling she says, "Well, I'm a liberated woman."

The Royal Treatment

The Royal Hotel is a funky old colonial building from the turn of the century with spacious but ugly rooms. There exists a random step in the middle of the floor, which seems to serve no purpose except to stub my toe. Brown and white checkered tiles cover the floor as well as the bathroom walls. The shower head is directly at chest level, but at least there's plenty of standing room in the wide tub.

Two purified bottles of water sit on the sink. Sara cracks one open and takes a swig, handing it to me to me while she unbuttons her shirt.

"I've been dying to get out of these old clothes. Salvador, do you mind if I jump in?"

"Help yourself," I say, turning my back while she continues to strip down. She leaves a pile of clothes on the floor and the bathroom door wide open. I duck out of the room to give her privacy. Sitting on the bed, I take my shoes off in disbelief. I hear the rushing water. Sorting through my roller bag, I find a fresh shirt.

"The hot water feels so good!" she calls out from the shower, and I imagine steamy droplets running down her naked body. She's inviting me in ... or is she? I strip down to my boxers, but my body does not move.

If I were in Los Angeles and met this woman at a party, there would be no question, no hesitation, but this is a foreign country. She already thinks I'm a pervert. I don't know, maybe the rules are different. I don't want to ruin my chances for later.

The water stops, and I freeze. After a moment, I hear

17

her steamy sigh, and I sigh back. Covered with a small white towel, she steps into the doorway.

"I left plenty of hot water for you," she says, drying her red curls. "This bathroom is luxurious compared to where I lived in Spain."

She sits on the bed beside me to slather hotel lotion on her legs. Mesmerized, I have to peel myself away and step into the steamy bathroom, shutting the door behind me.

I lather up with the same soap she used to rub all over her body just a moment ago. My cock grows in my hands while I close my eyes and imagine her standing behind me, reaching around. I hear the door open ... for real, the door opens. My hands busy themselves, pretending to soap up. Through the wet glass, I see her back is to me. She's leaning into the mirror and applying something to her face.

"Wow, it's steamy in here," she announces.

No kidding, I think.

"Doesn't the heat feel good after such a long trip?" she asks.

If she can carry on with her makeup routine, I tell myself, I can carry on with my shower routine. I shampoo, secretly hoping she's checking me out in the mirror, especially since my pronounced semi-erection would look flattering. I hope she catches a glimpse when I reach for a towel, but when I turn off the shower, she reaches in and hands one to me.

"Thanks."

When I'm all dressed, she's still fixing her face. I just stand there under her spell.

"Let's get on with it. The massage will help us loosen things up," she insists.

When we reach the marble steps at the outdoor lobby, a cabby holds a full-color, laminated brochure in my face. "I show you standing Buddha, sitting Buddha, and emerald

Buddha."

I tell Sara, "Looks interesting, but I don't think we should go with the first cabby we meet."

"I give you good price," he insists.

"Tal Rai?" Sara begins to bargain.

He makes an offer. She cuts the price in half. He meets her at 75%, and we agree to meet tomorrow at 10 o'clock in the morning.

"Today ... where you go?" he asks.

"No, thanks. We'll walk," I say, taking Sara's hand and crossing several lanes of traffic toward a manicured park.

It dawns on me that this is the first time I've ever been out of the country doing whatever the hell I feel like doing. I'm not reporting to anybody. In fact, no one even knows that I'm walking through a park in Bangkok with a beautiful Brazilian woman by my side.

We find ourselves ankle deep in a swarm of dirty pigeons. "Watch out," I caution, "they're scavenger rat-birds."

"Be nice; they're hungry," she says, buying cornmeal from a toothless bag lady.

The pigeons swarm the sidewalk around her feet. She has no place to step without kicking a few rapidly pecking birds. The old lady approaches me, but I shake my head, "No thanks. No. No!"

"It brings good luck," Sara says, throwing a few kernels at my feet.

"Ever heard of Avian Flu?" I ask, while increasing my pace. "The reality is that these birds carry mites and germs and diseases that could easily end your life."

Sara, struggling to walk in pace with me, says, "C'mon, they're just pigeons."

I pull a travel size bottle of hand sanitizer from my money belt and squirt some into her palm. She rubs her hands together and chides, "I don't know if this is killing germs or not, but it feels winter-fresh."

We venture beyond the vendors selling postcards, small statues, and fresh coconuts at the entrance to Wat Po. Inside, we find huge beast-headed guards made out of intricate mosaics standing in front of the ticket booth. Farther in, tall stupas adorn the burial grounds of rich or realized people from thousands of years ago.

In the main temple sits a life-sized, gold-covered Buddha, dwarfed by seven-foot candles and other gaudy altar decorations. Huge golden snakes hover above Buddha's head, as though he's wearing a cobra-hooded cloak.

Sara sits, and then kneels on the floor before the altar. I sit a comfortable distance away, watching locals light incense and make offerings of flowers and money. Just when I wonder how long this is going to take, Sara bows to Buddha, nods at me, and walks out. We put our shoes back on and walk down the courtyard, looking for the famous massage room.

A gaggle of massage students wearing lab coats take us to their leader. A transsexual-looking lady at the counter exchanges our nominal Thai Baht for two plastic cards with numbers. Sara requests the instructor, while I admit it's my first massage. The lady-boy declares they have the perfect person for me, who turns out to be a buff Thai guy wearing glasses.

I sit on the low, firm bed. Standing fans and barrels of steaming herb packs surround me. I tuck my money belt under my pillow and lie back, face up.

The horn-rimmed Hercules presses the heel of his hands into my feet, calves, and thighs. I gather he's taking visual cues from his teacher, a slender, graying Thai woman who, one bed over, is working on Sara's legs. Sara overflows with pleasurable moans.

The Thai masseur wiggles, moves, and then plasters my shins, quads, and hips. He uses his feet and his elbows, and I think, "This is not gentle stuff." When he digs his heels into my hamstrings, I let out a few yelps, to which he asks, "Pain?"

"Yes!" I exclaim, but he simply distributes the same pressure elsewhere. What did I ever do to him? Maybe he hates U.S. politics, and this is his chance to take it out on America. If it were any harder, I would cry, or leave, or break something, but his teacher is right there. She'd stop him if he were causing internal bleeding, wouldn't she?

He presses his palms into my groin, cutting off my circulation. The pressure of blood builds and throbs, but he keeps holding. When he finally releases, there's a warm rush of blood flushing through my major arteries. My muscles turn to jelly. I go dizzy. Whatever he does afterward puts me in this relaxed state of fear for my life.

Finally, he props me up, Indian style, and digs his elbows into my shoulders, completing the torture with several limp karate chops to the head.

Big relief.

Sara is also sitting up, eyes closed, looking as blissful as she did in the temple. We're both handed a little cup of herb juice with a straw and sent along on our merry way.

Sara declares that she's still high from the experience. We rest at a park bench to gather our bearings. "So, how was your first Thai Massage?"

"I don't usually consider having my muscles ripped clean from my bones a favorite pastime, but luckily, my brain pumped enough endorphins into my system that I was able to numb out."

"The more frequently you get them, the less resistance there is. Do you feel lighter now?"

"I'm elated that it's over and that I survived. Let's go celebrate with a cold beer."

"Sounds great," she says. "I'm starving."

3 Lava Lunch

We meander down several streets, passing savory smelling alleys with open-flame grills full of exotic animals, like mini squid, frogs, and sparrows on skewers. Curious, we lean in to inspect all our options, but since Sara's a vegetarian, and I'm afraid of negligent health code enforcement, we stroll into a street-side restaurant with red and white checkered tablecloths and no tourists in sight.

An old Thai man with a sad comb-over and golf pants cinched tight under his armpits brings us two faded menus, and then resumes wiping down the small bar in the back. There's a column down the left side of the menu with small out-of-focus photos, while on the right, all entrees are described in Thai.

"So what do you feel like?" I ask.

After a pregnant pause, Sara responds, "I'm fatigued. All the traveling has unwound something deep inside me..."

"I mean, what do you feel like eating?" I clarify.

"Oh." Laughter wells up from deep in her being. "Soup, I feel like soup. Do you prefer coconut or lemongrass?"

"Both," I say. "I'm hungry."

"Great. Let's get one Tom Kha and one Tom Yum, and I'd also like a Panang curry. If you get something vegetarian, we can share."

"As long as you'll order for me, get whatever you want. I'll eat anything ... well, almost."

Watching Sara negotiate with the old man in golf pants, you'd think they were having a political argument. They must not have the selections we've made. After a few minutes

23

of Sara's emphatic explanation of vegetarianism: no meat, no chicken, and no fish, the man nods and leaves us for the kitchen.

"So, what exactly did you decide on?"

"Beats me," she sighs. Content with the silence, she sinks into her chair.

I feel comfortable as well, but after a few minutes, I tight-walk the line between peaceful company and being a boring conversationalist. Finally, I break the silence, "So, what if this guru you're going to meet turns out to be another roadside charlatan?"

"Trust me, I'll know," she says, just as the owner brings two piping hot bowls of soup. She thanks the man and insists we pray before we eat. "It makes the food taste better."

She takes both my hands in hers and closes her eyes. She speaks a few sweet words to no God in particular. When she opens her eyes again, I'm taken by the green of her eyes. Her irises sparkle like sunlight streaking through a blue-grey sky.

After a few slow slurps off of the spoons, we're both coughing. Sara cautions me to pull out the Thai chilies. I pluck one off my tongue and agree. They're fucking hot! We scoop the little bastards out of our bowls and pile them onto a plate, making a substantial pile of little peppers and other red flecks.

The man seems to enjoy watching us. He brings a small platter of sliced lime and from a tall height squeezes juice into Sara's soup, and then he waits for her to taste it. She thanks him and orders a bottle of soda water and white rice. I guess the lime neutralizes the spice a little, but it still makes my mouth burn and eyes water.

Between spoonfuls of molten lava, Sara launches into an unbelievable tale about a young Spanish yogi who climbed a mountain to study with her master. He learned mantra, meditation, and pranayama (breathing practices).

"Then his master told him he had to return to Europe to teach, but that people in the West would not believe his wisdom unless he had gray hair. So when he came down the mountain only two years later, he had a long beard and a full head of gray hair."

"And you believe that story?" I ask.

"I know the man. He's the one that gave me my name."

"Oh," I say, coughing up a bit of fire.

The hideous plaid pants come to the rescue with rice, and we both serve ourselves big heaps of the soothing side dish.

"Salvador, I should probably tell you that the reason I'm going to India is to study Tantra yoga."

"Did you say Tantra?" I ask.

"Yes."

"What is that, exactly?" I press, still coughing.

She smiles, repositions herself, and after a pause says, "It's essentially a path toward enlightenment. Like any path, it has both philosophy and practices. Tantra is as vast and varied as Christianity, but instead of negating the body, it uses the body.

"You'll have to forgive my crude and rudimentary understanding, but I thought Tantra had something to do with sex."

"It does," she smiles.

Now I'm wondering if all this spicy food is making me horny. "Tell me more."

"Tantra teaches you to cultivate your natural drive for sex and direct it toward the ultimate love of spirit. The stronger the attraction and the sex drive, the more fuel you have to reach God."

Apparently, it's not only the food that's making me hot. "Do you have to believe in God to get there?" I ask.

"That's a good question. There are vastly different styles and practices within Tantra, but no organized religion around it. In a sense, it's like the opposite of religion, because as soon as you give power to the church or to the priest, then you've taken it from yourself. Everything I've ever studied had a strong leaning toward a direct and personal experience of the Divine. A lot of paths look like ancient religions, like there's a Hindu branch where you might transmute your lust into devotion for different Gods, like Shakti or Shiva, or the practitioners of Tibetan Buddhist Tantra might use transcendental sex to melt into the divine emptiness and connection with all that is. But the more honest answer to your question is: I don't know."

Dinner arrives. One dish is a mysterious curry with unrecognizable vegetables, which contrast with the distinctly square cubes of tofu. The other dish contains rice noodles flavored with a number of spices and herbs that don't seem to disappear when you chew them, thus the growing mound of inedibles at the center of our table.

During dinner, a little piece of rice falls down Sara's shirt and clings to her breast. She blushes and wipes it off. I'm stunned by this moment of concern for what she looks like. It occurs to me that most women are concerned about how they look most of the time. It is the very absence of this concern that makes Sara so beautiful. She catches me staring at her shirt and asks what I'm thinking.

"I'm just struck by how beautiful you are."

To which she says, "You mean how beautiful my breasts are."

We both laugh.

"Have you ever heard of Sting?" I ask.

"Of course. I love his music."

"What kind of Tantra does he practice?"

"I don't know. I've never met him," Sara admits, "but

I've heard about his five hour lovemaking sessions, and it reminds me of something my guru calls 'California Tantra,' where people manipulate creative energy for deeper orgasms or to save a bad sex life. I have to admit, I don't know much about the sexual aspects of Tantra. My training is with the white path, which is more subtle and philosophical.

"Not that Tantra theory isn't sexy. After only a few months of just breathing, I had my first whole body orgasms ... just by breathing and moving and sounding, and that's without any intercourse." She lowers her voice and says, "I've been celibate for the last two years."

"You haven't had sex with anyone in two years?" I repeat in disbelief.

"Not physically, no. It's all part of my practice, but I don't miss it. When the desire arises, I sublimate. I practice transmuting sexual desire into the desire to unite with God. I believe the ecstasy of spirit has more potential than the ecstasy of the body. Sometimes it feels like my guru is penetrating me with his teachings; but as I said, he has a long gray beard, and though he may be young in years, he's not my type."

"Maybe he has a disease that's making him age early?"

"If you heard our master's teachings, you wouldn't doubt anymore. See, our master's name is Das. He transitioned over a decade ago, and the one time I heard my guru channeling him, I got goose bumps. After my initiation, my guru told me about an ashram in India where a small group of devotees channel Master Das all the time. And my guru says he's still very much alive in their presence."

"Okay, so your teacher channels a dead guy?" I ask skeptically.

"In a sense. Nobody really dies. The teachings always live on."

"Right, but I don't know too many people who kind of die, and then hang around their students to keep teaching." I signal the owner for the bill.

"So, are you disappointed?"

"With what?" I ask.

"To hear that I'm celibate?"

"Me? No, I'm relieved," I say. "I don't think I could measure up to your Tantric master."

"Then is it still okay if I come back to your place to take a nap?"

"Yes, I can order a cot so we can sleep separate."

"Why would you want to do that?" she asks.

"I just thought ... never mind."

"Unless you're afraid of catching Avian Flu," she teases.

4 The Natives Are Restless

The sun is still sauntering across the sky by the time we return to the hotel. Sara undresses, completely naked ... well, except for her g-string and tee-shirt. She is naked under that. I strip down to my bulging boxers and plop down on my side of the bed. She slips under the covers and immediately relaxes into a deep sleep.

My sleep schedule's been wacky since I arrived in Thailand. I'm normally at work and nodding off at this hour, but not today. I can feel the heat off Sara's sleeping skin. To distract myself from the temptation of her fair and vulnerable body, I review the events leading up to this surreal moment.

After two hours of hiking through sweltering foothills, carrying bags of camera equipment behind a rented travel guide, I arrived with the film crew at a dusty clearing with several wooden shade structures with corrugated rooftops.

A tribe of colorful old ladies in funny headdresses, shaped like Grand Pubob caps, rose to their feet to greet us. They were clad from head to toe with red, blue, orange, and magenta patchwork material with stitched-on mirrors and beads.

They looked like a troupe of circus performers; but of course, they're too old for the circus. I would guess some of them to be as old as ninety. Then again, their living conditions are much harsher, so perhaps they age early. The women puffed perpetually on pipes. It looked like part of their outfits. In fact, it looked like part of their faces. Every exhale produced wispy clouds.

Our guide introduced us to the eldest tribe member first. Shy and curious, several women crowded around me while I set up the camera on a tripod. I frame and focus in on a hunchback lady who was unwrapping an elaborate technicolored dress. The patches were vibrant, but not contrasting, and it was crisscrossed with silver coins, symmetrically embroidered into the vest and dangling from the sleeves and skirt. It was beautiful workmanship to behold. Our translator told us it was a ceremonial gown used for a woman's rite of passage.

After the blond show hostess made a few introductions for the camera, she asks the guide, "What I want to know is: how much are these coins worth in American dollars?"

He scrutinizes them, then calculates in his head, and declared the value at approximately 1/8 of a cent.

This makes the show hostess squeal, "Who would want a ceremonial dress with cheap money sewn on it? Why would a woman want to advertise how broke she is, especially on her first day as a woman?"

The crew chuckled, some with her, some at her, and the little old lady was angered. She didn't understand the words but intuitively understood the insult. She replied in her language. The guide said a few words, and the conversation heated.

The hostess squawked, "What is she saying?" Then she ordered me to zoom in. "Oh, Lordy, look at her eyes. My God, look at those cataracts. She's got the worst cataracts I've ever seen. The poor old hag should consider surgery. I bet she doesn't even know that it's available."

She shouted in the lady's face, "You know they can fix your eyes?"

She cornered the old lady, trying to explain the surgery to her. It looked like a ridiculous version of adult peek-a-boo. I turned the camera off. She ordered me to zoom in. I refused. My buddy, Kurt, took the camera from me and after he steadied the transition, I said, "Leave the poor woman alone!"

"Leave her alone?" She snapped, "I'm trying to help."

"She was perfectly fine before you showed up to put her down," I said.

"Just look at her. She obviously needs help." The hostess defends.

"Oh, you're so full of yourself, it's a surprise you even noticed her," I said.

At first, she was dumbfounded, and I went on to tell her what I really thought of her self-indulgent, capitalist infomercial. I said her stupid show was a sad waste of resources and an embarrassing disgrace to America. To which she started screaming hysterically but unintelligibly.

The director yelled, "Cut! Everyone, take five."

The hostess stormed off to the nearest tree to smoke a Camel. The director followed her and put his arm around her.

Meanwhile, the crew was silent, trying hard not to congratulate me or cheer.

After a few minutes, she was in my face, shouting, "You're the one that has to leave. Get out of here. I don't want to see you again, ever."

The director arranged for someone to lead me back through the brush and instructed me to take a cab and meet him in the hotel lobby that night.

I hiked back to the road, laughing to myself and feeling relieved, because no matter what consequences awaited, I knew it would be better than having to work with that bitch.

That evening I met my boss in the hotel lobby for a couple of Mai Thais and, to my surprise, instead of punishing me, he thought it in his best interest give me an all-expense-paid vacation. Of course, I agreed not tell his wife that he was sleeping with the show hostess, and shook his hand when he slipped me a company credit card to use for the next two weeks. My only regret was not having the guts to ask him right then for a letter of recommendation.

    Sara looks so peaceful in deep sleep. The window is behind me, and the setting sun spreads a soft orange glow across her fair skin, except where my shoulder casts a shadow on her chin. She glows warm and magical. I wonder what she would do if I nuzzle into her. I could pretend I'm sleeping. Would she forgive me for one small kiss on the curve of her neck?

    She draws in a big sigh and stretches her fingers above her head. I try to look away, but I'm hypnotized. She catches me staring, and smiles. I smile back.

    "How long have I been out?"

    "I lost track of time," I lie.

    "Did I sleep through...? Is that the sunset? Huh. Jet lag." She rubs her face and rolls over.

    "Do you want to go back to sleep?" I ask.

    "Eventually, tonight, but I have my side of the bargain to uphold: we're going to Pat Pong."

    "We don't have to," I say. "I could go alone, if you want to sleep more."

    "And let you have all the fun? I don't think so."

    She sits up and stretches like a stapler, bending in half to touch her toes. I position my palm in the middle of her back. She curves up like a kitty cat and purrs, and then slinks onto the floor in front of her backpack, sorting through her portable closet for something to wear.

    The cab ride is relaxed and silent, a big contrast to the colorful activity outside. We watch bright neon signs alternate with dark narrow alleys. Pat Pong is the main strip of the red-light district. We recognize it by the well-lit, colorful rows of vendors and tourists. After paying the cab driver, we find ourselves in front of an overwhelming array of silk scarves.

The shop owner grabs the calculator, puts it in front of Sara and tempts, "Madam, which one you like?"

"Do you have purple? Like this color?" Sara points to a dress on a tourist nearby.

"Yes," she says and disappears into cardboard boxes under the sales booth. Producing a purple scarf with silver fringes she says, "You tell me how much you pay?"

"Would you take...?" She types some number into the calculator.

The shop owner, says, "Oh, madam, I cannot. You give me...." Typing in another number.

Sara puts the scarf down and says, "Thank you. I'm just looking."

The shop owner says, "I meet you halfway. You ask this much. I ask this much. You pay half-half. Okay?"

Another number is typed. I lean over to see what they're haggling over and am amazed to find she's asking $4 for a silk scarf that would be a bargain at $40 in any import boutique.

"No, thank you. I'll keep looking," Sara says.

"Okay. Okay, madam. Here. I give it to you only...."

Sara doesn't even look at the calculator. She's made up her mind to not take it.

"Are you sure?" I ask.

"Yeah, it's our first booth. Look down the street; every third vender might be selling the same scarf."

"Let's set a meeting place in case we get separated," I suggest.

Pointing to the golden arches on the corner, Sara asks "How about in front of McDonalds?"

"I hate Mickey Dee's," I say, "so try not to get lost, okay?"

We squeeze our way through the crowd to browse little booths filled with purses, watches, silver, jewelry, and shiny

33

bright flea market stuff at negotiable prices.

While Sara is bargaining for a little wooden Buddha, I notice three loud teenagers gesturing in front of a closed door. They hold posters with stick figure illustrations of different sex tricks. I read: "Pussy Galore. No Cover Charge." I scan the menu in absolute astonishment....

5 Sex Circus

Topless show...
Fire stick in pussy...
Pussy writing...
Pussy shooting banana...
Whistle blowing...

One of the kids in charge of marketing the sex show must have caught the shock on my face before barking, "We have ping-pong trick. We have sex with chicken, and we have blow darts. Come inside. Have a look."

"No, thank you," I say, trying to dismiss him with my hand.

Sara asks, "What does she do with the chicken?"

"Come inside. Have a look," he speaks in a singsong tone, waving his arm toward the door. I don't hear Sara's next question, on account of what I catch site of next door. Numerous dark-skinned women dance in glowing go-go shorts on a stage that looks like a boxing ring. A beautiful dancer with wide set eyes beckons me to come in. Excitement and embarrassment surge my system. I take Sara's hand and lead her back toward shopping.

"Don't you want to check it out?" she asks.

"This is the first bar we've seen. Every third bar could be selling the same merchandise," I joke. She slaps my shoulder.

We proceed to the next sales booth, which features an impressive array of weaponry, including Chinese throwing stars, razor claws, and brass knuckles. Sara makes eye contact with the almond-eyed shop owner, getting his nod of approval before she continues to fit a pair of brass knuckles onto her fist.

"A lot of these are illegal in Sao Paulo." She takes a few jabs toward me. This makes the store owner chuckle. "Ah, you like that?" she jokes, while slipping them off her fingers. I pick up a big Rambo-style blade. "My filmmaking buddy, Dean, would appreciate one of these. I'd like to bring him something back from my travels."

Sara inspects it, "How much are you willing to pay for it?"

"I don't know; $15 or $20?" I say, inspecting the half-wooden, half-sterling silver handle.

Indicating the Rambo Knife, Sara asks, "How much for this one?"

He offers the calculator and says, "How much you pay?"

"What's your name?"

"I'm Toto."

"Hi, Toto. I'm Sara. This is my friend Salvador. He's from America. He makes movies. He wants to buy this knife from you and bring it back to Hollywood. So, can you give me your best price?"

Thus, the game begins. They key in several numbers, each pushing the calculator back and forth. Finally, he hesitates before wrapping the knife in a sheet of newspaper.

"Okay!" Sara turns to me for cash. I pull a wad from my money belt, and she takes only the top bill, which is the equivalent of $5 US dollars. She hands it to Toto. They shake hands. My jaw drops when he hands her the equivalent of $3 change.

She gloats about her $2 purchase. "Bargaining is an art. You can't let them know what you're thinking, and you can't give in too fast."

"Homeland security would never let me bring that back

to the states. You want it?" I ask.

"Para Mim?" She hugs me in the middle of the aisle. "Obrigado!"

"What are you going to do with your new Rambo knife?"

"I'm going to cut apples and melons and passion fruit. You know in India everything's so polluted, if you don't boil or peel the fruit, you might puke it up later," she jokes.

"Oh, that's nice," I say. "You ready for a drink?"

I'm thinking that we can go into one of the open go-go bars but she takes my hand and pulls me through a door into the nearest sex show.

The bar is dark and stuffy. The music is loud and base. American Navy types, Japanese tourists, and Australian travelers populate the place. I order one rum and coke and one virgin lemonade from a skinny bartender with buckteeth.

Center stage, there are two women in black lingerie. One topless woman with dark lace stockings straddles the other one on a chair. They both writhe around, bouncing their perky boobs.

"Tell me if you feel the least bit uncomfortable and we can leave," I say to Sara.

"Oh, I'm uncomfortable all right, but that doesn't mean I want to leave," she says in good humor. "I'll let you know."

The topless woman pries herself off an enormous 14" strap-on worn by the woman in the seat. The music ends. They both bow. The room is a lazy shower of applause.

"Impressive," Sara says, playing with the ice in her lemonade. I'm regretting my decision to bring her to Pat Pong.

The dancers dismount the stage, circulate among the audience, and talk to tourists while sitting in their laps.

The next song is higher energy. Two new women come out, strutting their 6-inch heels, garter belts, and corsets. The dance routine is fast, limber, and semi-choreographed. The woman closest to us folds in half, takes hold of her ankles, and glares at me from between her legs. After a few more moves, she reaches her long pink fingernails into her crotchless panties and pulls out a ribbon. It's red, at first, but she continues pulling, hand over hand like a magician, and it changes to orange...yellow...green...

Both women are dancing around the room, trailing rainbow-colored streamers around the posts, chairs, and bar. When the last several feet of now-violet streamers are extracted, the audience wakes long enough to applaud.

"I have to admit, that's strangely beautiful." Sara shakes her head, clapping with the rest of the audience.

"It's definitely interesting," I say, putting my arm around Sara, in an attempt to deter other women from sitting on my lap.

By the third song, I have already polished off my drink. Three women come onstage, wearing tall combat boots and little military jackets. They light and puff on cigars. After a few quick dance moves to unfamiliar music with a strong build, the women position themselves on the floor, one of them nine inches away from our drinks. She points her high heels toward the sky, places the cigar in her pussy, and puffs away. A few lopsided smoke rings result. Sara buries her face in my armpit, as if we were watching a thriller movie she cannot bear to watch. She pulls my ear to her mouth and whispers something about the risks of cervical cancer.

I wave to let the bartender know we are leaving, throw some money on the counter, and we split before the song is over.

"I feel bad for dragging you here," I tell her.

"Get over it. I'm curious to see what the sex shows are all about. I just couldn't stomach watching some women risk their health for my drinking entertainment."

We go into a corner convenience store for bottled water

and poke at the strange food, like cuttlefish, chicken feet, and packaged pig snouts. On our way out, an overweight, older Mama-san, wearing a bar apron with fresh spills down the front, finds us in the street and says, "Where you come from?"

"America," Sara answers.

"Ahmalika." She broadens her toothy smile and says, "We have special show just for you." She holds out a menu listing a bunch of sex tricks. "You come see my girls?"

Sara looks at me, and nods, "Why not?"

We follow her, high speed, through the sidewalk venders, down an alley, and up a frontage road, parallel to the main drag.

I tell Sara, "This is Little Pat Pong. I remember seeing this on the map."

When the Mama-san begins to go upstairs, I balk. "It's okay. You follow me."

"No upstairs," I say.

"It's okay. You stay for one drink. One drink only. No cover charge."

"It'll be fine," Sara says.

"But we have no idea what they're going to do up there," I argue.

"I give you good deal, very cheap," the woman persists.

Sara dismisses my argument, "Let's just check it out." She turns to the Mama-san, "As long as there's no cover charge!"

We enter the dark saloon. There are two booths, one small bar table, a linoleum dance floor and a little bar in the back, all empty. She sits us down at the booth by the stage.

"Singha Gold? Or Singha?"

"Singha's fine for me," I say.

Sara asks, "Do you have Coca-Cola?"

"No, two Singha for sir?" says the Mama-san.

"How about red wine?" Sara asks.

"Okay. You like wine. We give you house special."

She disappears behind the bar into a back room. The music plays a thin and scratchy old eighties song, "Hit Me with Your Best Shot." A young Thai girl comes out wearing a string bikini and dancing. She looks about fourteen. A poodle is perched obediently at the next booth.

Mama-san returns with two cans of Singha, two glasses of red wine, and two shots of something blue. I try to send it back but she shouts, "You order house special, I give you house special," before walking away.

I scratch my head and laugh aloud, "Is it just me or is this weird?"

"It's definitely not just you," Sara laughs.

"Want to leave?" I ask.

"No, this is peaceful compared to the other club. We can at least finish one of our drinks."

Another young girl, probably a couple of years older than the dancer on stage, is fixing her lipstick in the mirror behind the bar.

I catch a glimpse of a skinny old man in the back room as he walks by in his pajamas. I get a creepy sense that this may be their house. The two girls look like they could be sisters, and it's sick to think, but the fat Mama-san might be their mother. They probably use the back room to turn tricks at night, but it might also be their shared bedroom. I decide not to share my creepy nepotistic thoughts with Sara.

When the song ends, a marching band version of Happy Birthday comes on. The bikini-clad girl brings out a bunch of balloons and places the strings in my hands. She is so focused on positioning my hand just right that she doesn't explain anything to me.

"What's this about?" I query.

"Maybe she thinks it's your birthday," Sara laughs.

They bring a small cake with burning candles to the

middle of the stage.

"No, my birthday's in November," I say to both the girl and Sara, but they don't hear me. All attention is now on the older sister as she straddles and squats over the white and blue frosted cake. She squints in concentration as she queefs on the candles, blowing them out one by one. I say, "Whoa. You see that? Whoa."

I try to applaud, but the young girl doesn't let me move my hand with the balloons. She repositions my hand and non-verbally insists I hold them out away from my body.

"I think that's where she wants you to hold them," Sara laughs.

The Mama-san enters and takes the cake off the floor so that the young girl can lay on her back in a strange yoga-like pose.

"What is she doing?" I ask Sara.

"It looks like Setu Bandha Sarvangasana, or bridge pose, but her hands aren't properly aligned," Sara says.

She's concentrating and squinting again, and I hear a soft phing. Phing. Something whizzes by me. Ka-Boom! a balloon pops, and echoes a bit in the small room.

"Holy shit! What the hell?" Another balloon pops and a little dart bounces onto the booth cushion beside me. There are a few more darts scattered by my side. "She's shooting darts at me."

I release the balloons, which float up to the old popcorn ceiling. Looking through my shielding hands, I see my assailant adjusting her angle so that she can continue blowing darts from her crotch toward the balloons on the ceiling. Sara's laughing so hard she spills her wine.

"Fuck, they're trying to kill us," I say, signaling to the Mama-san to ask for the bill. She ignores me. "They should caution the audience, or at least pass out protective eye gear."

Sara nods in agreement between guffaws and waves

both her hands attracting the Mama-san's attention.

When the music changes to an eighties rap song, the young girl lifts herself off the floor and makes room for her sister's little striptease.

"You spill your drink? I bring you one more?" Mama-san soaks the blood-colored fluid into a dirty dishrag.

"No, we're done," I say. "We're ready to go."

She pulls a slip of paper with Thai writing out of her apron and sets it in front of me. The only number on it equals about $155 US. I say, "This can't be right. We only ordered two drinks."

"You order two house specials and stay for show."

"But this is way too much. You said no cover charge."

"Okay, okay, I give you discount." She recalculates. The new bill is about $115 US.

"This is a scam!" I shout and stand up, causing Sara to stand up. The old man in the pajamas darts for the door, locks the dead bolt, and stands in front of it.

"You can't charge me for a special show. That's ridiculous," I say.

Now the woman is angry. "You come to my house, you spill drink, and you leave the show no finished. You pay more."

"No, I'm paying less because I didn't stay for the whole show." I pull half the amount she wants from my wallet and say, "This is all I have."

The woman takes the money and tries to calm us down, "Okay, okay, okay, I give you discount. One more drink, you stay for, I cut cake."

"No, thank you!"

The old man unlocks the door as we quickly move for the door.

"Good-bye," Sara says as we rush down the stairs.

"What a rip-off," I mutter.

"Well, now at least we know why *The Lonely Planet*

distinctly warns people not to go upstairs," Sara says as we make our way back through the alley.

6 Elephant and the Bearded Lady

Our walking route dumps us into a hospital parking lot on Suriwang Road. A couple of tuk-tuk drivers are standing around their vehicles arguing. An old man in a torn white tank top walks directly towards us trailing a baby elephant on a chain.

"Watch out," I say, urging Sara not to walk in front of the elephant. Sara reaches out to the massive beast and overflows with verbal adoration. I realize that I almost missed the miracle that this animal is. Now I notice its huge black eyelashes and curious trunk. The old man sells us a bag of peanuts for about 60 cents.

He shows Sara how to uncurl her fingers, and hold her palm flat for the elephant to find the peanuts. Sara squeals when Dumbo's slow-moving trunk fondles her shoulders.

"Look at that big metal chain around your neck. Poor guy, your feet are tired. You work hard, don't you?" Sara intimates, patting the elephant's forehead a few times. When the peanuts are all gone, Dumbo grows restless and Sara hugs him good-bye.

The tuk-tuk drivers are intrigued by the redheaded elephant hugger. "Madam, want a ride?" One driver calls.

"You ready to go back?" Sara asks me.

"No," I say. "It's too early. What else is there to do around here?"

A short man steps out from the shadows and asks, "You want Girly Show?"

Sara says, "No, I think we had enough of that for one

night."

"You like massage?" he asks.

"I love massage," she says.

He points to me, "You like girly show. I show you Thai massage with girly show."

He pulls a laminated full color brochure from the visor of his vehicle and hands it to me. Sara leans in to see the pictures of steamy western lesbian models in a hot tub.

"Oooh, la, la," Sara exclaims.

"Where is this?" I ask.

"I take you."

"Where, approximately?" I point toward the main strip and ask, "How far?"

The other driver jumps in and says, "Not far, half hour by tuk-tuk. One street with big spa, many massage. Ma Cheri, Mona Lisa, big spa have Superstar, girly bath, massage, and sucky and fucky. Anything you like. If madam wants, you get unisex."

I have to ask, "What's unisex?"

"Unisex. For madam."

Sara points to the two lesbians on the card. "Like bisexual? Uni-sex?"

"Yes, Ma Cheri better for madam."

"How much?" Sara asks.

"Usually 2,000 Baht. 2,000 for sir, 2,000 for madam. If you like Superstar, 4,000 Baht."

"That's a lot of Baht!" she says.

"It's very nice."

"Thank you, but no," I say and turn away.

"And how do you know I don't want a bubble bath from a hot lesbian?" Sara asks with her hands on her hips.

"I don't trust these guys," I say.

"They seem nice enough," Sara says, and we continue strolling.

"Didn't you read the *Lonely Planet*'s warning about all the scam artists? They clearly say, 'Never go to any upstairs bars or parlors.' I can only assume the same warning goes for a brothel across town. Who knows what these guys are up to? They could take us to the end of the river, take our money, and drop us off," I reason.

Sara says, "My intuition says that guy's harmless, just trying to make a buck, but if your vibration is worried about getting mugged, I don't want to be around you when you attract that."

"What's that supposed to mean?"

"I get that your intention is to avoid being robbed, mugged, or cheated."

"Don't forget sodomized," I chide.

"Right, but I've been traveling now for several years and I've never had a problem. Have you ever considered the possibility that if you focus on your fear ... that's what you'll end up with? It's a simple spiritual principle. Wherever you put your focus gets magnetized and attracts like energy. Think about our Thai massage today, you were afraid it was going to hurt, so what happened? You attracted the strongest guy in the room."

"Easy for you to say, you got an old lady, whereas I ended up with the Thai Schwarzenegger," I defend.

A well-groomed hostess with blood red lipstick slows Sara's pace by asking, "Madam, you married? He your husband?"

"No," Sara says. We stop in front of what looks like a traditional foot massage parlor. "He's my friend."

"Mister, you like hand massage?" The hostess asks, nodding her head and pulling my shoulder.

"What do you think Sara?" I ask. "Want to get hand and feet massages?"

Sara lowers her voice, "I think she means a hand job."

"No! Really?" I say, squinting from the bright neon foot in their window.

"She didn't ask me if I wanted one," Sara adds.

I look directly at the hostess, "You mean hand massage for me?" I point to my crotch. She smiles and nods, without a trace of embarrassment.

"You pick girl from my shop," the hostess urges.

Inside there are about nine women in tight black dresses wearing numbers. The girls are giggling and chatting in their own language, inviting me to select someone.

"I'm just looking," I announce.

"Looking is free," the hostess sings.

Sara asks, "Which one do you like?"

"Are you trying to pawn me off on another woman?" I ask.

"I want to see what kind of woman you're attracted to," she says.

I ask the hostess, "You have unisex?"

"For Madam? No, so sorry."

Sara jabs me and jokes, "Darn, I think number 56 is cute." Number 56 is medium build, angular-faced women, with a strong yet shy presence. She half-smiles at me.

The hostess catches wind of the flirtations and says, "Number 56 is very good. Best in Bangkok."

I feel a hot flush all through my body and say to Sara, "Let's get out of here."

"Why don't you stay out and see what the night has to offer, and I can head back to the hotel. I'm going to fall right to sleep, so you might as well."

It occurs to me that she's serious. I wave to the group, "Okay. Thank you, next time." We walk away, pretending to ignore the disappointed calls and complaints of the sexy women.

"I don't want you to resent me for making you miss out

on a good time in this crazy city," Sara says.

Walking toward a larger intersection, I stop in the street, pivot around toward her, and put my hands on her waist.

I stare directly at her and say, "I am having an awesome time." Then I tell myself to do it. Kiss her, right here in the middle of nowhere in particular, but the flicker of fear in her eyes stops me.

Instead I say, "I would rather be with you than anyone else in the world right now."

Her body tightens in my hands when she speaks, "Yes, right now. Everything feels great in the moment, but what about an hour from now when I'm sleeping and you're laying beside me with all that pent-up sexual energy, and I can't do anything about it. How are you going to feel then?"

I'm stunned at her bold but accurate accusation. She disarms me by caressing my shoulder, "I'm still jet lagged, and I want to rest up before arriving in Madurai. I wouldn't mind a little alone time."

"You're not upset or anything?" I ask.

"No, just tired. Remember, we have a date with Buddha tomorrow morning at ten," she says, hugging me. She hails a cab, and then leaves a wet, soft lip-print on my cheek.

At first, I feel like Dumbo, restless and out of peanuts while meandering down the busy street toward the main drag ... but then I feel a tug around my neck as if I'm being pulled by an invisible metal chain. Without thinking, I return in the direction of the foot massage parlor.

Number 56 is not as shy as she pretends. Immediately after closing the door to our little cubicle, she strips down to a lacy pair of brief shorts. Cheap plastic gels cover the ceiling lamps, which cast theatrical colors on her soft Asian skin. The brightest thing in the room is her crooked smile, which, at certain angles, could be confused for a grimace.

After a few attempts, I realize conversation is futile. The only words she seems to know are, "Sir, okay?" but she is deft at unbuttoning my pants and shirt and hanging them on the wall hook from a couple of mismatching hangers. I keep my boxers on, for the second time this evening, and perch uncomfortably on the futon, feeling the night on my skin. I run my hand down her arm and am surprised by how muscular her biceps are. I clear my throat and say, "You're very beautiful."

She moans and kisses my chest with multiple little kisses, like a bird pecking at seed. I close my eyes and lean back. Number 56 strokes the length of my body, which simultaneously produces a hard-on in my shorts and Sara's face is in my mind. Excitement and guilt surge through my veins.

Number 56 pulls down the elastic band of my boxers and strokes me rhythmically with her big hands, and though more and more blood is rushing to my cock, I start to fixate on her Adams apple. Disturbing flashes from the movie The Crying Game upset my pleasure. I have nothing in common with the lady whose lips are now around my cock. I scoot back. She follows me with her face. I pull her hand away, and she puts my hand on her little breast, which feels cold and oily. I wonder what she's hiding under her lacy little shorts, but ultimately decide that I don't really want to know.

"I'm sorry. I cannot."

"You have wife?"

"Yes," I say, figuring it will help preserve her Eastern practice of saving face. "I'll still pay you," I say, though I've already paid the Mama-san.

Once we are dressed, she tucks my generous tip into her short-pants and does not return my limp hug. I fear my quick departure will be like the walk of shame past the numbered women at the entrance. I worry they'll peg me as impotent or as a premature ejaculator. She bows to me and leads me past the entrance, which has only half the girls it did before. No one seems to notice my exit. I rush out into the street and hail a taxi to the Royal Hotel.

Without turning on the lights, I can tell the bed is empty and made. The pit of my stomach drops. Her luggage is gone. Have I been too trusting of this tramp? Has she run off with my stuff? Then I notice a metal frame for an empty cot in the corner of the room. I crane my neck to look behind the bed and in front of the sliding glass door; I find Sara's sleeping body curled up on a single mattress. Big sigh.

I undress completely this time and melt into bed. I lean over to inspect the moonlit glow of her ear, upper cheek, and temple. The rest of her face is covered with curls, her body with blankets. I settle back into the squeaky hotel bed, close my eyes but cannot sleep. My semi-erection turns into a full hard-on in the palm of my right hand. I imagine rolling down on top of Sara, sticking it into her, and taking two years of celibacy away from her while she sleeps. I'm ashamed at my cruel fantasy, but stroking myself in high gear. My mind is back at the brothel, where I'm slamming number 56 like a jackhammer, and she's so loud that two more women fight their way in to get theirs.

7 Crash Course in Chakras

The cabby is outside, excited to open our doors and escort us through a whirlwind of Buddhist temples, glittering mosaics, high ceilings, gold statuary, and crowds of tourists. Tour guides hold umbrellas into the clear sky while explaining the relevance of ancient artifacts in Thai-glish. We catch tidbits of interesting facts that echo exact words from *The Lonely Planet*.

Sara asks me if I feel any resonance with any of the Buddhas in each of the temples. I have to admit that I don't. Perhaps I'm too tired, too overwhelmed, and too skeptical.

"Would you like me to help you shift your energy?" she asks with an impish grin.

I consider coffee, a nap, or some noontime nookie. "What did you have in mind?" I ask.

"Ever had Reiki?"

"No," I respond.

Nor do I feel it is something I've been missing, but she looks at me with her sexy bright eyes full of positive anticipation.

"What do I have to do?" I ask.

"Relax and close your eyes."

I'm sitting on a mosaic bench next to a stupa when she places her hands above my head.

"Imagine I'm adjusting your energetic body or tuning your psychic antennas."

I hear her breathing as she sweeps and swirls her hands above my neck and shoulders. I feel a tingling. The little hairs on the back of my neck tickle. Warmth and calm wash over my frame. She sits beside me on the bench, asking, "What did you feel?"

"Not much," I lie.

Then there is a huge, ear-splitting "Ka-Boom!" Sara jumps straight up and screams even louder than the explosion. A few locals snicker, because her scream echoes in the otherwise-quiet temple. She squeezes me and laughs into my chest as one of the local guides explains that Buddhists often set off fireworks as an offering to show the magnitude of their devotion.

She recomposes herself and says, "Notice if you feel any different when we go into the meditation room."

I follow her from the shoe rack to a silent and somewhat stuffy temple. I sit and scan the scene. A number of Asians sit with closed eyes and varying degrees of straightness in their spine. Little golden papers are plastered all over the beautiful brass ornaments surrounding the altar. I watch the candles flicker for awhile and look into the half sleeping eyes of the Buddha statue. After some time, Sara bows and leaves. I follow her silently out of the temple walls toward the taxi.

"What did you feel when you looked at Buddha?" she asks.

"There's a hypnosis to it all, you know, people taking off their shoes, being quiet and even you asking me to be sensitive to experience energy. How do I know if what I feel is real or suggested?"

"Does it matter? If you experience it, you experience it."

Our cab driver asks us if we want to go back to the hotel.

I'm quick to reply, "I think I've had enough temple-touring for one day."

Sara proposes we go back to the hotel for a nap, but I

know if she gets nearly naked again in my presence, I'm going to explode.

"How about if we go back and you teach me some of that Tantra you've been talking about?" I offer.

She lights up, "Are you really interested?"

"Hell, yeah."

"In the sex or the spirituality?"

"Both," I lie.

"Good answer," she says. There's a long pause, and I can tell she's about to say something. Actually, not just anything; I think I know what she's going to say. "I don't think it's a good idea for us to have sex since I leave for India tomorrow at noon. Does that make sense?"

I nod, "Yeah, I sort of figured."

"But we could exchange energy, if you're willing to learn a Tantric exercise or two."

"Twist my arm, but I have to warn you, I'm not very flexible."

"Are you talking about your mind or your body?"

"Both."

"Wrong answer. You do not have to be flexible in your body, at least not for this. But if you can't open your mind and try new things, Tantra will be totally lost on you."

"I know, I was just kidding. I got Reikied today, didn't I? I was at least open to that."

"That was very big of you," she teases.

After settling a bit, Sara begins to prepare the room. She draws the curtains shut, which drastically dims the lighting. "It amazes me how loud Bangkok is, and we're three stories up!" she says, while fussing with the controls on the radio, which is connected to the master control center for the room.

At her fingertips, she holds the control for the lights,

Don't Drink the Punch

A/C, TV and radio. She tunes into an instrumental classic Thai station. At first, it sounds like background porno music, but after a few bars, it begins to sooth my anxious excitement.

She takes off her cargo pants and socks and crawls into the center of the bed. "Okay, you ready?" she asks, kneeling in her panties and patting the bed beside her as an invitation.

"What do I have to do?" I ask.

"First, Mr. Open-mind, I want you to Reiki me."

"I would, if I knew how."

"You don't have to know anything, just follow your intuition. I'm going to sit here with my eyes closed, and you're going to pretend like you're cleaning my aura."

"Okay, and how long do I have to do that for?"

"Until you're finished. You will know when you're done, and don't touch me. I mean it. I can tell if you're even thinking about it," Sara warns.

"No peeking," I say, moving my hands about. I'm thinking this makes for great foreplay, but eventually self-consciousness arises and I wonder what the hell I'm doing. After some time, the song ends. I think, saved by the bell.

"Okay," I say.

"Thank you. Wow! How was that? What did you feel?"

"I don't know. Different stuff, I suppose."

"You want to know what I felt?" she asks.

I nod.

"At first I felt incredibly sexual and sort of scared you were going to grope me, but I eventually relaxed, and it felt like you were just admiring me. That made me feel beautiful, I mean really gorgeous. Then it felt sort of silly and in the end you just stopped."

"Are you psychic or something? When you asked me what I was feeling, I was like ... I don't know, it wasn't really clear, but when you explained ... it was exactly what I felt," I say.

56

"Yeah, well, just practice listening to how you feel more, and you too can impress your friends with a new party trick."

"I'm serious," I reply.

"So am I. You want to lay down for the next exercise." Upon command, I fall straight back onto the bed.

"Wait. First, do you know what the chakras are?" Sara asks me.

"I've heard about them. I had a personal trainer at my gym who used to say, 'lift from your root chakra,' or something like that."

"Right. Well, there are seven main chakras, or energy centers and they are located up the sushumna, or central energy channel in the spine. They're not really in the body but they correlate to areas in the body like the tailbone, navel and forehead. I like to think of them as part of the subtle body."

"Like in the Matrix II, when Keanu Reeves reaches into Trinity to bring her back to life?"

"Right, that's Hollywood's version of subtle body for you. Anyway, when we bring our attention to those areas, it balances the body and brings our awareness out of the world of form and into the subtle realm. One of the most bonding things that you can do is practice this with another person. Don't worry. I'll talk you through it. First, you've got to get comfortable. You want to take off your pants?"

"I thought you'd never ask," I kid.

"We'll start spooning. Usually the man goes behind the woman, because he's bigger, but in this case, it's probably less distracting if I'm back here. Lie on your side facing the window, and close your eyes. Do you want to take anything else off?"

She wrestles around a bit to remove her t-shirt. So I decide, what the hell, I'll take mine off too. "I like having you curled up behind me," I say, feeling her cool, bare breasts on my back.

"It works out better this way. It's hard to give yoga instruction when there's a loaded gun at my back."

We laugh together, and then she tries to control her giggles and encourages me to settle back into my breathing.

"Notice how the belly rises when you inhale and falls when you exhale. Now, see if you can relax a little more. Do whatever you need to make yourself completely comfortable."

I sigh.

"Good. Sound is good. Feel free to yawn or moan. Now, drop your awareness down into your spine. Notice your hips and relax your buttocks. Find your tailbone. Visualize the color red. Red is basic, the beginning of the spectrum. Consider your basic needs and instincts. Know that they are provided for you. Food, water, and shelter flow to you as easily as fresh oxygen. Breath red energy into this area, releasing any concerns you might have about money or security...." As she goes on speaking, I notice the red, relaxed sensation is not just in my spine, but also all the way down my legs and at the bottoms of my feet.

After some time of breathing deeply together, she directs my awareness to my penis and balls and instructs me to breathe a bright orange light into the space below my belly button. Everything down there feels alive and exciting. It is sexual, but not aggressive. It's like the warmth I feel before an erection.

She tells me to visualize my pelvis as a bowl and to imagine it filling with sensual energy. Right when it feels like orange liquid is about to overflow and squirt out all over the sheets, she shifts my attention up to the solar plexus. There is a bright yellow sunburst radiating in all directions. I see it like the sun except that it's not blinding, just warm and strong. This is me, my soul. I am the sun and everything upon which it shines.

Reaching the heart, I become aware of my entire chest, not just the front, but also the space between my shoulder blades. She calls it the back door to my heart. I can feel Sara's heart beating behind me. It feels like love, exhilarating and bottomless. The visual is a gorgeous green field, like fields of tall grass without limits. Sara and I are melting into them.

When Sara instructs me to focus on my throat area, I balk. I don't want to leave this space. My field melts into a blue-green body of water. We're together still, standing at the shore, just holding hands. The clear water invites me, but I'm paralyzed. My body's a lead weight. I want to go in, but I'm stuck. Nothing's moving. Nothing's happening, and I'm feeling panic in the back of my throat. What am I afraid of? I don't understand it, and I want to scream.

I hear Sara encouraging me to focus on the space between my eyes, and the water surges into a huge wall rushing towards us, crashing down and smashing us into oblivion. I melt under a thick blanket of unconsciousness. After...I don't know how long, I hear voices, soft feminine laughter, but I can't tell who is laughing.

My vision blurs under a silky scarf that is tantalizing my naked skin. There are a number of women dancing around to the rhythm of drums and bells, all wearing beautiful sheer wraps, like gypsy sex nymphs from some fantasy harem.

I'm on my back, in a field of ashes, and can feel the cool earth around me. I am under an old oak tree by a fire at night. The stars are infinite, and an owl is perched out of sight. All I hear, above the fireside music, is the owl: Who? Who? Who? The repetition frustrates me.

A woman's voice shouts, "Phat!" and I suddenly bite hard through my lip. Teeth piercing through the other side, I experience no pain, just shock and fear. Blood pours down onto the pillows and there is a chunk of flesh. My tongue feels the metallic tasting flesh where my bottom lip used to be. My teeth protrude from my face, and the lip is gone.

Where did it go? Could the doctors sew it back on? Wait. I'm in Thailand. Do they have the technology to do that? Quick, somebody get ice.

I open my eyes and find myself back in the hotel bed, my lip still attached, and no signs of blood on the pillow. Relief...and it occurs to me that Sara is no longer behind me. I must have fallen asleep. The bathroom door is ajar and I can hear the sounds of bath water gently sloshing against the fiberglass sides of the tub.

I jump to my feet, faster than usual, and it takes a moment for my body to catch up.

I ask, "Are you okay?"

"I'm taking a bath. Come in, if you need to use it or want to talk."

I crack the door and stick my head in. Her warm, beautiful face shines back at me from the steamy tub. "The sleeping prince awakes," she says.

"What did you do to me?" I ask.

"Either I bored you out of your mind, or you're in desperate need of rest, but that's okay. I've been yearning for a bath. This is like my own little retreat. I'm so grateful to soak before I dive into the third world conditions tomorrow."

"Yeah?" I grab a towel and set it on the toilet seat where I can watch her soaking in bubbles.

"So you're pretty excited, huh?"

"I know my expectations can cloud my ability to live in the moment and lead to some serious disappointments, but I can't help being excited."

"What are you looking forward to most?" I ask.

"Everything. I mean, ever since I started on this path, my life has become brighter and juicier, and just when I think that it can't get any better, it always does. Like meeting you. This kind of magic happens to me all the time. I just can't wait to see what the next chapter holds."

"You know, I've never met a woman like you," I say.

"Thank you."

"I mean it, and you know what else? I never had an experience like that ... at least not without drugs. When I got out of bed my legs felt funny, like the ground was moving, like I was on a boat, and the solid stuff around me didn't make sense."

"Maybe it's jet lag," she says.

"No, I've been jet-lagged before. This is going to sound crazy, but I think it's love."

I'm relieved when she smiles and looks at me with a sparkle in her eyes.

"Fantastic," she says.

"Do you feel that way too?"

"Yes, every time I do Tantra."

I'm dashed, but she continues. "See, when I first met my guru, I thought, 'This is interesting philosophy. It helps engage my left-brain.' Sometimes I don't agree with everything he says, but we do the practice. The meditation feels so clear and undeniable. That's why I stayed for so long. It was not the guru but the direct and repeatable experience of love."

"And you think that's what just happened to me?" I look her straight in the eye.

"Do you want to join me?" she asks. "Before you answer that, let me ask you: would you be able to join me and not make it be sexual?"

"I think so," I say, trying to hide my excitement. I proceed to drop my trousers and tentatively step into the steaming Sara soup.

"So, at first it takes a while to settle into it."

"I know it's hot!" I yelp.

"No, I mean the Tantra. At first, there can be a lot of disappointment and frustration and waiting for something to happen. As you get acquainted with it, there's a sense of being swept into another world where revelation or epiphany is so easy to tap into. Most the time, though, it can be painful and confronting. You know?"

"Uh-huh...."

"Are you okay?" she asks.

"Do you always bathe in boiling water?"

"Afterwards we can take an ice cold shower. In Tantra, there's a dance with opposites. There's shadow and light. It's not either/or, it's both, and that's what's so mind-blowing and heart-opening," she says.

"Well, whatever it is, you must be pretty good at it."

"The ultimate experience of Tantra is independent of who you're practicing with," she says.

"But I've never felt this way with anyone else."

"You've never been in love?"

"I've been in love, lots of times, but this is different," I tell her.

"Exactly. This is different."

"Well, maybe I'm supposed to learn stuff from you. Maybe you're supposed to teach me stuff. What would happen if you stayed here another week, and we do more exercises together?"

"I'm honored, but my teacher is waiting for me in Madurai," she says.

"Maybe you don't need another teacher at all; maybe you are the teacher."

"I'm glad I created an opening for you. That's what my teachers do for me: they open doors to new states of being. And now that you've been initiated to the chakras, you'll always have that awareness with you," she says.

"Give me one logical reason why you can't stay," I

challenge.

"Thailand is not pulling me."

"But you just said you need to let go of expectations and stay open. What if going to Phuket with me is your next big adventure?" I offer.

"Hold on. Let me meditate on that." She closes her eyes for a split second. "Nope, sorry. I'm going to India, but you could come with me."

"Let me think about it ... tempting, but no."

She splashes me. "What happened to Mr. Stay-open-and-let-go-of-expectations?"

"I don't think it would be spontaneous. I think it would be stupid for me to follow you on your fantasy adventure. Dangerous, actually."

"Well, Tantra is not for everyone. In fact, it's often described as the most confronting path. If I thought I could achieve enlightenment through a gentler path such as Thai Chi or Zen gardening, I would take it. But I've found my path, or it found me, and I'm committed to see where it's taking me."

"Do you think we'll stay in touch?" I ask, trying to sound casual.

"Maybe. Correspondence from India is not that easy, especially while on pilgrimage."

"But afterward?"

"It's possible."

"Want me to scrub your back?" I ask, taking the little white hotel soap into my hand with the washcloth.

"Yes, please. I met a German guy in Portugal who told me that when he was in Bangkok, he went to one of those spas and got a Thai jelly fish massage."

"Sounds disgusting," I say.

"There's no actual jellyfish involved. It's just what he called it. They use hot oil and soapy water, but instead of using her hands to massage, she uses her whole naked body. He said it was unlike anything he'd ever experienced in his whole life, and the Germans can be pretty kinky. Of course, it was also full service where they sucked him and fucked him afterwards. He said that part's optional."

"So that's why you were so curious about those clubs last night," I say.

"I'm not excited about the prostitution bit, but I'm always into learning new massage techniques, and I want to make the most out of our last night together."

"So you are into girls, are you?"

"Beautiful people are beautiful people. I don't have a preference."

"I suspected that," I say.

"It's nice that you don't assume I'm straight."

"Well, when you decided you weren't going to sleep with me, I figured you must be gay."

She nibbles on my arm. "It was a lot easier practicing celibacy when I wasn't hanging out with someone I wanted to sleep with. Imagine that."

"Well, I don't think it's a good idea to sleep together," I say, "especially not at this point, with you leaving tomorrow."

She crinkles her eyebrows. "Are you being serious or sarcastic?"

"You've already made up your mind. I'm trying to justify the situation so that I feel better about the rejection."

"Are you feeling rejected?" she coddles. "I hear that Thai jellyfish massages are good for that. You want to try to track one down?"

"Hey, if I can restrain myself with the most beautiful woman in the world sitting with me in the tub, I think I can handle an oily prostitute rubbing herself on me."

"I would imagine it would be easier to control your impulses, since we're visiting the AIDS capital of the world."

"Thanks for reminding me," I say.

8 Thai Jellyfish Massage

Taxi rides in Thailand are as interesting as their destinations. A few blocks after clearing a sobriety check, where a teenage police officer with a machine gun shines a flashlight into our cab, we find ourselves behind a small Nissan pick-up. The truck is riding low from a full cargo of skin-tight dresses, bare legs, and big hair on about a dozen sexy women sitting on top of one another.

There is one woman fixing her lipstick trying to look good for the men passing in cars on either side. A police officer on a motorbike rides close behind. At first, I think he is like everyone else on the road, just trying to get a better look. Then I figure out that he's following close behind to make sure none of the prostitutes make a run for it when the paddy wagon comes to a stop.

I tell Sara that the Nissan is filled from a prostitution bust. The taxi man hears us and in near perfect English confirms my hypothesis.

"But I thought prostitution was legal in Bangkok." Sara leans forward for a better look.

"In some areas, yes. Some areas, no. No girlies allowed at Grand Palace. We keep the streets clean for royal visitor."

"Ah," Sara and I say in chorus.

"How many times you been to Thailand?"

"Only once before," Sara says.

"How many times have you been to the Mona Lisa?"

"This will be the first time," she answers.

"Girls at Mona Lisa, very beautiful!"

"Have you ever been?" I ask.

"Girls at Mona Lisa, very expensive," he says.

We pull into the big, almost empty parking lot of a huge building that looks like it could have been a car dealership.

A door attendant greets us at the entrance and leads us into the showroom. A tall glass window separates us from about 20 women dressed in various shades of peach. Sara takes her place behind me for the fishbowl selection process. A tall, heavy man with a shrunken suit approaches us. "How many girls you like?"

Sara asks how the pricing works and I begin to negotiate a bit. Since there are two of us that want a massage in the same room, I'm able to discount the total bill from about $100 to $75 US dollars.

A tall, chubby teenage girl, who I think is the Suit's daughter, leans over to me and asks, "Which girl you like?"

"Oh, I almost forgot. Do you have any 'unisex' girls?"

The Suit squints his eyes while he looks into the tank, lifts his chin and says, "Number 14 and 88 good for madam."

I zoom in on his suggestions, noticing they are the butchest ones in the room.

"Number 88 seems sweet," Sara says.

With images of last night's hooker in my head, I whisper, "Do you want to talk about this a little more? I don't like the selection, and I don't know if this place is all that clean."

"You don't have to pick a unisex girl. I just think it's best for me to stick to someone who might enjoy massaging me," she says without whispering. Two Japanese businessmen are escorted inside.

The chubby teenager opens a curtain to another display window, where there are a handful of women who appear to be napping. These women are, on the average, thinner and taller than the first bunch.

The Suit stops his conversation with the Japanese men to tell us, "Superstar. You pay more Baht. No discount."

"Got it. No one jumps out at me," I say and lead Sara's attention back to the first group.

"Number 22 is also unisex. You like?" The teenager entices. Number 22 is smaller and noticeably younger. She wears a short, peach skirt and matching peach bra. My girl is the most feminine in the room.

"Okay," I say. The deal is sealed.

The girls come out a side door and lead us up the industrial elevator to a corridor with mangy carpeting underfoot and a metal ceiling overhead. When we arrive at a gray door, Sara unties her Keds, and I notice that all the doors look alike, except the occupied rooms have high heel shoes sitting outside on the door matt.

Inside the room, there is one mirrored wall, a covered jacuzzi, a large cast iron bathtub, and a concrete floor with a shower drain built into it. My girl ties her hair up in a bun, strips off all her clothes, and runs the water. A maid knocks on the door and opens it with an inflatable pool raft and plastic mesh basket containing condoms, mints and lotions.

"You like drink?" the maid asks, unfazed by the nudity.

Sara asks, "How much are the drinks?"

"One drink comes with girl. No charge."

"What do you have?" Sara asks.

"Singha Gold, water, Coca Cola?"

"Do you have tea?" Sara says.

"Tea? No tea."

She settles for a soda, and I order a beer. I ask the girls if they want anything, but they don't respond, so I mime drinking and point to them, and this makes them giggle. I'm not sure if I've broken a custom, or if they just don't understand.

Once the maid leaves, Sara's girl, the unisex woman,

undresses and uses the mirror to arrange her hair into an avocado-green shower cap. She has more strength than flab on her big-boned frame.

When we're all undressed, the maid returns with two drinks and a remote control. I tip her and take a long slow swig. Up close, I can't tell if my girl is incredibly young or just young looking.

Sara clutches tight to her glass of warm Coke while she sits herself beside me on a bench, almost touching my thigh with her thigh. The unisex one turns on the television and changes a few channels to find the news. Her serious face glows with the blue of the tube.

"Okay?" she asks.

"No, I'd prefer no television," I say.

She turns it off, and I ask, "What is your name?"

They look at each other and giggle.

"I'm Sal. This is Sara. What is your name?"

The unisex one talks for both. I repeat each name once or even twice, but not having a frame of reference for Thai names, they don't stick. My girl sets the two rafts side by side on the concrete floor.

"Madam, ready?" She leads Sara over to an inflatable pool raft and lays her down on her belly.

"Madam, okay?" she asks, and Sara moans an affirmative. She uses the little plastic basket like an eggbeater to make suds in a warm bucket of water. I watch as her naked breasts jiggle with effort.

My girl gestures for me to come lay down. I position myself elbow to elbow with Sara. She smiles, half relaxed and, I suspect, half embarrassed.

"Tell me if you need anything," I say.

"Don't worry about me. I'm loving this," she reassures, while craning her neck out to kiss my nose. The unisex one pours a bucket of suds on top of Sara. Some splash over and hit me. With a few more splatters, Sara is covered with suds, and the unisex one lathers her own body up too.

I close my eyes and try to relax. My girl is doing the same while sitting on my butt. Warm soapy water spills over my back and legs, and I feel thin fingers moving around on my shoulders. The unisex one straddles Sara and massages her shoulders less than a foot from my face. From this distance, there's a hint of a moustache above her Cheshire grin. My girl's massage is somewhat weak, but anything would feel weak compared to yesterday's Thai massage, so I can't complain.

Both women begin slipping their breasts on our backs in big, fast circles. Sara's moaning from massage heaven, while I'm scoping the scene from the multiple angles offered by the mirrored walls. A deft knee digs into my ass. The unisex one straddles Sara's hamstrings, pressing her soft, inner thigh against the entire length of Sara's leg as she shimmies slowly down to her ankle.

Meanwhile, I'm not sure what my girl is doing, but it somehow feels clumsy compared to what the lesbian appears to be doing to Sara.

We're nonverbally instructed to flip over. I squint my eyes so I'm not blinded by the track lighting. The girl points to Sara's flat stomach as it is lathered with warm, foamy suds and says, "Madam look like superstar."

"Thank you," Sara says. I guess being called an expensive hooker by a cheap hooker is a compliment.

"Madam, no baby?" the big woman says as she rubs her breasts on Sara's tummy.

"Not yet," Sara says, as though calling out from far away. My girl pinches her flab, points at a c-section scar, and says, "I have baby."

To which the unisex one answers, "I have two baby."

"Wow. How old are you?" Sara tries to make conversation.

"She 18, I 20," the Unisex one says.

I'm thinking either she's lying or turning tricks in Bangkok is like drinking from the fountain of age.

That's about the last English word we hear from either of them for a while. They continue massaging while chattering amongst themselves in Thai. I interlace my fingers behind my head, propping up a bit to watch two big brown breasts sway from side to side over Sara's naked body.

My girl escorts me into the tub and employs a lime green washcloth to soap up my back and neck, and behind my ears. She strokes my slightly shy penis. I try to relax a little by watching Sara writhe under her woman's touch.

"Déjà vu," Sara says, sinking into the tub beside me.

"You've done this before?" I ask.

"We've done this before, earlier tonight. We were in the tub together."

"Oh, yeah," I say, though it feels like ages ago. "Well, I'm glad we're doing it again, because that gives me the opportunity to do something I was too afraid to do before," I say.

"What's that?" she begins to ask, but I lean in to kiss her before she's done. It's a real kiss, with tongue and passion, and of course, that's the moment the unisex one chooses to say, "Excuse me," and guides Sara into a big white terry cloth towel, sits her on the corner of the jacuzzi, and busily rubs moisturizer onto her legs.

My girl dries me off and then holds a condom a few inches from her face, between two fingers, as though it were a cigarette.

"You like?" she asks.

I turn to Sara and ask, "How do you feel?"

"Well, don't stop on my account. I mean, it would be nice to massage each other and make out while they do whatever they do."

I use a combination of mime and kindergarten vocabulary to both girls. "Okay, so. We...," I point to both Sara and myself and mock make-out with my own hand, "and you...," my hands fly all over my body in mock massage and on Sara's thighs. "Okay?"

She nods adamantly, in total agreement as though she understands, but I suspect she's pretending to understand because she fears being subjected to the humiliation of my repeating myself.

At that, Sara draws me in and says, "You are so much fun to be with." Soft kisses.

"That depends on who I'm with," I say scooting Sara toward the center of the bed where we can stretch out and lay down. We lay on our sides facing one another with our respective concubines caressing our backs on either side of us. More deep, wet kisses. I close my eyes and I can feel my girl reaching around and stroking my engorging package with her thin mechanical hands.

The girls are noisy with their little fake moans. Sara redirects all hands from her red birds nest to her milky breasts without breaking lip lock with me. My girl traces a little path of kisses southward until she's right about to give me head. Then Sara breaks our kiss and says, "Let me."

She takes my cock in her hand and strokes it. "Is this okay?"

"Better than okay." I nearly choke on my own pleasure. She proceeds to take the head of my penis in her mouth and nonverbally redirects the other women to play with my nipples, which my girl does, but the unisex one continues caressing Sara's breasts.

Sara is amazing with her mouth. She catches the unisex's hand between her legs, apparently one too many times, because she then grabs the woman's breast and squeezes it hard. The unisex looks shocked and a bit excited at this. She massages Sara's breasts even harder. My girl kisses my chest and neck, but before she reaches my face, Sara cuts in and kisses me square on the mouth. My lips are dry from heavy breathing but moisten quickly.

She says, "Where's that condom?"

"I don't know, I think...." Panic, excitement, thrill break my relaxed trance, and before I know it, Sara has the condom unwrapped and halfway rolled on me. She straddles me and squats on top, while using her hands to usher me into her. She teases at first, tilting her hips back and forth with several slow strokes. She then proceeds to ride me with the rhythm of a rock star.

The girls are thrown back for a moment, watching the intense transition, and then resume their tactile duties. At one point, the unisex woman is sucking Sara's breast while Sara is thrusting herself onto me. I direct my girl to do the same on the other side, and Sara takes the two women by the backs of their heads and presses them against her breasts and growls. The effect is awe-inspiring. She weans both women, leans in close and breathes hard in my ear. She convulses, wildly shuddering and moaning toward a breathtaking orgasm. At least I think it is an orgasm, because I can feel her shuddering throughout my body and throughout my girl's body. After I don't know how long, she collapses. I ask if she's ... but she shushes me.

I try to resume thrusting but she orders, "Don't move."

We melt deeply into silence for a few more moments, at least until the prostitutes grow restless.

Sara lifts her body off mine. I think, at first, she might just be changing positions, but she is making no attempt to continue.

"Mister no finish?" says my girl, looking at my still-raging erection.

"Should I let her finish me off?" I ask Sara.

"No," Sara says flatly. Something's askew, three women

to one man. There's no reason I should be left incomplete.

My frustration dissipates when Sara whispers into my ear, "I'll take care of you later."

"Promise?" I ask.

"I'd love nothing more," she says, standing up and stretching her legs.

"It's okay. No finish for me," I say, warding the prostitutes off my penis. I tip the girls handsomely and leave a small wrinkly bill in the room for the maid.

Despite all my reservations about coming into this place, everyone leaves mostly happy.

By the time we return to the hotel, we're tired from the 2 a.m. taxi ride. Sara packs up her things, while I shower off again.

When I come out, she's naked in bed, pretending to be asleep. As soon I slip in beside her, she disappears under the covers. She lays her head on my hip. I feel her humid breath on my balls as she slides her cool, flat hands over the length of my chest, arms, and thighs. Then her mouth presses gently against my shaft. I feel her curious tongue outlining my head, teasing me, until she takes me in her warm, wet mouth, rhythmically sucking.

She brings me to an edge, and then pauses. She resumes a new stroke, as arousing as the first. When I'm almost there, she changes positions. I'm frustrated, but since it's our first time together, I can't expect her to know how my body operates. When the third wave arrives, and she backs off a bit, I can't help but plead, "Don't stop!"

I've never been one to give directions in bed. Her persistence lifts me into an expansive bright space. Sara swallows, and rests her head to my chest. I run my fingers through her red curls and ask, "You have no idea what you're doing to me, do you?"

She smiles. After a few sweet moments, I feel sadness descend. "What time do you leave tomorrow?"

"In the afternoon, but I haven't gotten all my paperwork in order, so I've got to get up early."

"Where are your tickets?" I inquire.

"In the safe," she says and we are soon both fast asleep.

A Lesson in Non-Attachment

I awake with intense and frightful energy before sunrise. I don't remember my dream, except that it is urgent, like rushing to class late and unprepared for a final exam. I dress, open the safe, and leave the room, not knowing yet what I'm about to do.

When I return, nearly an hour later, I open the blinds. Sara glows in the predawn light. Something about this woman's skin glows in any light. Fully clothed, I lie back in bed and stroke the length of her arm a few times until she wakes.

"You up?" Her voice is groggy.

"Yeah, I couldn't sleep," I say.

"Well, if you close the blinds, it might help."

She presses a pillow in my direction. I push the pillow away from her beautiful eyes and ask, "Would it be too soon for me to tell you I love you?"

"Hmmm." She presses against me and kisses my lips. "If you waited just a few more hours it would be too late."

"And how do you feel about me?"

"Fantastic. I think our connection is magic. In the last seven months, I've met all kinds of people, and ours is by far the most memorable. Granted, I don't sleep with them all."

"So this is just another travel adventure for you?" I ask.

"No, this is magic. It's special, and when we say goodbye our bond will be released, but never gone," she says, now wide-awake.

"You're sure you have to leave?"

"Yes." She sits up. "I'm going to miss you."

"No you won't," I say.

"Of course, I will."

"Not if I come with you," I announce.

Silence.

Her gaze fixed downward into her lap, she speaks slowly. "I don't know if that's a good idea."

"Why not? I called Air India this morning and found out there are still seats left on your flight."

"To India? Are you sure?" she says, clapping her hands.

"Yes. If you want me to, because I'm certain I love you and don't want to lose you."

"You're serious?" She slides out of bed, bare breasts bouncing. "I don't know if love is going to be enough. Falling in love is the easy part. It's fun and feels fabulous, but going on a pilgrimage is a different thing altogether. One has to feel the calling and a certain level of commitment."

"I'm willing to try. We had fun yesterday, didn't we? I meant it when I said I think you're supposed to be my teacher. I could learn a lot from you."

"Last night was sweet and totally basic. What we did was harmless, and whether you know it or not, you had resistance. That's why you fell asleep." After slipping into her yoga pants, she hops back on the bed.

"I was tired," I say.

"And this journey is going to be very tiring. Besides, I'm not your teacher. Spirit is. We will be following a master, who may put you through experiences ten times more confronting than what happened for you last night. We might do absurd things that seem meaningless, and you must stay conscious through the whole process. Tantra is a fucking challenge. Trust me. I don't want you to resent me if you can't handle it."

"How can I resent you? I'm the one who wants to go."

"I don't know if you're ready for this. Hell, I don't know if I'm ready. I have no idea what's in store for me, and I'm scared shitless."

"All the more reason for me to come. I can support you and protect you as we go through it together."

"I don't need protection. I've never needed it before, and I've gotten along fine."

She shuts her eyes and sits silently on the corner of the bed for a moment. "There is something inside me crying out for your presence. I'd love to explore this juicy connection that we've discovered; yet, I don't want you to come for my sake. I only want you there if you're in pursuit of ultimate Truth."

"Look, Sara, I woke up this morning for the first time knowing what I had to do, because if I never got to see you again or listen to your quirky spiritual ideals, my heart would hemorrhage. Unlike you, I don't make fabulous connections all over the globe; I am a lonely and unhappy misfit. I have always been confused, lost in every relationship, looking for something specific, and I never knew what it was until I met you. You're like the part of me I didn't know was missing."

"Our connection is not an accident, this I know." A tear falls from her left eye and trickles down her cheek. "Who am I to turn away this gift?" She wipes her nose and face with the hotel bed sheets. "Do me a favor, though?"

"It depends on what it is," I say.

"Don't blame me when teachings get hard or if you discover things about yourself that you don't like. This work is designed to bring out the Truth, and I can't be responsible for what happens to you."

"Look, Sara, I don't care where the train is taking us. I just want to ride along with you as long as I can. If it turns out not to be my scene, I'll just say, 'It's been fun, this is my stop!' I've only got two weeks anyway, so I'll eventually have to say good-bye."

"And when that time comes, let's not make it a big deal. Let's try to savor every moment we have together, and accept whatever comes next. Do you think we can do that?" she asks.

I draw her into me, holding her face temptingly close to my lips and promise, "Yes, I'll be glad to savor you."

Thus, the journey begins. We knowingly plunge into the land of adversity, austerity, and crazy authoritarianism. I am a little concerned about confronting external challenges, such as typhoid, diarrhea, and leprosy, but I have no idea about the perils of the inward journey that await. There is no preparation for the land of shadow, desire, wrath, resistance, and ultimately, the unknown.

Act II
The Initiation

10 Blind Love Follows Blind Faith

Within seconds of being dropped off at the Bangkok Airport Hotel parking lot, another taxi pulls up, and a Sikh named Miranda jumps out. He's a thin, questionable character, with a turban and long fingernails. He throws both of our bags into the trunk, opens the back door, and ushers us in. At first, I think he is our driver; but after settling in, I see there's an unusually buff Thai guy behind the wheel. Miranda twists around from his shotgun seat and asks if we're excited to go on our trip.

"Yes, I'm so glad you could accommodate our last-minute requests so Salvador can join me," Sara says.

After a full morning of phone calls, failed faxes, and slow e-mails, Miranda is helping us finalize the necessary travel documents.

"Of course, it is much better this way. A young woman shouldn't travel without her husband," the Sikh Says.

"Oh, he's not my husband," she says, squeezing my thigh. "We're just good friends."

"Yes, well, in Thailand that's quite usual, but in India, perhaps it is better to tell people you are married," he says, pulling paperwork from his leather briefcase. "Let's attend to your papers, shall we?"

Sara reaches under her shirt and deep into her money belt to produce the green Brazilian passport. I stack my blue American booklet on top and hand them both over to Miranda. He peels a colorful printed sticker from its shiny backing and slaps it into each passport. "You will have no troubles at the customs office in Chennai. This is official paperwork," he says.

According to Sara, there's a big ethical distinction between buying black market papers and bribing official consulate workers who simply sell the same services underground in half the time, for twice the price.

Miranda meticulously holds each bill I give him up to the sunlight in the windshield to check if it's real. He then asks if we want to change US currency for rupees, promising to give us a great discount, because, of course, he couldn't use his rupees in Thailand.

"Well, what's your rate?" Sara asks.

"What rate do you expect to find there?" he deflects, as he pulls a fat envelope of cash out of his suitcase.

I cut in, "No, thank you."

"But we're going to need them at some point," Sara says.

"I've got travelers checks. I've got us covered."

He points at Sara, "For you, my friend, I can exchange rupees for Brazilian currency, if you like."

"I said no, thank you," I repeat, revealing my mistrust.

"When you're in a foreign country, my friend, you must learn to trust somebody." He snaps his briefcase shut.

"Now, if you like, my cab will take you to the airport." He instructs the driver in Thai, steps out of the car and leans into Sara's window saying, "Don't get into any trouble with the police. Remember: the American consulates don't know where you are."

During the tense seven-minute drive to the departure terminal, Sara admires her new visa and inspects the stamped pages of my passport before handing it back to me. "You've let your hair grow out; I like it better long." She runs her fingers through my thick, shaggy hair and tries to disarm me with an open mouth peck. I tip the driver as we pull up to the airport terminal.

"Here we are at the place where we first met. Isn't it romantic?" she says.

At the airport, we're all business: checking in, checking bags, paying airport tax and passing the security check.

The gate area is swarming with Indian men in business suits and women with colorful saris. It's like a little India, and Sara is in heaven. She's forgotten the whole taxi scene and is playing peek-a-boo with a toddler in her grandmother's lap. Both generations are dripping with gold earrings, bangles, necklaces and anklets. I pan the crowd finding lots of oily hair and red dots on foreheads.

When the boarding announcement is made, old and young rush madly for the plane. I get my first lesson in Indian culture: Personal Space 101. There is none.

The flight attendants wear purple saris with gold trim. I miss the entire oxygen mask and fasten-your-seat-belt routine because I'm busy explaining to Sara my suspicion that Miranda is part of an underground counterfeit operation.

"I'll admit, he was a bit creepy, but I have full confidence that the visas are official."

"I can't help but wonder what the hell we're getting ourselves into."

"That's the beauty of it; there's no way to know," she says.

"I'd like to get a better sense of what exactly I'm following you into," I say, summoning up my courage.

"Number one, you're not following me, because number two: I have no idea where we're going. I'm giving myself over to a higher power, and I will surrender to whatever the ashram is going to be like." She smiles slyly.

"This gets more intriguing by the minute. Are there any rules I need to know about?" I ask.

"The rules are on a need to know basis," she says, trying to hold a straight face.

"Oh, come on."

"Actually, I don't know what they are ... yet."

"And you've been preparing for this journey for over a year?" I ask.

"I wrote Swami-ji from my ashram in Spain, and he wrote back from India saying, 'When you get the calling to go on pilgrimage, leave your ego behind and come be with God.' Finally, last month the calling came, and they told me about their annual pilgrimage, so I rushed around making last-minute travel arrangements. When I asked how to prepare, he said, 'There is no preparation. Bring only cash and toiletries. You will be given clothes befitting a pilgrim when you arrive.'"

"What, do they expect you to travel naked?"

"Isn't it perfect? We're going on a Tantric pilgrimage, and we don't need clothes," she laughs.

The pilot comes over the loudspeaker and announces something in Hindi. The "Fasten Your Seat Belt" sign turns off, and I assume we're now free to roam about the cabin.

I continue, "Aren't you a little concerned for your safety?"

"I have faith."

"Faith in what?" I ask.

"God."

"I was afraid you were going to say that."

"Why are you so afraid of God?" she asks.

"I'm not. I'm afraid of God's followers. Do you realize more people on this planet have died in His name than for perhaps any other cause?"

"That's not true," she argues.

"Want to bet?" I challenge.

"What about old age?" she quips.

"I'm glad you don't gamble."

"I think you're afraid of the unknown." Within the confines of these uncomfortable coach seats she presses her body as close to mine as possible, and places her head on my chest.

"Isn't everybody?" I ask.

"God isn't unknown to everybody."

"I'll tell you what I'm afraid of ... it's this concept that some people know God and others don't, and that somehow makes them better than everyone else, and all the power structures and hierarchy that's built up around the industry of knowing God. I think that's the dangerous mentality that causes war."

Sara doesn't miss a beat. "I agree with that. Spiritual hierarchies can be very dangerous. That is the problem with the Catholic Church. Throughout Brazil, Catholics think that the Pope has the only direct line to God, and that he can judge people as saved or damned. In fact, that's the greatest bastardization of Jesus' teachings: that he is somehow the Son of God and everyone else isn't. That is why I don't want to be your teacher. There are enough followers in the world; I want you to experience Truth for yourself."

"And yet you're willing to follow this Indian Swami-ji. How is guru mentality different than blind faith?"

"It's different. I have a calling. A voice inside me is prompting me to go. Call it intuition or purpose or whatever you want, but it's real, and I'm willing to surrender to it, not because anyone is telling me to, or because I know what will result, but because it comes from a deep place within," she says.

"Well, I can't argue with that."

"No, but you're trying, aren't you?" she smiles.

"As long as you still question what is being taught. I imagine you'll have to listen to whatever he says and ask yourself if it's a rational thing to do."

"You don't get it, do you? This work does not happen in the mind. It cannot be rationalized. That's why they call it

'Crazy Wisdom'; it comes from a higher source."

"Right. Well, I guess it's a good thing that I'm coming with you. Somebody's got to be the voice of reason."

"You didn't sound so reasonable this morning."

"That's because your beauty drives me out of my mind."

I laugh. We both do.

"Okay, so what's the difference between being seduced by a sexy woman and hypnotized by a charismatic spiritual teacher?"

"Nothing at all. They're both totally irrational," I say.

"Oh, look," Sara says, pointing out the window. I squish against her and behold a vast fluffy blanket of clouds carrying us.

After a pause, I admit, "You know, I don't even know what an ashram is."

"Technically an ashram is any place where people do yoga and also sleep, but since we'll be on pilgrimage, we'll be sleeping on the road. We'll be traveling by bus or car or foot ... the ashram becomes the people we're with. They are our spiritual community, or 'Sangha,' as they say in Buddhism. The teacher is Travel itself. That's the real guru, moving through space, so you can see who you are, unclouded by all your stuff."

"Wouldn't you sometimes just crave a place to rest, a place to call home?" I ask.

"I have that place. It's in my body. I check in with it at least once a day. That's yoga," she says.

"Right. You're going to teach me some of that, aren't you?" I ask.

"If you like," she says.

"Sure, that's why I'm here. I want a crash course in everything Eastern. I don't want to be asking a bunch of stupid questions."

"That's the ego that doesn't want to look dumb; but in fact, you have a huge advantage. 'Beginner's mind' means you're not wrapped up like I am, always thinking you know it all. In matters of the spirit, it's best to come empty. Everything you've learned is probably wrong anyway."

Sara spots the stewardess in the aisle and squeals, "Oooh, food!"

We're both starving, having been too busy making travel plans to think of eating breakfast. "False alarm. They're just handing out headphones. What's showing?"

The in-flight magazine features a number of Bollywood films, each with a colorful cast of thousands. The feature presentation is nothing we've ever heard of, but it is described as a huge, epic with gorgeous silk saris, big dance scenes, weddings, and wars. "Do you want to see it?" she asks.

"I think I have enough entertainment right here," I say.

When the stewardess finally brings the food, she glares at my tray table and says, "Sorry, Sir, vegetarians are served first."

After a short, silent prayer, Sara peels the tin lid off her little dinner and offers, "You can share my nan (Indian flat bread) if you like."

She digs her blunt utensils into a delicious-smelling curry with a variety of exotic vegetables. I look around to find everyone else is being served or already eating. The entire plane is full of vegetarians.

By the time my mutton is delivered, I'm so hungry I practically inhale it.

"I hope you enjoyed it. That's the last flesh-food you'll be eating for a while. The pilgrimage will be strictly vegetarian," Sara informs, while the stewardess comes around collecting remains.

"Just as well. I've heard horror stories about people eating rat in India."

I look over to a very pale Indian woman sitting cross-legged in her seat, between two empty seats, unmoving, as if she's in some sort of a deep trance. I point her out to Sara and say, "She looks very spiritual. She must be on some type of special yogic diet."

She has a plate in front of her brimming with something like strange ratatouille.

"Where?" Sara cranes her neck. "Oh. God!" she exclaims, covering her mouth and turning to look out the window.

"What?" I ask.

"She's sick."

"Oh, you mean, that ratatouille didn't quite make it to her barf bag?" I take another look. "I guess she's probably not really in meditation then, is she?"

"Don't stare," Sara says, still looking out the window.

"I can't help it. It's like a compelling episode of Disaster-piece Theatre."

No laughter.

"It sucks to travel alone when you're sick. I know. I've been there," Sara whispers turning her back toward me.

I remind her, "You're not alone anymore."

11 1st Impressions, 2nd Thoughts

After landing, I hurry off the plane into the nearest bathroom. It's labeled 'Refuse.' I regret my decision not to use the blue water bowl on board, which at least offered toilet paper. I manage to relieve myself over a squatter's hole in the wet concrete floor, without soiling any of my clothes, while holding my breath through the whole process.

Afterwards, I find Sara holding my place in the customs line. The overhead monitors periodically display blinking notices, which cause the crowd to rush from one line to another. I turn to the guy standing behind me in a business suit and ask if this line is okay for foreigners.

"All lines go to same place," he says.

"Why did everyone just switch lanes?" I ask.

"For exercise."

"I see," I say. "And do you know the proper time here?" He looks at his watch and says he thinks it's 4:30. That's strange. My watch is set for seven sharp. He double-checks with the guy standing beside him who insists it's 5:30.

"No, no, no, I set my watch on the airplane when the flight attendant made the announcement," the first man says.

"Ah, but my cellular has a satellite clock," the other argues.

"So does mine, it is just not functioning," the first one continues.

I turn to Sara and ask her if she's ever heard of a time change in which there is a half hour difference.

"No, but if there is such a thing, India would be the

89

place for it. Don't worry. We won't be using our watches anymore."

Sara slides by the customs official with a smile and a Namaste, but when it's my turn at the Formica desk, the official suit stops me and pours into every detail. First he checks my passport, then my visa, and when he can't find anything wrong, he looks at the in-flight custom declaration form and says, "Where you staying, sir?"

"Um, I'm coming from Bangkok," I say.

"No, where you stay in India?" he asks.

"Well, I'm going on pilgrimage so...."

He cuts me off. "Name. Address. We need address of hotel where you stay."

"I don't know exactly. I'm staying at an ashram."

He looks over at his associate or supervisor who stops what he's doing, comes over and looks at my papers. "Whose ashram, sir?"

"I don't know what it's called," I say, hoping that playing dumb will do the trick.

"Are you going to Matha Amritanandamayi Math?" He asks with a raised eyebrow.

"What? Oh, yes. Yes, that's it," I say, having no clue what he just asked.

He scribbles something on my paper, tears at the perforated line, staples and stamps. "She's in Kerala. This is long difficult travel for you."

"Yes, I know," I said, and I thank him.

He waves. "Go now," and whispers, "Jai Ma."

Not far beyond customs, we encounter a total zoo of taxi drivers and families and hawkers. Everyone is waving frantically and screaming out to each other. Sara spots a small brown man holding a cardboard box panel scribbled with 'SARASWATI'. He lugs Sara's pack through the parking lot.

"Saraswati, welcome, my sister!" A smiling Dutch

woman in a pure white robe steps out of a big, dirty vehicle and pulls Sara into a hug. They entertain this whole body embrace for an awkwardly long time. "I am Sri Durga," she says, looking over Sara's shoulder. "My master sent me to pick you up and run a few errands before returning to the ashram."

"Let me introduce you to my new husband, Salvador."

"Welcome," she bows to me, just as they do in Thailand. "I didn't realize you were married."

"I'm not, but the Indian customs official said that I should tell everyone that I am."

"Not a bad idea. Is Salvador joining us on pilgrimage?"

"Yes. I wrote the ashram this morning to notify you of our change in plans."

"We seldom get e-mail, only when we come into town." She turns to me with a warm smile. "Anyway, you must be a very advanced soul to be called to pilgrimage on such short notice."

I smile, but keep my mouth shut as we pile into the back seat of the boxy Indian-made utility vehicle called a Tata. Ganapathi, the little brown driver, is fast and furious when we dart past a running stream of hawkers, bikers, bullock carts, goat-herders, and barefoot school kids in uniforms walking along the road. My overall impression after about an hour of driving is that India is colorful, dusty, and chaotic.

At the nucleus of chaos, a technicolor temple towers above all other buildings of Madurai. The driver stops in the middle of the street and drops us off. We follow Sri Durga past the street side vendors selling bangles, sequin-encrusted purses, and pillowcases. We step down into the ruins of an ancient stone temple, which has been converted into a bustling marketplace.

It takes a few moments for my eyes to adjust to see the dark sandstone walls. I behold a huge stone carving of a dark goddess with a hooked sword in one hand and a decapitated head in the other. Draped with a brilliant sari, she wears bright yellow marigolds around her neck. Sri Durga stops, dips her finger into a heap of red powder near the goddess's feet, then smears the powder onto her forehead. After bowing, she turns to us and says, "Saraswati, meet Kali."

Sara gasps, closes her eyes and bows. She stains her forehead in the same fashion as Sri Durga. Afraid of not doing it right, I decide to step back and admire the goddess's fierce face from a distance. I also notice all the local people staring at us as they mill around the building. We hurry after Sri Durga, who rushes past numerous vendors as they thrust various items in our direction and call out: "Sister. Hello, sir. Sir?"

We do our best to ignore everyone until we arrive at a small strip of tailors and clothing vendors. There are about a dozen old, foot-pedaled Singer sewing machines, run by barefoot tailors who bump elbows as they work. This is what I imagine the inside of a sweatshop must look like. Sri Durga chats with the ringleader as though they are old friends. They negotiate price in half English and half Tamil, pulling out two bar stools for Sara and me to sit on.

The barefoot tailors are all working on various stages of decorative umbrellas. We are told it's a special order for a big wedding this weekend. Sri Durga insists that our pilgrim suits be prioritized, " ... so at least they can attend Puja (worship) tonight." The request is received with an ambiguous head bobble, which I'm told doesn't mean yes and doesn't mean no.

A short man with fat fingers steps out from behind his booth to measure my shoulders, my arms, waist, and inseam. While Sara is being measured, several workers bark loudly, causing our tailor to back away, making room for an elder woman to hobble up to Sara and run a tape-measure around her breasts. Sara shoots me a glance, and I shake my head in disbelief of the sexual repression in this country. What a contrast to the freedom of Bangkok.

The vendor nervously propositions Sara, "Madam, would you like to sit down and take a chai?"

Sri Durga jumps in, "No, thanks. It's too hot for chai." Then she gives the tailor measurements for two more pilgrims scheduled to arrive tomorrow.

Outside of the market, filthy young children who try to sell us small-ticket items, fake jewelry, sweets, and hand-made crafts mob us. I don't have any Indian coins to offer.

"Now, you must be hungry. I know a restaurant where you can eat and take a chai," Sri Durga says.

"I thought it was too hot for chai?" replies Sara.

"It's never too hot for chai. I just didn't want to keep that man from finishing our order. He's already very busy, looking for any excuse not to finish his work." She leads us into a clean, bright, air-conditioned restaurant. "This is one of my favorite chai stops in town."

Everyone inside turns to stare. We are the only Westerners in sight. Sri Durga orders for us and warns us that the soap is unsanitary at the big communal sink where we wash our hands. We use bottled water to rinse off enormous banana leafs which are set before us like place mats. A barefoot boy scoops rice and curry directly onto them. Sri Durga reminds us to eat with our right hand. She doesn't have to remind us what the left hand is used for.

During our messy, spicy, but delicious lunch, Sri Durga notices our shoes and asks us if we brought sandals.

"We will be going to many different temples, and because you have to leave your shoes at the entrance, perhaps it's better to wear something that slips on and off easily."

"But these have good ankle support for long walks," I defend, "and have you ever noticed how mosquitoes love to bite ankles? It's like they prefer ankle meat," I joke.

"I brought anti-malaria pills from the clinic. Should I start them?" Sara asks.

"I started mine before I left for Thailand," I say.

"We've never lost a pilgrim to malaria. This is my 7th year on pilgrimage, and if you keep your mind clean, your body will stay healthy as well," she says, with a snippy pride.

For dessert, we drink from little tin cups filled with sweet hot milk and palm sugar. When the bill comes, I reach for my money belt. "Do they take credit cards?" I ask.

"Let me," Sri Durga offers. "I'll take you to the bank after this."

"No, really, I'll put it on my card."

"Do you even know the conversion rate?" she asks.

"No," I admit.

"Well, the total for our food, including dessert, is about the equivalent of 40 US cents each. I think I can afford it. And I'll order a few more bottles of water and snacks for the road. You can pay for my dinner when we come back through town in a few days."

We follow Sri Durga past a number of severely-disfigured beggars and up to the third floor of a marble building. A man in a full military uniform opens the glass doors.

"What is the US exchange rate?" Sri Durga asks the clerk.

I produce several American Express Travelers Checks and lay them on the counter, while Sara irons out several crinkled Euro bills.

I hand the guy my passport and he takes it into the back room to authenticate. The decorated door attendant reenters with a chilled Coca Cola bottle and a straw for each of us. I whisper a reminder for Sara to use the straw for sanitary purposes.

The curious assistant wants to know where we're from and what we do for a living.

I answer him, "I'm a cameraman for a film crew."

He stares at me blankly.

Sara adds, "He makes films, in America."

"An America flim maker!" he explodes, and then repeats it to his friend who has returned with the passport and cash. He exclaims, "You make flims!"

I try to tell him it's pronounced "films," but he insists, "I love American flims!"

"How is your name?" He looks at my passport.

"Sal Levine," I say. He's very excited, repeating it as though I am Tom Cruise. I try to tell him that no one's ever heard of me, but he isn't about to be disappointed.

"I'll look for you in American flims!" the assistant says. "Here's my card. You remember me." He hands me a plain white card with his name on it and shakes my hand.

We step back onto the busy street. Between auto rickshaws, a paraplegic beggar rolls by on a makeshift skateboard. Sri Durga hands him a few rupees. We stop before a tan shoe cobbler who sits with wide-open hips, holding a new shoe steady between his own bare feet while he hammers tiny nails into the leather. His cart is overflowing with freshly-made leather sandals for men and women.

"It's strange they won't eat cow but don't have a problem using the leather for shoes," I marvel.

Sri Durga looks down at her own sandals and defends, "I'm sure there are lots of cows that die of natural causes."

Walking away on about $6 US of new leather, we come across a toothless woman holding an ill-looking baby, swaddled in a fly-infested blanket on her hip. She flaunts a pet monkey that's crawling up her dress. She opens her mouth and outstretches her hand, begging Sara for money. We don't have any small change. Sri Durga tells us not to give money to single mothers. "They end up using their babies to beg. You can buy them food or clothes, but don't give them money."

The woman pulls on my sleeve and points to a nearby

stand with grocery items. She mimes feeding milk to the baby, and then gestures to a can of powdered milk in the store. Sara asks the storekeeper for a can. When he tries to charge her the equivalent of $50 US, Sara slams the can down exclaiming, "It's a scam!"

"They're obviously in it together," I say, ignoring the pleading mother and the shopkeeper as we walk back to the car.

Sri Durga puts kirtan (devotional chanting) on the stereo and sits in meditation while we drive out of town. Sara and I take our posts at opposite windows, spreading out in the back seat. We're wide-eyed, watching the bustling city dissolve into a tropical landscape.

I imagine shooting the scenery with my camera as it whizzes past. Palm trees, rice paddies, oxen pulling hay carts. The rivers are running and everything's in bloom. Apparently, it's been a heavy monsoon season. The roads are devastated with countless potholes. At times, we are bouncing along at two miles an hour, and at other times we are flying at ninety. It seems that every other vehicle is intentionally trying to run us off the road. Periodically, we slow down for a cow to cross.

12 *Not in Kansas Anymore*

Miles outside of nowhere, surrounded by nothing, we turn onto a bumpy path through a forgotten village where goats and chickens scramble out from under our grill. Sri Durga says, "This is where Master Das used to live and work as a potter before he renounced work and went into Samadhi (enlightenment)."

It appears that automobiles are a new and rare sight for the little naked kids who run out of their huts to welcome us. They wave while their mothers or grandmothers stand by smiling. The sun has nearly completed its journey across the sky. The brown skin of the friendly villagers glows in the last of the day's sunlight, or perhaps these people always radiate the warm glow of a simple life.

We rumble over a half mile of eroded terrain and finally arrive at a several acre compound with a number of thatched roof structures.

Sri Durga informs us that we are just in time for satsang (holy service). She shows us to our temporary living quarters and tells us she'll be back with some robes we can borrow until ours are ready. "Can you wash up and be ready for the meditation within a half hour?"

"Of course," Sara says, before I even understand what she's asking of us. We have just traveled around the globe, I have no idea what time it is, here, or in my country of origin, and my body is shutting down at the mere sight of a bed.

The room is stark and utilitarian. A mosquito net hangs from a permanent hook in a bamboo crossbeam above a thin double mattress. I untie the mesh and fumble around with the tangled net. Sara washes her face with water from a tank in the corner of the room where there's also a dirty hole in the ground pretending to be a toilet. I climb under the net and sprawl out on the lumpy mattress.

I watch Sara bathing with baby-wipes in front of me. I'm feeling dirty and disgusting from the dust and diesel fumes, but too tired to do anything about it. I hear a knock and Sara bounds to the door. Sri Durga offers Sara a couple of white robes.

"This one's mine. It should fit you, and this one I borrowed from Prabhu. I hope it fits Salvador."

"Thanks," Sara says.

I whine from the bed, "Do we have to go?"

Sri Durga calls back, "Do what you like. We'll wake you for sunset satsang if you need to rest now."

"We're coming," Sara says, bringing in the robes as Sri Durga hurries off.

"Why don't we take the evening to relax a little instead of rushing off to yoga class?" I suggest.

"Feel free to stay. I won't hold it against you," she says, slipping into her robe.

"All right, give me a moment to put on my dress," I joke.

I splash water on my face and follow her a few hundred feet to an elaborately-adorned meditation hall.

The water does absolutely nothing to prevent me from falling asleep during the twenty-minute silent sitting. Someone rings a wake-up gong, which sends my heart racing. Everyone chants, "Aum...Aum...Aum..."

The second phase of satsang is about 30 minutes of droning devotional song. Strange and redundant tones transport me into the twilight zone. It's an episode wherein a dozen Western bodies dressed in Eastern robes are belting out sounds that I didn't know the human mouth was capable of making. The chanting concludes, and we sit silently for a few moments.

The third phase of the evening is a spiritual lecture led by a fat and uncommonly happy man who is followed into the room by two little Indian boys. He takes his seat at the front of the room. He has a gray/yellow beard and wears orange robes.

The Indian Santa Claus clears his throat, laughs and says, *"Welcome to our newcomers. Formal introductions will be made tomorrow. We have others who are still arriving. Let's start at the beginning, shall we? There are so many texts, with vastly differing ideas about the creation of this universe. How does one know what to believe? Big Bang? Adam and Eve? Time is moving backward? Tantric texts don't even agree, so let's back up before the beginning. Before time, space and causation, there is only Brahman. Brahman is the infinite, absolute reality, beyond all quality or attributes. Brahman is the source of all consciousness.*

"I'm speaking from Vedanta philosophy, because I don't really understand Brahman. To understand anything is to confine it in consciousness, and since Brahman is the infinite, it cannot be comprehended. He is also known to many Tantrikas as Shiva, the whole of the universe in seed form. Brahman as lord Shiva is in ecstatic union with Shakti."

Boom! Swami-ji throws a book on the floor. It scares the shit out of me. *"Let's say that's the Big Bang, the coming together of Mother and Father which produces everything on this worldly plane. He is pure consciousness and space, and she is his polarity. Shakti is dressed in energy and form. She is everything made manifest, even the mind.*

"When Mother dances with Shiva, they are seemingly inseparable. She expands her vibration and encases Shiva in divine union. Thus, he reflects her brilliance. He is a perfect mirror. Just as looking at one's reflection makes it nearly impossible to see the actual mirror, Shiva seems invisible and

inseparable from Shakti. Shakti's infinite creativity has the tendency to obscure his consciousness. This is Maya. It's the illusion that's all around you, everywhere you turn. The pillow you're sitting on, the clothes you're wearing ... it's all Maya.

"And who's experiencing the Maya? You are, with the limited consciousness filtered by your mind. Mind and matter appear to be separate, but they are one, and if you are a spiritual seeker, you'll seek to re-unite with Mother and Father as they are. It's like an eternal game of hide and seek. It is that simple.

"Your objective is to see through the illusion to pure consciousness, to awaken to your true nature, while you are still wrapped in the body of illusion. Got it?

"Another favorite bedtime story for the Tantrika is the one where lord Shiva is dreaming and the whole play of the existence is but his dream, including this very moment. We are all in Shiva's dream. Shiva grew bored of being infinite and alone, so he invented Maya, to keep him engrossed in the divine play of infinite possibilities. Yet, God is not asleep; we are. What happens when we awaken from this dream?

"Do we discover we are not this ego-personality that we thought we were, or is there another dream within the dream? Perhaps the true awakening is into a dreamless sleep?"

Swami-ji stops to take a drink of water. *"It's fun stuff, this creation theory. Some Tantrikas believe that all of creation happens within the body. The Bible says that God created the world in seven days. When Shakti enters the body in the form of kundalini, she is dressed as the serpent energy that slips in from the crown and slithers past the third eye, throat, heart, solar plexus, sex, and coils up to rest at the sacral plexus. On the seventh day, having completed her creation, she rests, dormant at the base of the spine. She stays there as long as you are fascinated by the physical. When your life force is resting at your lowest chakra, you cannot experience your oneness with all.*

"We could have fun with this one. In order to realize your true nature, the serpent energy must rise again to unite with Shiva. Lady Kundalini must find her way up your spine, as though it were a tree trunk, and she must slither up through the crown chakra to merge with absolute consciousness. Perhaps that's the forbidden fruit.

"Of course this is just one of our pet theories. Don't mistake any of it for Truth. For that matter, don't take too seriously anything said here, unless you experience it directly. That is the only true source of knowledge. Got it?"

He nods to one of his little Indian helpers who jumps to his feet and retrieves a burning ghee lamp. Swami-ji holds it above the group. Everyone, myself included, scoops smoke from the flame, and washes it over their face.

The other boy retrieves a basket from the altar and hands it to Swami-ji, who holds it up and says a few words in Sanskrit. He then extracts a piece of Prasad (sacred dessert) and gives it back to the boy, who walks around serving everyone a sugary, flaky pastry. I don't know what it's made from, but it's delicious. When the basket comes back around to Swami-ji, he takes a second piece, spilling crumbs into his beard.

Finally, we are instructed to maintain our silence throughout the evening. *"Take the teachings with us into a deep and sudden sleep,"* which is exactly what I do.

13 Ejaculation Control or Mind Control?

The pre-dawn call to meditation is an obnoxious, ongoing bell and singsong chant: "Om Namo Shivaya sunrise satsang. Om Namo Shivaya sunrise satsang!"

Sara is already up, standing stark naked on the other side of the mosquito net. She nudges me and invites me to help her in the shower.

"How can I resist?" I ask, as I widen the exit to the mosquito net and follow her to the bathroom.

"All you have to do is hold the purified water up here, so I can wash my yoni, okay?"

I take the 10-gallon jug off the stand, elevate one leg on the ridge of the shower, and prop it on my knee.

"Like this?" I ask.

"A little closer," she says, pressing the little spicket for water. "Usually I don't mind taking showers with the well water, but redheads are prone to yeast infections, and I don't want an itchy yoni on my first day."

"Yeah, that's no fun," I say, mesmerized by her rubbing a washcloth between her soft, white thighs. She catches me staring and smiles.

After finishing she says, "I'll thank you later." I set the water jug back on the stand as she wraps herself in a towel.

In the meditation hall, Sri Durga talks on meditation:

"We practice stilling the mind, consistently, progressively, so that we eventually can conquer it. The preparation of meditation is nothing more than a technique, a simple discipline to prepare us for more magic later. In Tantra, as you know, we are not trying to transcend the body. Instead, we are creating space for God to descend into us.

"So think of this practice as a way to prepare the house and make it nice for an honorable guest to visit. Perhaps if your house is calm and beautiful, your guest will like to stay a little longer.

"You see, in the beginning, the mind is very messy. The thoughts are bouncing around. In fact, Swami-ji says that thoughts are like monkeys swinging from tree to tree, and for the uninitiated, the monkey is drunk and stung by a scorpion. Meditation is the way to tame the monkey mind."

She reviews the basic instructions for meditation. I straighten my spine, relax my body and focus on my breath. It's impossible to act like an 'independent, impartial observer.' Just by paying attention to my breath, it seems to deepen. When my body is relaxed enough, we are told to begin mantra meditation in silent repetition, but since I've not been initiated, I'm instructed to hear: 'So' on the inhale. 'Hum' on the exhale. 'So' in, 'Hum' out. 'So, Hum.'

What does 'So-Hum' mean?

'So,' am I doing it right? 'Hum.' How long are we going to do it?

'So,' Sara's naked in the shower. 'Hum.' When are we going to make love again?

'So,' what was Swami-ji's talk about last night?

'So-Hum.' My knees hurt.

'So-Hum.' What is Mother going to say when she hears I quit my job?

'So-Hum.' I need to remember to ask for a letter of recommendation from my former boss.

'So-Hum.' I'm in Hawaii, filming a political rally. Al Gore is speaking on the environmental crisis. Now, there's a man who's got something to say. Why am I thinking about Al Gore?

'So-Hum.' I should be thinking about David Koresh. I can't believe he convinced all the mothers in his cult to agree to let their 12-year-old daughters sleep with him. Oh, I almost forgot to think 'So-Hum.'

My thinking spins out in a zillion other directions, random thoughts. I don't even see that I'm lost in thought until Sri Durga strikes the gong, and the whole room breaks out into resonating "Aum...Aum...Aum...."

Afterward, both my legs feel like rubber pincushions, and the chanting proves no less inane than the night before.

When the chanting stops, we continue sitting in silence as Swami-ji enters looking even happier than last night. *"No lecture today, only darshan,"* he says, and devotees line up for a ritualized Q&A session. They sit before him, one at a time, pouring out their hearts' concerns, while he dispenses advice.

I find this more interesting than the Jerry Springer show. Everyone else simply sits around in a contemplative stupor.

Amrita, a voluptuous Aussie woman with dirty blond hair, sits before Swami-ji and admits she can't stop thinking about her ex-boyfriend.

Swami-ji asks, *"Is the love a mutual flow of give and take, or is it one-sided?"*

"In bed, it was mutual. Master, it was the best sex I ever had." Her voice cracks.

"And it will remain that way. It is the best you are capable of, as long as you feel you are searching, longing, and thirsting for a lost experience, but you can experience so much more if you are willing to let that go, become whole, and open yourself to the experience of true merging in the moment. What is the nature of your relationship now?"

"You know, Master, we're on again, off again."

"And in this moment, you are off again, correct?" Swami-ji says.

"Well, technically, yes," Amrita answers.

"There's nothing technical about it. If you're off, you are off, and you must now kill him. Burn his body, release his spirit, mourn his death, and get on with your life, metaphorically speaking. Do you understand?"

"But it's so painful," she argues.

"I didn't say it would be easy. Do you think the monk who finds Buddha in the road is going to find it easy to kill him?"

"No," says Amrita.

"No, but how else can that monk continue on his path toward liberation. You got it?" Swami-ji concludes.

"Yes." With that, she smiles, bows at his feet, and goes to the back of the room to meditate.

After a few more questions from various devotees, Sara takes her place on stage and bows at Swami-ji's feet.

"My problem, Swami-ji, is that I think I know too much. I've been very blessed on the path of yoga, but I'm very new to it."

"Who says you're new to it?" Swami-ji asks.

"I only started five years ago...," she says.

"In this life," Swami-ji corrects.

"Yes, in this life, and everyone tells me I'm such a good teacher that it's hard for me to empty myself and start over as a student. Even today, when Sri Durga gave instructions for meditation, I witnessed my ego satisfied with my meditation practice, telling myself I'm already there," Sara says.

"Now, before you came to me, did you think you knew what I would say?"

"Well, I had an idea."

"Good. I want you to sit and contemplate the teaching you imagined I would give." He nods at her.

Sara bows down to his feet, and then sits out of earshot to resume her meditation.

No one moves forward. Swami-ji glances in my direction, and I feel a hand on my back gently pushing me forward. Without knowing who touched me, I awkwardly find myself before Swami-ji's feet.

I admit, "I don't know what I'm supposed to say or do here."

"You're welcome to let go of the notion that you're supposed to say or do anything," Swami-ji says.

"That's good," I say, opening the door to an awkward silence.

"I called you up because you're sharing the same bed as Saraswati, are you not?"

"I am."

"Do you feel that's in your highest good?" he asks.

"Absolutely," I blurt.

"Would you be willing to sleep separately?"

"Probably not," I say defensively.

"So then do you know what I'm going to ask of you?"

"Oh, please don't," I say, thinking I'm doomed if he asks us to refrain from sex.

"When you make love, do your best not to ejaculate, at least not yet. Can you do that Salvador?"

"So we can still have sex?" I say, somewhat intrigued by the challenge, "I guess I can try it."

"Can you guess why I'm asking you to save your seed?" he asks.

"Because you don't want me to have too much fun?" I ask, sending him into a fit of belly chuckles.

"That's good," he says, composing himself. *"Preserving the chi is an ancient practice that comes from Tibetan and Taoist doctors who've studied the effects of male ejaculation for centuries. They have exhaustive documentation on how it taxes the kidneys and depletes the entire body of vital energy. The prana (energy) preserved in the seed is the*

very fuel that it takes to break through to enlightenment. By retaining it, you'll not only have more energy to devote toward the divine realm, but you'll live much longer. Think about it, what happens immediately after ejaculation?"

When I realize it is not a rhetorical question, I debate between the smartass answer, "I smoke a cigarette," and the truth. I offer the latter, "I usually fall asleep."

"Do you know why that is?" Swami-ji tests.

"Because I'm tired."

"Or, because of your resistance to the subtle realm that is only available in a state of sheer ecstasy. Orgasm is an egoless state, and if you are too strongly identified with your ego, you will not be able to stay conscious during the vulnerable and expansive state afterward."

"Not to worry, we will train you. We will condition your mind and body to sustain greater states of love. Eventually, you'll distinguish between subtle orgasms and the gross physical ejaculation. In time, your orgasms will propel you to the space between Heaven and Earth. In the beginning, however, you must simply practice preserving the chi."

He pauses to scratch his beard, and then adds, *"The immediate benefit is that you will connect with Saraswati on a whole new level. She will find you more attentive and attractive than ever before. Every moment becomes a gift, because you are no longer building towards one grand moment that's more important than any other moment. Got it?"*

"Fair enough," I say, bowing.

How hard can it be? After all, he's a nice enough old guy and I like the advice he's given everyone else.

14 Sign on the Dotted Line

At the close of satsang, Swami-ji offers to give Sara and me an orientation. We wait for him on the steps of the meditation hall while he attends to several students. The rest of the disciples introduce themselves as they file past us on the way out. I have a hard time pronouncing all the Sanskrit names, let alone memorizing them, except for this one bloke, a burned-out British hippy with a full head of gray hair pulled back in a ponytail.

"It's cool, man. Just call me Bud," he says. "So you brought a bit of the Americas here, did you?"

It occurs to me that Brazil is considered part of America. "Yeah, where are you from?" I ask.

"The great English isle. Bath to be specific," Bud says.

"What brings you to India?" I ask.

"The Beatles. What else?"

"But I thought the Beatles were from Liverpool," I say.

"Yes, of course, but the source of all their inspiration is here, in India. In fact, between all four Beatles, 32 songs were channeled while they were here studying transcendental meditation. So if I'm ever truly going to make it as a legendary rock star, I reckon this is the place to be," he offers playfully.

"Well, then, carry on." Bud walks off with a nod and a grin.

The jolly Swami-ji proudly tours us around, explaining how the buildings are raised to protect from flooding during monsoon season, and the walls are made of dried and compressed cow dung.

"No shit!" I say, but he corrects me.

"In India, it's 'Holy shit.' Even their dung is considered very auspicious for construction."

In the distance stands a rocky hill that is being mined for granite. It looks and sounds like a volcano, with its periodic dynamite explosions that rattle the ground and produce subsequent plumes of smoke and dust.

The dormitory is a long hall with cheap metal-frame bunks, a folding card table, and some chairs. I ask how many disciples stay there, but he corrects me. "Devotees. We're not disciples. We're practitioners of devotion, and I believe at the moment there are half a dozen."

We pass through several smelly shade structures made to protect the animals: two cows; three goats; one skinny, long-nosed puppy; and numerous chickens being chased around by two horny roosters. We walk past a beautiful tree in the corner of the property. Sara rushes forward, bows to it with one hand on the trunk, as though feeling its warmth. That's when I notice bells and ribbons tied to it.

Swami-ji says, "There is an Amma in this tree. I had a Vastu Shastra expert (Indian Feng Shui consultant) survey the land, and he confirmed it."

"What's an Amma?" I ask.

"Divine Mother," Swami-ji says. "Like Amma Chi."

"Oh, right," I say, pretending to understand.

Swami-ji escorts us into the most finished room on the property. It has a high ceiling, a low bed, and a huge tub. He calls it a "Tantric boudoir" and uses it for private initiations, Pujas, and healing sessions. Silk fabrics drape the walls, and incense burns on the altar. Though beautiful, it strikes me as a strange contrast to the austerity of the rest of the ashram.

The final stop brings us to a little office with a library nook. Sri Durga prepares our registration papers behind a reception desk while Swami-ji sinks into a loveseat with a dog-eared copy of *The Tantra Sutras* in hand. We browse shelves of English books on every area of metaphysics: angels, auras, astral travel, chakras, channeling, cleansing, devils, demons, Dakas, Dakinis, divination, groups, and ghosts, just to name a few. Sri Durga produces two stacks of papers and beckons us to sign the admission agreements.

Sara flips to the last page and signs, just like that. She returns to the library, plops herself at the feet of Swami-ji's loveseat and continues reading a book called *The Ultimate Guide to Teaching Tantra*. I stand at the front counter, reviewing the contract, but frustrated by the poor translation. I blurt, "What's the bottom line?"

Sri Durga clears her throat, puts on reading glasses and thumbs through the text. "I don't remember everything, but mostly they're liability release forms and agreements of confidentiality, copyright laws, no promises, no guarantees, we reserve the right to deny you service, etc. It's basically written to protect the ashram and preserve the secrecy of the teachings."

"But of course," I say, partially in jest, but she's not smiling. "You know, I'll be returning to Los Angeles in about ten days. I'm starting film school at USC."

"So I've heard. We don't usually take residence for less than two months, but my master feels your situation is unique, so we're willing to take a ten-day agreement, and extend it if you like."

"I appreciate that," I say.

"We do ask that you pay the minimum two-month donation, even if you'll be staying for less."

After Sri Durga calculates the currency exchange, I discover that a two-month stay is the same price I'd pay if I were to make a lifetime commitment to this joint. Coincidentally, it's also about approximately the same price I'd pay to spend the rest of my vacation in some touristy hotel on the beaches of Thailand.

Don't Drink the Punch

I pull out the company plastic and silently thank my unfaithful boss as Sri Durga presses it against carbon paper.

"Now, let's see what we have," Swami-ji barks from across the room. I take my contract over to him. He squints at the cover page. "Ah, Levine. I didn't think you were born a Salvador. Are your parents both Jewish?" he asks.

"Yes, sir," I answer.

"And are they still alive?" he asks, setting the contracts onto the loveseat beside him.

"No, my father passed away several years ago," I say.

"Sit down for a moment, Salvador."

I position myself on the floor next to Sara.

"It's good for a man to live without concern for what his father thinks."

"Yes, but it's my mother I've always been worried about."

From the folds of his robe, he produces a little note pad. "Where were you born?"

"San Bernardino. That's in Southern California."

"Do you know the exact time of your birth?"

"The exact time? I'm not positive, but I think it's something like 7:30 in the morning," I guess.

"Can we find out for sure?"

"If you want to e-mail Mother."

"That can be arranged. Now what questions do you have for me?"

After a moment, I ask, "Are their certain rules that we should be aware of? I don't want to be disrespectful by not knowing the ashram etiquette."

"Ah, my boy," he laughs and turns to Sara. "Where did you find this one?" He turns back to me, and says, "The minute we make rules, we'd have to find ways to break them. Everything around here tends to find its natural rhythm and order. That's how we continue to grow. People play out their natural duties, and we often make decisions by consensus. The most important thing is that you take responsibility for yourself. Trust your body to find the Truth. You'll be asked to do a great number of things, and everything is optional. Now, other than leaving your mother's e-mail address with Sri Durga, do you have anything else you need to complete, any unfinished business outside of the ashram?"

"My ticket's pretty flexible for my flight home. It's an open-jaw, but I do need to call them and book my flight back when we know what airport I'll be departing from. Is that the kind of unfinished business you're referring to?"

"Is there anything else?"

"I don't think so," I say, though I feel like it's a trick question.

"Well, think about it. It's vital that you complete all karmic cycles before we depart. We want you to separate from the outside world as much as possible. You have the advantage of not being able to understand the local language, but you can still be influenced by the thoughts of lesser vibrations around you. You see, words and thoughts are like energy forms. They have a way of jumping from person to person. People think they originate their thoughts, but really, they just receive them, and they pass them around, like a disease. That's why yogis live in caves and ashrams, to stay away from the outside world. We purify our minds and surround ourselves with only the highest vibration. Now the most important thing for you and Sara is to observe the ego. Got it?"

"Got it," Sara says, with her hands to her heart.

I hesitate to ask, "Uh, exactly, what does that mean?"

"Let me remind you that you are equipped with the most powerful supercomputer on the planet. Your mind is faster than any NASA rocket ship. The least bit of stimulation is likely to send it off into orbit. There is nothing that can defeat its power unless you learn to use it against itself, to trick the mind with the mind.

"Start by observing the mind. Notice how it operates. In time, we will learn other tools, but right now, simply witness it, as though you are playing a very intense game of cat and mouse. Watch the thoughts. Remove yourself enough to notice what it's doing. Detach yourself from all judgments. Experience whatever your body is doing, and at the same time, observe it as objectively as possible.

"I think you get it. Now, let's go fill the belly."

While stepping out of the library, Sara takes my hand. It feels small and cool in mine. It is silent reassurance that I've made the right decision. Being with her feels so damn right.

15 Ashram Life

After collectively blessing the food, we line up with metal bowls and cups and each receive a scoop of yellow vegetarian stuff. We all sit together cross-legged on several tatami mats on the floor outside. The food is warm, nourishing, and mild.

It feels like I'm back at Camp Hess Kramer, a Jewish Summer program in Malibu. I "observe" the same sort of happiness that came with being away from my parents as a kid. Only the mess hall here is quiet. There is no silverware clinking against plates or squawking school kids. Also, this camp has stranger counselors and temple rituals than I remember.

Near the end of our meal, someone pours piping hot chai into our cups. One sip and I burn my tongue. My eyes narrow, my teeth clench, and I feel a flush of anger. I hear Swami-ji's voice in my head instructing me to "observe the anger." The burning sensation fades into numbness on my tongue.

Heads turn curiously to gaze up the street. I hear an engine and crunching gravel before a taxi drives into sight and pulls through the fenced entrance of the ashram. Sri Durga runs up to greet a yellow cab, complete with an advertisement of some Ayervedic face cream on the door.

A beautiful Indian couple emerges from the taxi while the cabby unloads a ridiculous amount of luggage. The man is a clean-cut, middle age Indian guy in western clothing, who I overhear is named Raj. His bride, Jivana, appears to be under twenty. She is wearing an expensive silk sari. She looks tired and a bit overwhelmed. I imagine that's what I looked like when we first arrived. Though I feel for her, I'm oddly relieved about not being the newcomers anymore.

The scrawny driver struggles with their luggage. While watching the young couple being led into their room, Amrita leans over to gossip with Sara. I overhear her saying, "Their marriage was arranged. The man tried, at first, to find someone he loved, but could not. His mother hired a Vedic astrologer to find a Hindi woman that would make a good match. She's a bit young, but her family has money, and the astrologer declared they have near perfect compatibility. The problem is they have no sexual chemistry, so he insisted that she come here to learn about her sensuality."

Sri Durga assigns people to do karma yoga (self-less service). She appoints Sara to clean up in the kitchen and me to help Prabhu in the field.

I find Prabhu in the little mango grove behind the kitchen. He throws a hoe into my hand and leads me through the brush to where a path used to be. Prabhu is a healthy, broad-chested man with dark dreadlocks. I hear a hint of a South American accent, but he's too busy observing his ego to reveal himself much in conversation. I'm guessing he's about my age, early 40s.

The recent rains watered the weeds and created erosion so that the path is but imaginary now. I hoe at one end of the path and he at the other, presumably to prevent my talking to him. I rhythmically pluck weeds and find myself fantasizing about Sara again. I imagine going for a little walk with her into the fields. I'd love to show her all these exotic plants and bugs, especially these fat, black worms with orange racing stripes. I wonder if they will turn into the big, black butterflies I see fluttering around.

I notice the rhythm of last night's chanting looping through my head: Om Shrim Reem Kreem Glum Gum

Ganapata-yeah Namaha.

At first, I'm excited about being able to remember it, and then I'm not able to stop it. Om Shrim Reem Kreem Glum Gum Ganapata-yeah Namaha.

I wonder to what extent the chanting is used to brainwash people.

From the corner of my eye, I catch a long blue plume of a peacock as it dashes into the nearby brush. Wow. Maybe the chanting summoned him. I walk over to Prabhu to ask if he saw it, and notice he's chanting the same mantra I am.

Prabhu smiles and shrugs as if he saw it but simply can't be bothered. A half an hour later when my path meets his, he nods and gestures for me to walk along the trail that we've just renovated. We follow it all the way out to a huge water well made of stone with crumbling mortar. As we approach, something scurries in with a splash. Prabhu chucks a pebble in its direction, which pulls me out of my daydream.

"Why are you here?" Prabhu asks in a deep, scratchy voice. He clears his throat.

"What do you mean? Here on Earth?" I try to kid.

"On pilgrimage." The scratchiness has gone away.

"I'm not really sure; it just seemed like the thing to do," I say. He looks away with no comment.

"Why are you here?" I ask.

"I am finished with the illusion, and I'm ready for liberation."

"I see," I lie.

"Do you love her?" he asks, despite himself.

"Sara?" I ask, and have to think about it. "I didn't know love could be like this. It like a thin layer of something has lifted; I see colors now, where the world was black and white; and when I'm with her, I think, 'this is what it means to be alive.' When she was going to leave me to come here, it would've been like letting life walk out on me."

He asks, "So, are you here for her, or to taste the animating force within her?"

"I haven't thought about it," I say honestly.

"Well, think about it," he says, nodding good-bye while he walks away.

I look down into the well and notice two little black eyes peeking out above the mossy water, a turtle. I smile to myself, stretch my sore arms, and then follow the freshly-hoed path back to the mango grove. I feel proud of the trail we created. Unlike digital film editing, manual labor feels good to my body. I notice lightness in my being as I continue to my dorm.

Back at the room, I find Sara sprawled on the floor in her undergarments. She dries her wet hair in a streak of sunlight that splashes through the northwest-facing window.

"I like the afternoon program at this Tantric retreat center," I flirt, staring at her uninhibited beauty.

"The water's still on if you want to shower," she says and resumes rubbing moisturizer into her soft white skin.

"Can I ravish your body after I wash up?" I ask, leaning down to kiss her.

"You can ravish me now if you like," she says.

"I've been playing in the mud for the last two hours."

"It's just Mother Earth."

"Let me at least rinse off," I say.

She instructs me on how to run the shower and how to shut it off, which includes turning a valve on the outside water tower. After a cold rinse, I return to find Sara has taken off her panties and is lying naked on her belly, reading *Autobiography of a Yogi*. I lay my towel down beside her and position my head close to her perfectly rounded bottom. She turns over, props herself up and rests my head on her lap. Her red pubic hairs look brassy in the sunlight.

"Can I read to you?" she asks.

"Sure," I say, moving my face closer to her pussy and inhale deeply. She smells like woman, delicious. Not easily following the riddle-like words of Paramhansa Yogananda, I finger her fine curls, and she doesn't stop me. A few more inhales. She smells like the ocean: sweet, salty air. She squirms and presses her pubic bone against my chin.

"Want to try something?" she asks, setting the book aside.

"With you?" I query, kissing her nether-lips.

"Yes, with me." She guides my head away from her sex. "Sit up like you're in meditation and put your spine against my spine."

I do. "Is this going to hurt?" I tease.

"No, just breathe."

"Just breathe?"

"Yeah." She exhales.

"Well, what's the alternative?"

"What do you mean?" she asks.

"If I don't breathe, I die. Right?" I feel her back vibrating while she laughs.

Composing herself, she says, "Observe the breath. Just notice what happens at the top of each breath and at the bottom."

Immediately my breathing deepens. I smell the mango cream lotion on her skin. I feel the air in my throat and my lungs expand. When they deflate, it feels like I'm melting. They fill again, so naturally, stretching the space between my ribs. My lungs inflate, not only in front of me but also behind me, where my back rests against hers.

One breath blends into the next, without a top or a bottom. I catch myself holding my breath, looking for the top. I release and empty out, but there is still air in me. It's like a false bottom. I tune into what her body is doing, and our bodies fall into sync. Everything is effortless.

After I don't know how long, the room feels funny. Everything is bright. The walls breathe along with us. Moved by a force of magnetism, I turn to embrace her. Pulling her in, I wordlessly lower her onto her side and bring my body as close to her as possible. Our embrace has a life of its own. Our chemistry takes over. I slide inside her easily, and she gasps with pleasure. She bears down, contracting around me. I try to remember Swami-ji's advice, but it's as though she's milking me with her tight, hot pussy. She shudders, arches her back, and quivers out of control.

Between breaths, she looks straight at me and into me with rapture on her face, sending me to the point of no return.

"Wait!" I say, pulling out and trying without success to stop the imminent. I'm flooding with love and falling through space. At the bottom of my landing, I smell sweet salt on her neck, and she smiles through a tangle of curls.

"I didn't want to cum," I say.

She smiles. "Well, I'm glad you did."

"But Swami-ji told me not to," I tell her.

"Did he say don't ejaculate, or don't orgasm?" she poses.

"I don't know." I admit. "What's the difference?"

"It doesn't matter, now, he's not here," she whispers between kisses.

"That's a good thing," I say, and use the corner of my towel to sop my juices off her taught belly.

There is a knock at the door. Uh-oh. Now we're really in trouble.

16 Initiation by Fire

"Just a minute," Sara calls.

I spring up, pull my shorts off the top of my suitcase, throw them on, and poke my head out the door.

It's Sri Durga, smiling knowingly and holding a tall stack of robes on each of her outstretched arms.

"These are his," she says transferring one pile onto one of my arms, "and these are hers," doing the same on the other arm. "There's one orange robe in there for each of you. You'll be guided on when to wear it. Satsang starts a half hour after dinner." She pauses and looks around. "It smells like sex in here. I suggest you take another shower."

"So sex is dirty now, is it?" Sara says, walking up to the door, naked, to receive her new robes.

Sri Durga smiles, not afraid to stare at Sara's body. "We're doing a special Agni Puja (fire ceremony) tonight, to initiate you before the pilgrimage. It's best to be wearing your own energy for this."

I thank her and shut the door.

Outside, the last of the sun dips behind the horizon. I'm surprised to find that there are a number of barefoot villagers trekking down the road toward the meditation hall. They are also dressed in white and wearing beads.

The hall is packed with twice as many people as last night. Even Ganapathi, the driver, and farm workers are dressed for the occasion.

Swami-ji sits on a deer-hide rug. He is behind a huge

121

metal wok, situated on a cinder block structure called an Agni pit.

The two little boys from last night circumambulate the room. One holds a bowl of burning incense while the other wafts it with a peacock feather.

The anticipation is palpable. Amrita, to my right, is swaying side to side, and Prabhu, in the corner, appears to be twitching. Swami-ji lights a ghee lamp and dedicates the light to purify our hearts for the journey upon which we're about to embark.

He passes it in the direction of the newlyweds who sit directly across from us. He welcomes them and congratulates them for recognizing their commitment to each other is a deep commitment to the divine.

I look over at the petrified young bride, Jivana, whose eyes are glued to the floor. The groom smiles broadly and nods at Swami-ji. Sri Durga begins a call and response chant, and though I do not understand a word, the energy is impressive.

Swami-ji lights several white camphor beads on a bronze platter and dumps them with a flamboyant gesture into the pit. Poof! The ti pi of kindling is aflame. We continue singing over the snaps and crackles.

At the end of every phrase, we exclaim: "Swa-ha!" (Ashes!) Swami-ji flings something flammable into the fire. "Swa-ha! We chant mantra to honor the Sun. Swa-ha! Moon. Swa-ha! Mars. Swa-ha! Mercury. Swa-ha! Saturn. Swa-ha! Venus. Swa-ha! And other heavenly bodies. Swa-ha! Swa-ha! Swa-ha!"

With each mantra, we throw a different offering: chickpeas, lentils, and black-eyed beans. Saturn is my favorite, because the sesame seeds crackle and pop in the fire.

I haven't been around an open fire in years. I'd forgotten how mesmerizing it is. Memories of beach parties by the Santa Monica pier flood back to me: girls, marshmallows, and beer. That's a sort of a California ritual, isn't it?

Swami-ji's fearlessness hypnotizes me. He reaches directly into the fire to situate the offerings: bananas, coconuts, and fresh, fragrant jasmine buds, which bloom and curl up in the raging flames. I do notice a suspicious lack of hair on his forearms and fingers. As the night progresses, my eyes become bleary from the smoke. Everyone's eyes are bloodshot, but they're warm and happy.

My lids grow heavy and the smoke is thick in my lungs. The chanting drones and becomes muffled. I'm in that misty place between memory and fantasy. I look across the heat waves, and the faces on the devotees across from me melt and twist with song. When I turn back to the fire, there's a strange puff of blue-black smoke that lingers in the air above the fire. It doesn't blow away. I do a double take, but it's still there.

Swami-ji reaches his hairless hand right through the cloud to make an offering, and it has no affect on the smoky emanation. The music grows louder, and other people squint their eyes as the strange cloud morphs into the outline of an elephant.

I whisper, "Look," to Sara, and she nods in agreement. Two big ears and a trunk off to the right begin to appear. What I do not tell her is that I think it looked at me, not just a smoke formation pointed toward me, but a little elephant that saw me. Maybe I'm high from the smoke and the sage. The chanting picks up before it softens again on the last several stanzas.

At the end of the ceremony, we call out, "Swaha," "Swaha," "Swaha," throwing the last bit of every offering into the sacrificial fire. Swami-ji holds up the original lamp, and the villagers scoop smoke, covering their eyes, and they file out. Parents carry their sleeping children back to the village.

Once all of the visitors leave, Swami-ji hands two small bowls of powder to Sri Durga. He stands, stretches out, and sits back into his normal throne in front of the altar.

All attention is on Swami-ji as he reads in Sanskrit. He translates into English a teaching about absolving the guilt that separates us from Source.

He reminds me of our old Rabbi, preaching to the synagogue during the high holidays. A line forms in front of him. I'm transported back to the one time I went with a friend to Catholic mass, and everyone lined up to receive the "body of Christ" under their tongue. In this ritual, instead of giving out wafers, Swami-ji marks each devotee's forehead with white ash, yellow sandalwood paste, and red cum-cum powder. This is our initiation.

Swami-ji also gives each pilgrim a personalized prayer. He speaks, and they repeat aloud, but I'm so warm and slaphappy from the fire ceremony, I can't make much sense of it.

At the point of initiation, I repeat something to the effect of: *"Oh, adorable Lord, forgive me for everything I've done knowingly or unknowingly against you. I vow to pursue ultimate Truth, despite whatever illusions present themselves, no matter how convincing. Free me from ignorance, greed, lust, guilt, or anything that separates me from you. I am your servant, your knight, your pawn, your lover, your king. I am yours beyond definition, forever seeking the source of our union."*

Swami-ji's ring finger is cool and penetrating when it presses between my eyebrows. It seems to linger internally, eternally or infernally. He transmits several syllables into my mind, and I find that they repeat themselves over and over in my head.

At the end of the ceremony, he says to everyone, *"I trust you have gotten whatever you were ready to get tonight."*

He lifts a burning lamp, and we draw more light into our eyes.

Sara and I drag our sleepy bodies back to the bedroom.

She steps out of her robes, and I say, "I'm glad I'm not the only one who made a mess of my new threads."

We both smell like sage and burnt beans and whatever the hell else we threw in there.

Plopping onto the bed she says, "The smoke is purifying. I want to stay in this sweet energy all night. I want to marinate in it until the morning." She's serious, so we tuck our naked and smoky bodies under the bed sheets and mosquito mesh.

Her skin feels soft and cool under my long strokes. I slide my hand down from her neck, shoulder, ribs, hip, and bottom. Her entire body is pressed against mine for warmth. I continue stroking in one direction, for the sheer pleasure of how the length of her body feels under my hand. It's like petting a cat, mindless, cozy, and reassuring. I don't expect the cat to pet back.

17 Magic Bus

At 4:30 a.m. we awake to a cacophony of Indian music blaring and echoing around the compound while roosters and dogs cry out in competition. Apocalyptic end-time images flash across the screen of my mind. I leap out of bed and look out the window into the pre-dawn darkness.

"What the hell is that?" I ask.

Sara sits up and shakes her head. "I think it's someone's idea of music."

From the bathroom window, I ascertain that the sound amplified from a nearby village, a mile away. I give up trying to recognize order or rhythm, because of the poor speaker quality, static, and echo distortion.

"And so someone, somewhere is enjoying this, while the rest of us have to suffer?" I ask.

"Maybe it's a wedding," she says, her breasts revealed. Her legs tangled in bed sheets beneath a gossamer canopy like a mythical princess. I maneuver myself back into bed beside her and she slides her cool flat hand against my chest and lower abdomen.

"They decide wedding times based on astrology, not out of courtesy to the neighbors." She kisses me, and her hand discovers my excitement for her. "So did you have any sexy dreams last night?"

"I was too tired," I admit.

"Really? I thought you were trying to play with me as I was drifting off."

"Don't blame me for fondling you in your sleep; I can't

keep my hands off you."

"Tell me about one of your sexual fantasies," she says, stroking me.

"What do you mean? Like when I fantasize about fucking you forcefully?" I ask.

"Yeah?" She says, putting her mouth around my nipple and sucking. "Where?"

"In your pussy." She bites. "I mean, yoni."

"Where? I mean, where are we?" she asks and slides her head across my chest to suck the other nipple.

"Oh, uh, anywhere. I don't care. I just see your creamy skin and breasts and legs spread. You asked for a fantasy. That's what I fantasize about."

"Yeah, but that's easy. You can have that any day."

"Really?" I ask, with rising energy. "What if I want it today?"

I take one of her wrists and pin it down to the bed while I roll over on top of her. She wiggles, and I pin the other one down. "How about if I want that every day?"

"Oh! Mmmmm," she manages through her surprise. I press my lips against hers, feeling her melt under my weight.

"Why don't you tell me about your fantasies?" I encourage.

"Well, I sometimes fantasize about being fucked forcefully in some strange ashram in exotic India."

She lifts her head and kisses me deeply.

I gather her elbows closer in order to hold both of her wrists behind her head with my left hand. "Are yogis allowed to say, 'fucking'?"

"I'm sorry, I mean engaging in divine union," she laughs.

"That's better." I say positioning myself between her legs and command, "Now spread 'em." She does.

"Wider." She straddles her legs so wide they touch

either side of the bed. "Good. Now you know what I do to naughty yogi's who use words like 'fucking'."

"Oh, Master, what do you do?" She teases.

I use my left hand to spread her outer lips and stroke my fingers hard against her wet inner lips. Her breathing quickens. I press my cock into the crease between her inner thigh and her slippery slit, and she moans. "Oh, please."

"Please what?"

"Please, more," she says, and I stroke myself with her juices, poking the head of my cock only an inch into her.

She lifts her hips, writhing and wanting. "Please, please."

I continue to tease, and she becomes more active and accurate with her upward thrusts. The rhythm takes over, like something external, moving through me, and I pass it onto her with each thrust.

"Ah. Ah. Ah. Ah...," she says with each exhale; then, "Tell me when you're about to cum, and I'll stop you," she whispers.

As soon as I'm at the crest of my pleasure I say, "OK stop." She freezes, then reaches around and presses her finger into my perineum. She's breathing. I'm breathing. Neither of us is moving, and it feels good to be encased in her.

Before I lose my erection, we resume our pleasurable groove. She thrashes around with uncontrollable pleasure, I'm sure she's coming, and before I come, I try to think of other things, but alas, I'm swept under. I shudder, roll my eyes back, and afterwards she covers me with kisses.

I ask her, "How was your orgasm?"

"I didn't," she whispers.

"I was sure I felt your muscles, you know."

"It was an incredible experience, but it was not an orgasm, per se," she says.

"Oh, man; I'm sorry," I say.

"It was exciting to be ravished by you," she comforts me, but I feel totally let down, or like I let her down. I came too fast.

Sara insists she's not attached. "We are practicing new things; we can try it again soon."

We hold each other in silence until the bell ringer is chirping his song: "Om Namo Shivaya, Morning Satsang!"

We step out into the brisk morning and fall into stride with other white-clad bodies moving toward the meditation hall. I think my major accomplishment will be to catch up on my sleep during meditation without letting on. I awake to hear the following words in Swami-ji's voice:

"Now that you've been initiated by fire, your lessons will become increasingly challenging. You will transcend every test only to the degree that you remember who you are."

I open my eyes to find Swami-ji still meditating. He lifts his lids and half-smiles at me before going back under.

By the end of meditation, my kneecaps feel like they're going to pop off and roll away. I join in on the "aums" and feel a little less anxious during the chanting. Did I imagine Swami-ji speaking? Did he see me and smile, or did I imagine that too? After chanting, Swami-ji launches into a little lecture:

"Your success in this pilgrimage is in direct proportion to the clarity of your intention. We suggest one intention above all: intend to directly experience the divine in this incarnation. That is liberation, Samadhi, Moksha, Self-realization, enlightenment, nirvana. Call it whatever you want. In my experience, it's the only thing worth intending for.

"And the path to attainment is the same as with mastering any craft: practice, practice, and practice. That paves the runway, and then, one day, the practice is complete, and your body-mind will lift into flight. This is why we practice, every sunrise and every sunset, transcending the ego and

staying open to Truth.

"*To deepen your practice, you must observe Mauna (Silence) unless you're guided to speak. This means, no leaking one's energy with idle talk. Avoid all eye contact and non-verbal communication except when we are in ritual. Pilgrimage is a deeply personal journey into the Self. You do not need to share your experiences with anyone else in order to validate it. If you leak energy with conversation, you will not have the necessary energy to reach enlightenment, especially since most conversation is about the past or the future, which activates the mind. Refrain from speaking about anything other than what's alive in you in this very moment. Besides, if you are busy talking, you will not hear the master when he speaks.*

"*Of course, if you are assigned a task that requires speaking, feel free to speak on the task at hand, or if you have questions of me, but with fellow devotees, it's not necessary. I know I've been lax on this before, as my personality has a strong preference for talking, but I encourage you to do as I say, not as I do.*

"*There are several other logistics that will help ensure our success on this journey. Stay together at all times. We will be traveling at a rapid pace. We must be discrete about our spiritual practices. Most local Indians are not ready for these teachings, thus we are misunderstood and even feared. Don't let that infiltrate your faith. We will be going to various temples and perhaps even visiting other teachers. Don't be distracted by their empty rituals. Remember, your commitment is to Truth. Do exactly as you are guided to do.*

"*Most importantly, everything is your teacher. Don't be attached to where you think your next teachings should come from.*" Swami-ji shows many teeth. "*Any questions?*"

I pretend I don't have a million.

"Good then, we leave after brunch. Pack only the essentials: three white robes, one orange one, toiletries, money, and necessary papers.

Sara justifies packing a huge bag of baby wipes that she bought in Bangkok and her dog-eared copy of *Autobiography of a Yogi* by saying, "They're all necessary papers."

We put our essentials together in her duffle bag and leave the rest in my roller bag.

After brunch, we wash the dishes and counters, sweep the floors, and clean the grounds.

Within two hours, the bus is packed with everybody's luggage strapped to the roof. It's unlike any vehicle I've ever been on. Our driver, Ganapathi, seems honored to be working for a spiritual cause, but doesn't speak a lick of English.

Swami-ji climbs onto a thin mattress with tie-died sheets which is rigged into the back of the bus. He insists the bed is not just for his comfort; but for the duration of the pilgrimage, it's for anyone who falls sick, needs a rest, or wants to make love.

Bud holds up his chai and says, "I hereby dub this vehicle the Magic Bus." Sara stifles a laugh when I give him a high five. That old 60's song is now permanently lodged in my brain.

Ganapathi tests the shocks on the bumpy half-mile road through the village. The villagers all come out to see us off. It's not just the children this time. The toothless grandparents lean out of their huts, and the men stop working in the fields to wave and wish us luck on our pilgrimage.

Act III
The Pilgrimage

18 Ganesha Governs the Root

We're rumbling along a half-paved, half-pothole-ridden road, honking at every car we pass. Ganapathi darts from one near-death encounter to another without even breaking a sweat. Despite all known laws of physics, the Magic Bus appears to shape-shift, squeezing into impossible spaces to accommodate our survival.

Every couple of hours someone shouts, "Pee break," and we pull over by the nearest bush or tree so the women can find a semi-concealed area to squat, hidden from the local bikers and goat herders.

We men are not so shy; we pee in open sight, as is the tradition along Indian roads. Still, I'm surprised when Swami-ji pulls his penis out from under his orange robes to piss on the street without a shred of shame. He doesn't even bother turning his back to the oncoming traffic.

I watch through the window as we pass picturesque stretches of land with all kinds of paddies, plantations, and palm trees. The suntanned children in the passing villages are often naked, chasing rubber tires down the street with sticks, while their teenaged mothers burden huge workloads upon their heads.

Around sunset, we pull into the best-lit, most well-attended and highest quality vegetarian restaurant we can find, which isn't saying much, considering the standards of the shantytowns from which we have to choose. We parade past the main dining hall through the glass doors at the back of the restaurant. People don't even pretend not to stare at us, the

Westerners wearing white. An elderly holy man cups his hands at his heart and says, "Jai Krishna," while bobbling his head. I smile and move out of his way.

Our group occupies almost the entire back room. I ask Swami-ji if there are a lot of Hari Krishna's in this area. He laughs and says, "Not likely. When they see a bunch of Westerners on pilgrimage, they naturally assume we are Hari Krishnas. I let them assume whatever they want, because if I tell them we are Tantrikas, they might not serve us; in fact they'd most likely kick us out."

"Why's that?" I ask.

"Tantra is like devil worship to them. The Hindu priests call it witchcraft. All they know is it involves sex, alcohol, and human sacrifice. Isn't that right, Jivana?"

"I do not know, Swami-ji. Is that what it involves?" Jivana says, looking up from her banana leaf, while a hunchbacked woman doles out rice.

"Raj, what would Jivana's mother say if she found out you were studying Tantra?"

"She would hang herself, that is, after she had me shot."

"See," Swami-ji says, massaging his rice into a rainbow of different curries.

"Tantra is feared for two reasons: first, because it is so powerful, and the social class system could not afford to allow people to realize the Truth; and second, because of the sex."

Swami-ji roles a clump of rice into a ball and pops it into his mouth before he continues. "You see, Tantra predates Hinduism. It was widely practiced in villages and tribes before organized religion. At that time it was mostly Goddess worship."

Raj says, "That's why we've come to you. We cannot find these teachings anywhere else in India."

Prabhu interrupts, "Excuse me, Swami-ji, is this a discussion, or are we still in Mauna?"

Kamala Devi

"Well, it is sunset. Why not make this your lecture for the evening? Or if you prefer, we can eat in silence and discourse later."

I, for one, am relieved not to be driving in silence, but Prabhu frowns on talking while eating, so we shut up and slurp our spicy food.

I order more rice and fan my face from all the fire, to which Swami-ji says, "At the ashram, we use recipes that are more satvik (pure). Chili and spice make the mind active and you become distracted from meditation. When on pilgrimage, however, I let you eat spicy, because I have no control over the sanitary conditions of the kitchen and the spice kills germs."

Swami-ji takes the bill to the overstaffed counter. While they stamp, staple, and check the bill in triplicate, I stare at the posters on the walls. There is one framed picture of Lakshmi (Goddess of fortune), one of Saraswati (Goddess of wisdom), and then some guru I don't recognize (founding father of restaurant?).

Each deity in a poster has colorful powder plastered not only on their foreheads but on their hands and feet as well. On our way out, I notice a little metal statue of Ganesha (Elephant God) by a bowl of cum-cum powder, where workers can pray to him and stain their forehead before starting work each day.

Driving through the darkness, I decide God must've endowed our driver with more cones and rods than the rest of the human race, because he stares endlessly into blinding oncoming lights, without blinking. Reflection-less bikers appear inches before our grill. The drivers in oncoming traffic often turn their high beams down until they're just in front of us, and then they flash their brights right into our eyes with a loud honk as they pass.

Out of respect for the holy bovine, Ganapathi often dims his lights when he sees the red-eye reflection of a cow sitting on the side of the road. To sum it up, driving in South

India is one narrowly-avoided head-on collision after another.

Swami-ji finally says to me, "One can either get an ulcer watching the road or get some sleep."

Ironically, when I close my eyes, the death-defying swerving feels soothing, like a rocking cradle, especially when Sara's relaxed arms hold me in a sleepy embrace. Her presence makes even the uncomfortable vinyl-covered springs feel like home.

At sunrise, we pull over onto a dirt shoulder for meditation, or to fall back asleep, as in my case. After three "aums" comes the chanting, during which Bud teaches numerous Slokas (verses of Sanskrit scripture) in praise of lord Ganesha.

Afterward, with Swami-ji's encouragement, Bud continues to speak with an uncharacteristic knowledge and authority. Swami-ji offers Bud his stool in the front of the bus so he can give the lecture. Bud becomes animated, as though he is telling a joke.

"You know how Ganesha became the remover of obstacles? Every child throughout India can tell you about the God with the elephant head. It's simple. Shiva was away at battle, and our Divine Mother Shakti wanted some privacy to take a bath, so out of dirt she fashioned a son. She breathed life into him, because she is the creative force in the universe, and she can make anything she wants. Then, she asked her son to guard her bathhouse. He was not to let anyone in, no matter what, but he was no match for Shiva, who came home from battle and wanted to be with his wife. That's when he..." Bud does the international sign-language gesture for slicing someone's head off, and then limply replaces his arm by his side.

"Needless to say, Shakti was very upset to find her son slain, so Shiva sent his army to bring back the head of the first

sleeping animal that was facing the North. When they returned with the head of a young elephant, Shiva put the head back on the boy's body and bestowed him with a special boone. He declared that everyone who wants success in any new project can achieve it if they first pray to Ganesha. We will now go to a sacred Ganesha temple to ask for his blessing as we begin our pilgrimage. You are to pray for him to remove any obstacles to your attaining Nirvana. Got it?"

Our driver navigates through the countryside, and within 15 minutes we appear in the midst of another loud, chaotic town, with a towering temple that spans an entire city block.

Swami-ji says, "Remove your shoes and leave them in the bus. Stay together. Follow Bud, and be open to his transmissions."

We walk the dirt path, past a number of postcard and souvenir venders. There are people of all ages begging outside the temple. Inside, the floors are worn smooth, polished by the bare feet of millions of pilgrims over the centuries. There's an old woman with a deformed arm making an elaborate mandala (circular model of the cosmos) on the ground with different-colored sands.

"See, Ganesha is made of earth. The elephant is totally grounded, and your mission is to let Ganesha ground you. Open your root. Get connected to Mother Earth. Feel what you've got going on down there, not just between your legs, but also at the base of the spine. I don't mean to think about what happens in your head. Let that go. Feel from way down there while we walk."

Sara lines up right behind Bud, placing her bare feet in his very footsteps. Sri Durga brings up the end, right behind me. We arrive outside an enclosed shrine and are instructed to sit on the earth and wait for Bud to return.

"Hey," I whisper to Sri Durga.

"What is it?" she asks in half tone.

"What's with Bud? Isn't he supposed to be silent like us? Why's he doing all the talking?"

"He's not. The master is. He's just speaking through Bud's body."

Sara reaches over to take my hand and says, "Remember, I told you our master left his body over ten years ago?"

"But I thought Swami-ji did the channeling," I say.

Sri Durga explains, "He did, for the first few years, and then there came a point during one of the pilgrimages when the master felt that Swami-ji's teachings had begun to stagnate, so the only way to teach Swami-ji new things was to move through the mind-body complex of other devotees. I was the first one to channel after Swami-ji, but now there's no telling who will be the best vibrational match for the master to come through."

"No shit? Are you serious?" I ask.

"Dead serious," she says, slapping me on the thigh.

"So, Swami-ji is no longer our teacher?" I ask.

"He's a student like you and me, and he's our translator and tour guide, in charge of our health and safety. So if you have any questions, feel free to ask either of us."

"Got it," I say.

Bud returns to announce, *"We'll now allow a Brahmin priest to do a Puja for us. Stay present, without thinking about anything. Let go of your mind."*

All the devotees file into this larger shrine, tended by a massive Brahmin, wearing a white dhoti (traditional wrap) tied around his waist like a Sumo wrestler. He has a white string hanging diagonally across his torso from one shoulder, and wears a number of ashen stripes on his bare chest, neck, and arms. The baby-faced priest lights up at the sight of our grand entrance. In broken English, he tells us the history of how the wooden sculpture was made out of one huge tree.

While he talks, fondness rushes my system. I can't tell if it's for Ganesha or his elephant-like devotee. Swami-ji places a folded bill on the donation tray, which prompts the priest to chant on our behalf. He barks a fast singsong in Sanskrit, like an auctioneer, while throwing flowers and powders at the statue's feet. He concludes by touching each of us between the eyebrows with cum-cum powder. Bud scoops smoke off the priest's lamp, sweeping it over his body to cleanse himself.

We follow Bud while he circumambulates the deity three times, placing his hand on the back of the statue each time while chanting, *"Aum Gum Ganapata-yea Namaha."*

The priest is pleased by our practice. I think he assumes we belong to some kind of cult, and then it occurs to me that his assumption would be accurate. When I place my hand on the back of the statue, the muscles in my lower back begin to spasm. Sri Durga's cool hand on my shoulder gently encourages me to move on. I open my eyes to find everyone has already left the building.

We step back and sit on the ground leaning back against the wall at the perimeter of the little temple. In my mind's eye, a huge dark door opens to let in light. Ganesha is a doorway. I wonder what that means. After some time of feeling warm sunlight on my face, Bud resumes his teachings.

"It seems impossible that a human could survive with the head of an elephant, and do you know how Ganesha gets around? On a little rat. That's right, this bastard child was made from dirt, has an elephant head, and rides around on a little rat, and, in order to have success in anything spiritual, you have to pray to him. Does that make any sense to you? I hope not, because it's not supposed to make sense. If you're committed to this spiritual path, the first thing you have to do is let go of having everything make sense all the time.

"Let's say that you were Ganesha and you were given

this job of protecting your mother, and so no one's going to get to her without getting a piece of you first. So the only way for Shiva and Shakti to come together is for your daddy to cut off your head. Since their cosmic connection represents the ultimate cosmic union, your losing your head is a small sacrifice to pay for this scale of liberation.

"*Besides that, what you become is even better. You see, Ganesha is part human, part animal, part God. Have you ever looked at an elephant up close? The trunk is like a great, big, prehensile lingam, and the mouth represents a perfect yoni. Ganesha is part male, part female.*

"*If you believe in Ganesha, it means you're willing to accept the impossible. It's a way to acknowledge the magical and delve into the mystical. Know what I mean? From here on out, it's a dead man's party, so leave your ego and mind at the door. Where we're going, you don't need them, but you can pick them back up on the way out, if you want.*"

We exit from the same door we came in, each bending to touch the earth at the temple entrance in reverent gratitude. We pile back into the Magic Bus and ride to a local hotel which is attached to a vegetarian restaurant.

That night, after Sara curls up against me and falls asleep with her head on my chest, I look up at the leak-stained ceiling in the dingy hotel, and chuckle at the concept of Ganesha as God. Here I am, on pilgrimage with a bunch of spiritual freaks, following a disembodied dead guy and praying to Dumbo.

In my amusement, I drift off on a lumpy mattress to the sound of bloodthirsty mosquitoes buzzing around a drippy faucet. I sleep soundly, without even a premonition about the disorienting, life-altering, death-defying experience that is soon to unfold.

19 Nazi Health Clinic

Bud's silver ponytail looks debonair against the orange robe he's now wearing. He's grown more comfortable using his arms when he channels. If it weren't for his humorous, passionate teaching style, I might've been disappointed with the dark, faded, and often-crude sculptures that are enshrined within the various local Hindu temples we visit.

Though admission into Hindu Temples is forbidden, even illegal for Westerners, we seem to bypass guards and priests by Bud's grace. We follow his inspired steps, clockwise through the carved pillars. Each temple displays unique art and statuary surrounding the inner sanctum. At the centre of every exotic temple is the garbha griha (womb chamber), where the main deity resides. Bud demonstrates deep emotional resonance to the significance of every statue.

When he bows at the feet of a deity, I often worry that he's going to kiss and embrace them. There is such love and reverence in his eyes when he speaks that Sara and Amrita often find themselves in tears. We stop to meditate before various venerated deities.

Meditation in the temple is qualitatively different from meditation on the bus or in the hotel rooms. Ironically, temples are anything but quiet. There are fast-talking priests, crying babies, and beggars with drums or bugles. At the very least, there's the constant "tink-tink" of ankle bells worn by every woman above the age of two. Despite the distractions, I find my concentration strong and thoughts clear.

143

Don't Drink the Punch

Once we happen upon a lively Puja to the bronze statue of Goddess Durga. A crowd of Indian pilgrims gathers around the shrine to watch as two priests shower Durga with offerings. She sits tall on the back of a lion, holding various weapons in each of her ten hands. One priest stands on a pedestal while the other priest hands him buckets of milk, honey, fresh fruit, nectar, and coconut milk which he pours down her fierce and curvy body. An ear-splitting brass bell rings continuously until the ultimate moment when they rinse her with buckets of purified water.

At the conclusion, the bell-ringer gathers up a pail from Goddess Durga's feet which collects the liquid overflow from the Goddess's body, and he splashes the messy fluid over everyone in the crowd. The cool spray tingles on my cheek. People place their hands together to receive from the priest, who doles out a drink of Goddess juice. Sara pushes herself closer, receiving some liquid, holds it to her mouth, then dries her hands by wiping them through her hair and down over her breasts before walking away.

I see her blissful smile and do the same. The juice is gritty pink in color and tastes like brick. I take my spot on the floor against the wall and pretend to meditate while secretly praying I don't contract dysentery, cholera, or parasites.

That evening, my appetite is non-existent. The mild touch of diarrhea I've been tolerating since my arrival in this God-forsaken land has ballooned to full, explosive proportions. Throughout the night, I alternate between being too hot for covers and shivering in a puddle of my own clammy sweat. Sara rubs my feet and brings me cool towels dipped in purified water, but this only makes me feel guilty for keeping her awake.

"I'm just going to rest and gather my strength for tomorrow," I croak, after the call to morning satsang.

"Be sure to drink a lot of fluids," she says, kissing me

and setting a water bottle within reach.

On the first couple days, I'm glad to be excused from the repetition of sunrise/sunset satsangs, which take place on the rooftop or in Swami-ji's suite; but after being incapacitated in bed for the whole day, I actually miss and appreciate the addictive nature of the master's teachings.

On the third day, I bundle up and go with Sara to satsang. At the end of Bud's enlightened rant, he holds darshan. I go first, because of my condition. I tell him I think drinking holy water from the Durga Puja made me sick, but he insists it's spiritually impossible for the nectar of a Goddess to have done anything but purify me.

He looks at me as though he is a doctor trying to diagnose his subject. *"Perhaps the teachings are putting you through purification. Truth is like medicine, and sometimes, when the body has resistance, it has to purge first. In their Peyote or Ayawasca journeys, the Native Americans often purge before they journey to new territory. Trust the process. Your stuff has got to come up, to come out, especially in the root chakra. See, Lady Kundalini is clearing through your base, and that's powerful stuff.*

"When energy rises and hits a block in the body, it's like, 'Bam!' The body doesn't budge at first, but light will find a way. Whether back pain, blindness or impotence, it happens to all of us in different ways. In fact, that's the very nature of illness: resistance to Truth.

"What do you think happens when you try to run high voltage through a dense body with bad habits? It's simple electricity. There's too much amperage through low wattage wires. You've got to ground the energy. That's what this is. That's why we go barefoot into these temples and bow to the feet of the deity. The entire pilgrimage is designed to help you handle higher and more subtle levels of energy. You're slowly aligning with your God-force. Soon you'll tap into the part of

you that is already whole. Here, sit tall. Close your eyes...."

He presses his ring finger through my congested forehead into a tiny point in deep space. That's the last thing I remember before waking up in a puddle of sweat in my hotel bed a few hours later.

My body still aches. My head still hurts. My nose still runs. Sara impresses me with her devotion. She brings cum-cum back from the temple and anoints my forehead, bows at my feet, and even gives me Reiki treatments. She suggests I visit a doctor, but I tell myself I'm getting better. I think I'll be back to my old self in no time.

At night, she reassures me that we'll make passionate monkey love when I'm better. It's nice to hear, but doesn't help the brief, achy, burpy, fear-filled sleep I snag between frequent trips to the toilet.

My dreams are unnerving images of deep-sea fishing in wild open waters where I am wrestling, fighting, struggling to pull in a huge fish, like Moby Dick. He is bigger than I can handle, bigger than my little boat.

One day, when everyone is away at sunrise satsang, I figure someone must have called for a local doctor, because I wake up to find a huge Indian guy in a yellow robe sitting at the foot of my bed. I can hardly keep my eyes open to see what he looks like. I feel his heavy hand on my forehead, and he asks me what I want. He speaks in perfect English, without a trace of accent. He actually sounds like ... I know this sounds strange, but if my voice weren't so sick ... he'd sound just like me.

I say, "I want to feel better."

"Is that all?" he asks, as though he's expecting a more enlightened answer like "Truth" or "Buddhahood." As though he has the power to grant me whatever I want.

I say, "What do you mean?"

"What's your heart's desire?" he inquires.

"I want to be with Sara," I say.

"Ah. On this, stay clear."

I am not sure if he meant I should stay clear about my heart's desire or steer clear of Sara.

"What do you mean?"

"If you do not satisfy this desire before you leave, you will be incomplete. You will have to come back again, and it will be even more difficult. Get clear now, and remember what you came here for." With that, he is gone.

After a few moments of groggily trying to piece together his riddle, Sara rushes in. She flicks the light switch, bows, and kisses my feet as she's taken to doing since I've been sick. Then asks how I'm feeling.

"Uh, I had the weirdest dream," I manage to say through a dry throat.

"What was it about?" she asks.

I reach for my empty water bottle, "Hold on. I need some water."

I sit up.

"I'll get it," she says.

"No, I've got to get up anyway," I tell her.

I steady myself against her and kiss her head just above her ear, on my way to the bathroom.

"How was satsang?" I ask, while relieving myself.

She tells me, while I struggle to open a new bottle of water. I tip my head back to take a drink, and I hear, "Thunk! Crack!"

"Salvador, did you slip?"

I'm propped up against a broken fiberglass sink, sitting on the cold tile floor.

"Huh?" I ask, realizing I had passed out. "I'm okay," I say, finding a little blood on the back of my head where I hit the counter. "Good thing it wasn't a wrought iron sink."

"Come on, we're taking you to a health clinic," she says, helping me stand.

Swami-ji packs up all the pilgrims. I wrap myself in a hotel blanket and we ride the Magic Bus to the nearest hospital to satisfy my desperate need of medical attention. The massive two-story cinder block building looks as if it could double for a Nazi death camp. Iron bars cover the windows, barbed wire fortifies the perimeter, and the walls are garishly painted with five-foot swastikas.

Sara helps me hobble up the stairs to the reception counter. Swami-ji comes along to translate, but the nurse at the front desk speaks near-perfect English. She hands me a 3x5 card and asks me to write my name and my father's full name. I write, "Sal Levine" and "Lawrence Levine," and I am instructed to sit in the waiting room.

Sara inspects the painted swastikas on the walls. Swami-ji says, "They are sacred Indian symbols from ancient times, way before Histler took them and bastardized them."

"Histler? You said Histler. You mean Hitler?" I ask.

"Yes; anyway, they represent eternity. He loved iconography. He was an artist, a brilliant mind gone astray."

"More like an evil mind," I say.

"Beware of thinking anyone is evil. That's an absolute term. It's a judgment. You don't want to close your doors on truth because you've passed judgments. You're here to push beyond all concepts of good and bad, wrong or right."

A nurse comes in and sticks a thermometer under my tongue. Sara points at framed photographs on the walls, which contain a graphic portrayal of various surgeries in progress. Within one frame, there are amputations of leprosy, removal of breast tumors, and treatment of elephantitis. At first, my stomach turns, and I judge the display as grotesque; but after some contemplation, I grasp that these photos are like diplomas, displayed in an effort to instill confidence in the mind of the waiting patient. A simple certificate of the doctor's education would have no meaning for an illiterate lower cast person, whereas graphic proof of their experience in the operating room is far more impressive.

Sara supports me into a semi-private consultation room where I sit on a springy metal cot. A young, fast-moving female doctor, who's unconcerned with tongue depressors or blood pressure pumps, comes in and greets us. After itemizing my symptoms: fever, chills, headache, body ache, insomnia, and fatigue, she asks if I'm having difficulty urinating. Without waiting for the answer, she orders the nurse to take a blood sample.

Before I know it, there's a needle in my elbow crease drawing thick red life force out of my arm. That's when Swami-ji appears in the doorway and negotiates an additional HIV test.

The doctor reaches into her desk drawer and pulls out a plastic package. She unwraps a kit that looks like a mini pregnancy test. She gives me a simple finger prick and tells me to wait ten minutes. Upon witnessing this fast, new HIV-screening technology, Swami-ji sends Sara to the bus to bring everyone in for the same procedure. Bundled up in my hotel blanket, I sit back on my wire frame cot and watch each member of our group come in to get pricked, taped, and ushered to the waiting room, holding a number that corresponds to their test.

It's a comic display of human individuality: Swami-ji cracks jokes to the nurse in her language; Sara is grateful; Bud is impressed; Amrita cries; Raj is somewhat shifty; Jivana, dutiful; Prabhu, reaction-less; and the poor driver, Ganapathi, looks shocked and overwhelmed, as if someone forgot to tell him why he was coming in to the room.

The Sangha is relieved when every test comes back negative, except mine. I have malaria.

The doctor returns saying, "I'm surprised you've gone this long and are still doing so well. Malaria can cause kidney failure, coma, and, in extreme cases, death. I'm prescribing basic Malarone, four times per day for three days, and an antibiotic two times per day for your respiratory congestion. There's also a multivitamin that's high in iron; but if you are not vegetarian, you must be sure to eat meat."

Swami-ji interjects, "We are on pilgrimage. That is not a possibility."

"Okay, okay. At least eat more fatty substances, like dahl, lentil, and sweet-cakes, more food in general. The food in America is much fattier than our food. In your condition, you need the energy." I nod and smile at the fond similarity between this Indian doctor and my Jewish grandmother. Is this kind of compulsive nurturing a universal feminine trait, or does she somehow know I am Jewish and missing Mother?

"What I don't understand is, how could I get malaria, if I've been taking anti-malarial pills religiously since before I left home," I say.

"How do your bowels evacuate?" the doctor inquires.

"Pardon me?"

"Your elimination?" she says.

"Oh, you mean, Delhi Belly? Yeah, that's standard," I laugh.

"Then you've been expelling the medicine every day, and the pills do you no good," she explains. "I'll prescribe charcoal to help the diarrhea. I recommend you check into the hospital upstairs, where my nurse can hook you up to an I.V."

"That is also not possible," Swami-ji says.

"Okay, okay. The nurse will be down in a moment," the doctor says and rushes out.

"Why not?" I ask Swami-ji.

"Health standards aren't the same here as in the States. You're likely to catch something worse than malaria upstairs."

"Oh," I say. Looking at the dried bloodstain splattered on the floor, I decide not to argue.

The nurse comes back and hands me a clear I.V. bag, which I take with my right hand, and then she asks for my other arm. Without further instructions, she pokes a huge needle into the top of my hand, hooks up the I.V., tapes it down, and then demonstrates how to hold the bag up with my right hand.

"Great. So, how long do I have to do this?" I ask.

"Until empty," the nurse says.

After filling the four prescriptions, the final bill comes to $7.30 US. That includes the doctor's visit, the I.V., and all ten HIV tests.

That night, I'm relieved of most symptoms, except, of course, my incurable love for Sara. I sit beside her during sunset satsang. I've also grown quite fond of Bud, especially when he's tapped into something. I'm not sure what it is that he's tapped into, but I'm disappointed to find that he's talking less and less lately.

In his last speech he says, *"Enlightenment is a mind-blowing trap, man. A paradox, where there is a vast expansion in which one realizes their connection to the whole of existence, and yet, all of existence is unaware of you, because you don't really exist...."* He trails off, muttering something about not being able to share it or explain it because, *"Ultimately, all words only point in the direction of the object, but the object appears to move upon the pointing."*

Bud is thus content to sit silently and contemplate the moving object of his meditation, while Swami-ji fills in the lecture by reading from Tantric texts.

Afterward, I remind Swami-ji that I have only a couple days before I have to depart for Bangkok from one of the major cities.

Bud takes the opportunity to blurt out, *"There is something for us to experience in Goa."* Laughing hysterically, he adds, *"But is Goa ready for us?"* That's one of the last things he says before shutting up for good.

20 Snake Charming

Sara's thrilled to discover that Goa is an old Portuguese colony, like Sao Paulo, her hometown. My first impression of Goa is that it is a haven for hippies. At least that's how it appears from the mattress in the back of the Magic Bus, where I'm curled up with my stolen hotel blanket. My stomach is still doing somersaults from the Malarone, sweet cakes, and diesel fumes, when we pull into a gas station.

Swami-ji cranes his neck at the window and calls to a freckle-faced Scandinavian woman in a bikini top who's gassing up a fluorescent pink scooter. Her dreadlocked boyfriend with a fuzzy hat and matching jacket says, "Jai Bhagwan."

"Jai Bhagwan," Swami-ji laughs. "Where do we catch the ferry?"

"No more ferry, man. They built a bridge. Just keep heading down this highway, and you'll get to the other side."

"Brilliant," Swami-ji smiles and gives a one-handed Namaste as we board the bus.

After crossing a beautiful but polluted body of water, we whirl past all kinds of interesting shops. Colorful tapestries and tee shirts, tie-dye handbags, and beach towels are displayed from lush, tropical coconut trees in banana fields.

Before sunset, we pull into a big parking lot overlooking the beach to meditate. Meditation feels nice for the first time. I find it more relaxing than boring. Well, it was a little boring.

Who am I kidding? The last ten minutes were

unbearably boring, but some of the chanting is now sounding familiar, and the fresh salt air frees me from the grips of nausea.

For dinner, we follow Amrita down a narrow trail made by tourists on the eroded cliff. We walk through a cave-like entrance with a mosaic of seashells past an open-air bar to a patio built into the cliff. There are pillows on the floor for chairs and tree stumps and large toadstools for tables.

We wash our hands with foamy soap at the oversized iron sink fixed to the base of a willow tree. Nora Jones is playing over the loudspeaker. Amrita sings along while we are seated. She looks radiant. I've always seen her as attractive, but there's something extra special about her today. She positions herself in lotus in the seat next to Swami-ji. She is in the corner of the patio with her back to the beach, projecting her voice as though in a music video: "*Come away with me....*"

I smile to myself thinking that "The red pill makes you taller, the blue pill makes you small," would be more appropriate lyrics considering the *Alice in Wonderland* surroundings.

An oversized English menu makes its way into my hand. After figuring out what it is, I catch myself staring at it, without any regard for what to order. I realize an English menu is an infrequent luxury, especially one with tofu scrambles and wheat-grass smoothies.

I scan the beach scene from over the guardrail and spy a motley bunch of guys standing around an ironing board smoking cigarettes and playing cards. They must be gambling. Affectionate lovers share a blanket on the sand, a sight I haven't seen since the States. Several European tourists are video recording tide pools. My heart aches for my absent camera. It's the only thing I've missed on this trip.

I can't believe it's almost over. Maybe that's why I'm feeling so much better; my body knows I'll be returning to a safe, clean, and rational world soon. I admire the pre-sunset glow on Sara's soft face. We smile at one another, and I turn away. I don't want to let her know I'm thinking about leaving. If I want to enjoy my last day with her, I can't let myself think about leaving. Not now, it's too painful.

Still looking away, I find myself falling into fascination with Amrita's melodious voice. The song ends and she addresses the Sangha: *"We came here to move through our sexual blocks. This is the perfect place to mend the wounds created by a sexually dormant and unconscious culture. Social constructs about sexuality block and pervert the natural flow of Kundalini. She gets so confused here,"* Amrita grabs her breast with one hand and her privates under the table with her other, *"that she never makes it here."* Her hand floats from her breast to point at the heavens above her head. *"Mixed messages about sex often corrupt the most natural act into something kinky and dirty, so there's a tremendous healing that needs to happen for us to realign with our birthright, which is pleasure and bliss."*

Amrita takes a few deep breaths and decides to pause, as if knowing an almond-eyed Goan is about to enter to take our order. He arrives and shows a nervous curiosity about our group. After repeating everyone's order, he asks, "Why are you walking around in white clothes?"

Swami-ji replies, "We are the pure of heart."

The waiter cocks his head and walks away. I notice that most of the men on the beach are wearing Western clothes. The tourists, who come on vacation from other parts of India, mostly still wear longhies or dhotis. We may be the only white-clad spiritual pilgrims in town.

A tall, dark and, according to Sara, handsome Israeli comes out to greet us. He is wearing designer jeans, several gold chains, and a Rolex watch. I cannot tell whether it's a copy or the real thing. He introduces himself as the owner of the bar.

Don't Drink the Punch

"My sannyasin (renunciate) name is Arjun, but my friends call me Armani. I'm a long-time student of Osho's."

"Ah, so you've heard about Tantra?" Swami-ji asks.

"Tantra? Yes, I've read *Sex and Super Consciousness*, and *Sex Matters*, but there is much I do not understand."

"Well, do you believe the Bhagwan was the original Tantrika?" Swami-ji tests him.

"No, there are many teachings before him, many practices. He simply popularized them, made them available."

"Exactly, and we are followers of another such teacher."

"Oh. I think it's complicated, no?"

"Can be, yes, but with the help of a master...," Swami-ji smiles and moves his arm around Amrita, "it can also be very simple."

Armani declares, "That's what I like, simplicity. Osho makes everything simple. So, tell me. Tell me about your Tantra. You want a drink from the bar?"

"We've already ordered chai," says Swami-ji.

"Good. Good. Drinks are on the house," Armani announces to the group.

Amrita begins, *"Tantra is essentially simple Mr. Arjun-Armani, but humans are constantly complicating things. The mind must complicate things because it's not so stimulated by the obvious. But the Truth is infinitely simple. You see, sex is the primary force in the material universe. It's the force that creates everything we see.*

"What makes two atoms form a molecule? Attraction, the positive and the negative charges, the masculine and the feminine polarities. All contrast is simply interplay of opposites, which, in its essence, is sex. That's what perpetuates existence."

"True. True," Armani says, taking off his Gucci sunglasses, "but I have to ask, if everything is sex, then sex loses its appeal a bit, doesn't it?"

"Exactly. The advanced practitioners are not run by desire for sex, and therein lies liberation. Most humans spend many lifetimes wrestling with these desires."

Armani sits on the guardrail beside Amrita and leans in to make his point. "Are you saying desire and sex are obstacles to enlightenment?"

"Quite the contrary: sex is the pathway to Self-realization. However, there's a de-fascination that must occur before one can use sex as a tool toward Tantric truth. There are constructs and conceptions that need to be deprogrammed, in both the body and the mind. Sometimes that work means indulging in orgiastic acts for the purpose of exploring and illuminating one's shadowy desires. This is where Osho's teachings were most often misunderstood.

"You see, Osho implored his followers to exercise their sexual fantasies and demons in order to transcend that which unconsciously runs them. Unfortunately, many lost sight of the purpose. They got trapped in the labyrinth of desire.

"Each sexual act can give birth to a new desire, which generates more karmic bondage. It's a slippery footing, but with discipline and practice, it is possible to become a true sexual libertine. The objective is to hold a steady erection without a wavering mind. Sex becomes the meditation. Fantasy falls away, and the lover is present to behold the Beloved. The body, in this profound state of reverence, is the perfect instrument for devotion. That's real yoga, purifying the body of the poison of passion during one incarnation in order to transmute it into the elixir of enlightenment."

Armani prostrates on the ground in front of Amrita's table. "Oh, Master, how long is your stay in Goa?"

"I'm here now and have not seen beyond that," Amrita answers.

"Would it be possible to arrange a public satsang in your audience?" Armani stands and brushes himself off.

"What did you have in mind?" Swami-ji intercedes.

"The people here need your teachings. I feel it. They're hungry for someone like you. I can manage your publicity. Can you teach at 10:00 a.m. this Sunday?" Armani pleads, revealing himself as the type to mix business and pleasure.

"It is not possible. We do satsang at sunrise or sunset only," Swami-ji insists.

"Then we'll do it at sunset! Saturday is a big drinking night and no one's up at sunrise around here, unless they're still up from the night before," Armani jokes.

When the waiter returns with our food, Amrita tells the Sangha, *"During eating contemplation, I want you to observe and enjoy fully the aroma and flavor of every morsel. Taste as if it were your first meal."*

My attention is overwhelmed by the arrival of my tofu scramble. Next to my plate, there is a bundle of silverware in a cloth napkin.

"Check it out. I got a fork!" I shout, like a blind man who has been given a cane. My outburst may be inappropriate, but it's authentic.

Amrita laughs and says, *"Tell me, Mr. Arjun-Armani, do you not appreciate the simple pleasure of eating with your hands?"*

"In my country," he says, "it is customary to eat with a fork and a knife, and we eat certain dishes with bread. Since we serve many Westerners here, they seem to prefer the silverware."

Amrita speaks with a full mouth, *"Well, I find the metallic taste a distraction; it's far more sensual to feel my food with my fingers before I put it in my mouth."* She hums a little while chewing a handful of dhal. *"It increases the pleasure in my mouth."*

I set my fork down and start scooping my scrambles up with my fingers. Anything to increase my pleasure on this glorious day, after being sick for so long. Sara scoots closer to me and rubs her hand on my thigh under the table.

Amrita continues, *"It's not just; there is also something Tantric about being in touch with what comes out of your body, the fluids and odors that the body produces. And, of course, when you're in a country which traditionally does not use toilet paper, you become intimately acquainted with all the body's functions. Do not shy away, Mr. Arjun-Armani, it's real. It's raw and human. That's what Tantra is. A true Tantrika sees no separation between the sacred and the mundane. How can one expect to ascend to the heights of heaven without first building a foundation in the realm of shit and piss?"*

A light breeze kicks up after sunset. The plates are cleared, and Armani pays our bill. "I've made arrangements for you to stay at my hotel down the road. I hope you'll be my guests and honor us with a public satsang."

21 Grad School in Goa

Armani's modern, cinder block hotel features a huge banquet hall. When Amrita sees it, she plops herself down in the center of the room and asks not to be disturbed. Swami-ji explains that the master is downloading new teachings to her. After our tour of the premises, we return to the hall. Amrita reemerges from her meditation, and with an air of authority, announces, "I've received instructions to lead a ritual, which will be superior to a public satsang. We'll need your help hosting a Tantric Chakra Puja.

Amrita points to Armani and says, "I'll meet with you privately to demonstrate and discuss the possibilities, but in the meantime, can you arrange to have our meals prepared and served to us here, so we won't be disturbed for two days?"

"It's my honor," Armani says, falling on the floor before her. At first, I think they are reenacting some kind of kinky role-play, but it occurs to me that behavior like this is not unusual in the context of this group.

I'm stoked when I find out our room has clean sheets and a western toilet! My body is back, my mind is clear, I feel good, but I'm still terminally in love. While still dressed and spooning on the bed, I caress the curve of Sara's hip. She draws my hand up to her heart. Holding it to her chest, she twists her torso to gaze into my face. "It's wonderful to have you back. How do you feel?"

"It's good to be back. I'm ready to cash in on some of that monkey love you promised," I say, squeezing her thigh.

"I can tell," she says pressing her hips against the bulge in my pilgrim pants. "But, I'm wondering if it isn't better for us to hold off."

"What's wrong? Are you on your period?" I ask.

At this, Sara giggles, and then laughs hysterically. She tries to speak a few times, but only shakes her head and laughs more.

Irritated, I ask her, "What the hell is so funny?"

"I'm sorry; I finished my period last week. Didn't you notice my bloating, cramping, and blood everywhere?"

"I was sick," I say, pulling my arm from under her. "I didn't notice anything."

"I know, that's why you should save your strength...."

"I'm plenty strong now," I argue.

"Well, you could've died, you know. Energetically, it's not a good idea to use your life force right now. Ejaculation strains the kidneys, and your liver is already doing double time with the Malarone," she insists.

"That has nothing to do with us tonight. If you don't want to sleep with me, that's fine, but don't try to make it medical," I refute.

"I'm sorry. It's just that sex creates such powerful desires, and that may distract us from what we're here to do. You heard Amrita. A lot of practitioners lose their purpose when they take sex casually," Sara says.

"Who's taking sex casually? I never made love to anyone with my body and soul the way I've made love with you. Didn't I tell you that like five cities ago?"

"I just don't feel like making love," Sara says.

"Fine," I snap.

"You're cool with that?" she asks, apologetically.

"Yeah, it's fine," I say, rolling away, turning my back so she doesn't see my bruised ego.

She curls up behind me and says, "I know you're

leaving tomorrow, and I'm afraid making love will make it more painful than it already is."

I stand up and take off my shirt. "That's very rational sounding for a woman who lives in the moment."

"I'm serious," she says.

"So am I," I say, bending to kiss her lips. When I try to take it deeper, she turns her cheek. "Tonight might be the last night we ever have together. Are you just going to turn away from me?" I ask.

"You have no idea how hard it was for me to sleep beside you when you were out of commission," she whispers into my ear. "I was just lying there, all those nights, beside you, my beloved. I yearned to give you my body and take away your illness, but there was nothing I could do."

I kiss her nose tenderly, and then go check out the bathroom. "How about taking one last shower with me?" I ask, while kicking off my pants and stepping into the shower stall.

"Is it hot?"

"Come and find out," I beckon, lathering myself while she peels off her robes and piles them into the sink. I rinse and watch as black grime swirls down the drain. Then make way for Sara to step in and savor the relaxation of our first warm shower after a week's worth of traveling through oily temples and dirty roads. I massage her small, slippery body with soap in one hand. Not knowing how long the heat will last, I cover armpits and ankles first and then slow down as I caress her breasts and buttocks. She melts with moans and sighs.

After we are both rinsed and wrapped in beach towels she says, "Now what were we fighting about?"

"You were telling me that I am your beloved, and how badly you wanted to give me your body," I say.

"It's true. I look at you and it's like looking into another dimension. I see a perfect mirror. You're like my masculine counterpart." She tucks the corners of the mosquito net under the mattress while I lock the door.

Soon, we're naked in the orange glow of the outside lights, arranging ourselves under the covers. She spoons me and half whispers, "When I lay beside you, I have a yearning to be inside you. When you were sick, I had time to really be with that. At night, I imagined that my hunger for you was part of a greater emptiness. Then I breathed into the emptiness until I felt full again. This is how I've been fulfilling myself each night."

What does one say to that? I push my face into my pillow and try to hold back what I know is coming next.

I finally ask, "Would you make love to me tonight if I changed my mind about leaving tomorrow?"

"But your film school is starting soon. No?"

"I could skip it this year?" I say.

"Can you do that?" she asks.

"Actually, the question is: would you sleep with me if I did?" I turn to look into her beautiful face.

"Hypothetically or for real?" she asks.

"I can't imagine that hypothetical sex would be very satisfying," I say, and she presses her laughter into my chest. Then she props her head up on her elbow, becoming serious. "So you'd give up all your future plans, your films and your school, just for one night with me?"

"Well, to be fair I'd want more than just one night, but yes. If given a choice between love now, or fame in the future, I'd give it all up to wake up beside you," I say.

"I know what's going on. Can I call you on it?" Sara asks, crinkling her forehead in concern.

"Go ahead," I say, thinking that this is one of the things I love about being with her; people don't go around "calling me" on things.

"You want to stay now because the master broke through to Amrita, who is transmitting teachings about the Sex

Chakra, and it's too irresistible to pass up."

"Maybe that's part of it," I admit, "or it could be that the medicine is having a weird effect on my head, or maybe it's the salt air, but who cares. This stuff is deeper than any film course I've ever taken and more real than any film I could ever create."

"Have you thought about this?" she asks.

"It's all I've been thinking about. When a man nearly dies of malaria in a third world country, he thinks about a lot of things. I looked at my whole life and looked at it hard. Did you know that for the last five years I've been working for a travel show but have never had an intercultural experience? It's enough to make me question my direction and all the decisions I've made. I'm always taking the next logical step and doing what's expected, and if it gets tough I take the easy way out.

"I've been applying for grad school for so long that I've forgotten why I even want to go in the first place. Sure I'll gain technical skills and make contacts, and build my credibility, but for what? So I can make movies for other people? So I can help them tell their stories?"

"Good film comments on the richness of life, and I haven't begun to live yet ... until I met you. I've loved more and learned more with you than in all my past experiences combined. If I go back now, I'll end up helping everyone else tell their life stories; but if I stay, I have at least a chance of truly creating my own."

"I'm honored to have you stay," she says, squeezing me with all her might, "but I'd rather we just hold each other tonight instead of making love, if that's okay?"

"Woman, you drive a tough bargain, but I accept."

We drift off in each other's arms, sleeping to the serenade of a cricket and gecko choir.

22 *Sensual Scavenger Hunt*

The sunrise wake-up call drags us out of bed and into the practice hall for a new kind of meditation. Amrita instructs us to stand up and shake our bodies to warm up. At first, I welcome the sensation of not sitting. "We should do this every day," I think. She loosely guides us to shake each body part in turn, from the ankles, knees, hips, torso, shoulders, hands and head. The room warms from the heat of breath and moving bodies. Then we're instructed to bring more subtle awareness into different parts of the body such as genitals, labia, and lingam. Amrita guides us to feel the heart's beating within our rib cage, between our lungs.

My body is generating heat and my breath shortens. Soon, all the shaking seems ridiculously inane, strange and surreal. After about 45 minutes of wondering when it will be over, we are finally instructed to stop, to sit still, and to observe how the energy remains in action within a still vessel.

Amrita instructs us to sit in yab-yum, which means I sit Indian style and Sara straddles my lap. Amrita demonstrates a number of complicated open-eye breathing techniques, while sitting on Bud's lap. During these exercises, I'm so focused on the warm energy rising in waves up my spine that I hardly notice my legs going numb. I wonder if Sara feels it too. Maybe this is something she feels all the time.

After about twenty minutes, Amrita invites us to switch partners. A little confused by what she means, I see Sri Durga getting off of Prabhu's lap. *"Women will now find a new Shiva to partner with."* I look over at Jivana who is holding fast to

Raj's neck.

"It's okay," Raj tells Jivana. "It's just a meditation."

"Don't worry, Jivana, Salvador doesn't bite," Amrita chimes in, urging Jivana to move to me so that she can take her place on Raj's lap.

I hide my own discomfort with the instructions, while Jivana situates herself upon my lap. At first, I feel rejected that she did not want to be with me; but then, through the breathing, I feel a welling tenderness, like I want to hold her, protect her, and tell her it's going to be okay. When I finally stop thinking about it, I can actually feel waves of energy in her spine, similar to Sara's, except they're cooler and quicker. I'm amazed at the distinction between the two.

The women rotate again, and I find Sri Durga's energy is soft and maternal. In fact, she reminds me of Mother. Perhaps it's just because she's the oldest woman in the group.

Finally, I pair with Amrita, whose energy nearly knocks me out. She digs her heel into my ass twice to wake me up.

We circle up for the master's satsang. Amrita demonstrates an exquisite ease in her body, yet there is a tone in her voice that is somewhat harsh and lands strangely on my ears. She takes a few, deep, whole body breaths before she begins:

"There is a common mistake most humans make in their search for the divine. It's a compulsive looking upward. God is so constantly elevated. He's up there," she waves her hand above her crown, *"in the unobtainable heavens or higher realms. God is so elevated that everything on the earthly plane becomes profane. This unnatural divide between spirit and the flesh is a violent act against God. Humans are thus cut off from their true carnal knowing of light and Truth.*

"There are entire cultures that are cut off and schizophrenic because their natural physical senses are damned and denied. When you open your eyes and learn to

observe, you'll eventually realize that the beauty of the human body is every bit as astounding as the perplexing array of heavenly bodies above. We are visible evidence of infinite intelligence, and as Tantrikas, we shall celebrate ourselves as such.

"We will host a Chakra Puja for the larger community of Goa. It's an ancient Tantric ritual, which acknowledges our embodied divinity. You will spend the bulk of the day in preparation for this practice. You will be assigned karma yoga to serve the community and asked to contemplate your sacred sensuality."

Each couple is given a shopping list to help prepare for the event. We are also given a stack of invitational flyers, with instructions to recruit other "open-hearted couples" we encounter on the streets. We are reminded not to get lost in the doing: *"Your contemplation is to experience divinity while engaging your senses and serving your Sangha."*

During the mini-bus taxi ride to a beach called Calangute, Sara says, "I've practiced several Chakra Pujas in Madrid and always dreamt about the day I'd share this ecstatic experience with my true beloved. Tonight is the answer to my prayers."

She strokes my face gently and nuzzles my neck. She looks down at her list and raises her eyebrows. "Ready to have some fun?"

As the dazzling sun glistens off the gorgeous blue-green coast, we digress into vacation mode, meandering through the sloped and busy market, hand-in-hand, chatting about whatever the hell we feel like. It's a total lapse from our silence. I'm free-associating, cracking jokes, and loving life. Like on Friday nights, after a long hard week of work, I feel recklessly drunk, except it's sustainable. And I'm not worried about puking all over my date or having a hangover the next day.

Don't Drink the Punch

Some items are easy to cross off our list: cardamom seeds, red and white candles, musk, essential oils, coconut oil, patchouli and sandalwood incense. Then we stroll into a hip, indoor/outdoor German bakery to post a flyer on the wall. We decide to take a chai and strategize the rest of our scavenger hunt: ritual ash, thirty silk blindfolds, a violet 60-watt light bulb, bindis, and fresh flowers that haven't completely bloomed.

At the back of the café, there's a triangular stage with an African-looking guy playing a didgeridoo. A dark-skinned woman of undetermined ethnic origin accompanies him by undulating behind a conga drum.

"Why do you think it's so sexually liberal here compared to the rest of India?" Sara asks.

"Maybe it's the influx of foreigners who use it as a resort destination," I guess.

"Do you think it could have to do with the Portuguese influence? Like in Brazil, the women are more rebellious or liberated than anywhere else in South America."

I shrug my shoulders, distracted by the tan hippy chick at the next table. She wears a bikini top and dons a huge bandage on her lower back, partly covered by surf shorts. She's bragging to a couple of stoners about how she avoided deportation when her visa ran out.

Sara turns to check them out and asks the woman if she just got a new tattoo.

"Yeah, you want to see?"

We crowd around while the hippy chick carefully divulges a jagged black tribal pattern that spans to her hips.

"Whoa, man, that's chronic!" says Stoner number one.

"Did it hurt?" asks Stoner number two.

"The artist is from New Zealand. He studied with the Maoris," she brags.

"It's gorgeous," Sara concludes. I look again and think

it looks puffy and painful, but such is art: always subjective. After the chick tucks away her tat, Sara asks, "Do any of you have plans tonight?"

"You're looking at it," says the long curly-haired stoner, holding up his beer. "You?"

Sara counts out four flyers as she speaks. "We just rolled into town. We're studying with a Tantric master and are offering a Chakra Puja tonight if any of you want to come."

"What is Tantra?" the Hippy chick with the fresh ink inquires.

"Oh that's some freaky shit," Stoner number two offers. "Check this out." He trails his forearm across his beak-like nose, before continuing, "My brother used to work in Uttar Pradesh, and he was walking past a cemetery on his way home from lunch, and he heard some moaning and shit. When he looked around a little, he found a naked bum huddled over a dead body, eating human entrails! And my brother is always the Good Samaritan, so he threw his left-over food at the naked dude, which angered him at first and caused him to cast some wicked spell. But when the sadhu realized my brother was only trying to feed him, he insisted that my brother rush home to his loved ones.

"When my bro gets home, he finds his wife covered in blood in the back yard. Apparently, she tripped in the garden and was impaled by a rusty rake and had to go to the hospital for stitches and shots, and she ended up getting tetanus."

"No Shit!" Stoner number one says, pulling his long black locks into a ponytail and revealing his hairy shoulders.

"Then check it out. My brother goes back to find the sadhu and brings him a blanket and some chai and asks him to help his wife, and when he comes back home, she's like 100% better without one sign of a puncture wound. I can't say my brother ever made friends with the guy, but he did find out that he was into Tantra. There are all kinds of lost souls like this guy wandering around the cemeteries looking for dead bodies to possess."

"Did he say what kind of Tantra he practiced?" Sara asks.

"Beats me," the big nose stoner shrugs. "It's enough for me to want to stay away from it all together."

"Right, well, I promise we won't be serving any entrails for dinner," Sara says, handing each person a flyer and trying to keep the conversation friendly.

"Right on!" the stoner with hairy shoulders points at the flyer. "Armani is hosting your Puja. He throws the best raves in town!"

23 Hot Monkey Love

With only a few items left on our list, we decide to forage the fields for flowers instead of buying them in some shop. We head out in the direction of the nearest banana grove and use our Rambo knife to cut a few sad-looking lilies. Pulmaria blooms fall from the trees, but have no stems, so they're hard to gather into a bouquet.

I point out a colorful moss that appears to be in bloom, but we laugh at the idea of bringing moss back for the altar.

"What is a Chakra Puja anyway?" I ask, while I follow Sara deeper into the banana grove, crunching dried mango leaves underfoot.

"You'll find out tonight."

"Yeah, but any clues as to what I can expect?" I ask.

"Only that you should have no expectations."

"Clever woman," I respond.

"Sssh!" she exclaims and points at a colorful bird perched above us.

"Polly want a cracker?" I say and scare the bird away. She hits me in the chest, and then kisses me. "Just tell me one thing about it," I plead.

"Well, every Chakra Puja is different, but the one thing you can count on is that we'll begin in a circle formation, and the women will sit on the left side of the men. In fact, that's how 'Left Hand Tantra' got its name."

"And all along, I thought it was called that because the right hand was busy." She shoots me a funny look. "I'm kidding. I've never even heard of 'Left Hand Tantra.' I had hardly heard of any kind of Tantra before I met you," I remind her.

Soon we're out of view of the road, and I'm overtaken by the spontaneous inspiration to take Sara's Rambo knife to cut down a fresh banana leaf.

"It looks like a place mat," she says. "Why do you need a place mat?"

I push her against the trunk of a big banyan tree and set down all our shopping bags.

"I'm going to have a picnic," I say, placing the leaf at her feet and dropping to my knees.

"I see," she says, helping me navigate through her robes so that I can find her sex with my mouth. After a delicious but brief moment of hot connection, she stops me.

"Stay here," she instructs, takes my knife, and goes around wildly cutting more banana leaves as if she's Jane of the Jungle.

"What are you doing?" I ask.

"You'll see," she says, throwing them in a pile in the center of our little clearing, then guiding me onto our makeshift banana leaf bed.

I take our flower collection from the trunk of the banyan tree and sprinkle the flowers around the perimeter of our bed. Sara adds a few final touches to my flower arrangement, then I help her undress. She pulls my soft and surprised penis out from under my cotton robes. A few wet kisses and he's stiff. I stretch my head back and look upward at the dizzying pattern of leaves and branches and dappled sun. When the excitement becomes urgent, she slows her stroking and lets me catch my breath. I'm lying back with my eyes closed listening to the ruckus of wild birds.

It's as though we've crawled inside an aviary to make love. She resumes, and after some time, my mouth dries from breathing so deeply. I yearn to drink of her juice. I wet my lips and rotate around for the 69 position. She protests with a sharp little moan, but soon her moaning becomes louder, longer, and more loving. My hands grab at her soft white thighs while I hungrily push my tongue into her folds and suck on her little lips.

When I open my eyes, I see the face of a red and yellow speckled lily staring at me. I fixate on the little speckles of this wild flower, which remind me of the red cum-cum powder given out by priests in the temples. Sara senses my distraction and slows.

"What is it?" she asks.

I sit up, reach for the lily, rip a corner of the flower off and place it symmetrically between her eyebrows.

"Namaste," she says, and takes the flower from me to select another perfect piece of the petal to rip. She holds the little dot delicately and licks the back of it, chanting "Om Namo Shivaya," as she presses it to my forehead.

"Thank you," I say, with my palms pressed to my chest. I take her onto my lap in yab-yum and our mouths melt together.

"It's funny, I feel at peace with my decision to stay. In fact, I think I'd be content to sit here and kiss you, just like this, for the rest of my life."

"Me too," she says with another kiss, and I regret when she pulls away.

Now she's inspired by a new desire. She guides me down, laying my back flat against the leaf-clad earth. She passes her cool hands over my warm body in several long strokes. It feels good to just lay back and breathe. She reaches around, gathering flowers from all directions like a dancing little wood nymph. She secures her sitting position between my legs. Then slowly, lovingly, places each flower petal, one at a time, around my relaxing penis.

"What are you doing?" I ask through my smile.

"I'm decorating my Shiva," she says.

I know how silly it probably looks, a grown man with flowers in his pubic hair, but we're in the middle of a banana field, and nobody's going to find us here. If it pleases her, it pleases me. And when she kisses and licks her creation, it especially pleases me.

Brought out by the natural setting, I feel my animal nature take over. It's something fierce and primal.

I pull her to me and roll on top of her. The flowers fall from my body to hers and spill onto the green leaf below us. She grasps at my body. The chemistry of our sexes rubbing together is intoxicating. I slip inside. It's like coming home. I find a deep, sweet rhythm, like a groove, and she's all breath. We tap into a force that's moving our bodies in a cosmic dance.

With each inspired stroke, a moan rises from within her. Like a bird she calls, "Caw. Caw. Caw!" I find myself flying. Soaring above our bodies, beyond the treetops, I'm coasting on the ocean breeze. "Caw. Caw." With each cry, I'm pumping my wings, and I see the blue-green shore and sail along the glorious cliffs. An impending climax brings me back.

"Hold still!" I say.

"What?" She freezes.

"Like that. Perfectly still." I breathe deep and it happens: a fluttering contraction, light but pleasurable, pulses through the base of my lingam.

"Did you feel that?" I ask.

She smiles and lifts her hips unto me. "What was it?"

"I think I just climaxed without coming." I say.

"Want to try to do it again?" she asks, writhing against my stillness until a new wave of pleasure rolls in, rushing, and splashing through us both. She rides me to a new height: her orgasm. I am wet from her ecstatic spray. She trembles in my arms, then relaxes, and our breath finds its rhythm. I let fresh air fill my lungs and, still hard, I resume the dance. New, invigorating energy moves through me as I reach even deeper into her. I almost climax again, but stop. Nothing happens.

She suggests I save myself for the Chakra Puja tonight, and teaches me how to draw the energy upward through my body by breathing up my spine. Then we circulate it through our bodies by focusing from the root to the skull, and back again. Together we breathe from the surface of our skin down to the depths of our bone marrow, without even questioning what the hell that means.

24 Chakra Puja

Back in the practice hall, before the anticipated Chakra Puja, we decorate the hall with all the items purchased and found during everyone's scavenger hunt.

Amrita leads us through about an hour of advanced breathing and kundalini rising exercises, then sits on the floor with all the devotees in a close circle. She reaches out for Swami-ji's hand on one side, Prabhu's hand on the other and wordlessly encourages everyone to complete the circle.

"This is where the dance begins. You are each a supportive angel, creating a conscious container for each participant's heart to burst into spontaneous love. In order for that devotion to erupt safely, it's going to take your total presence. I'm going to ask for your help throughout the night, and I want you to stay out of your ego, out of your head, and in total service. If we do our jobs, the participants will be so enraptured in a deep Tantric trance that they won't even notice the work you're doing to create their experience. This is true karma yoga. It's your offering to the divine tonight."

She smiles and then draws Prabhu's hand to her lips and kisses it. Without words, he kisses the hand of the person whose hand he's holding on his other side, and they continue to pass the kiss all the way around until it completes the circuit.

In a more direct tone, she continues. "Now, Raj is in charge of lights and music. The dimmer's on the wall. There's a stack of CDs that Armani and I have already selected. Jivana is in charge of the ritual feast."

Jivana bows dutifully.

Don't Drink the Punch

"All the women are to help Jivana serve these delectables to our guests."

Swami-ji interrupts, "It is not advised that you take any of the medicine we are serving. This journey is for our extended Sangha. It's not your time to partake."

"Thank you," Amrita says to Swami-ji, and adds, "We will have an opportunity to indulge in other ways afterward. Prabhu, you are to do nothing other than hold space for the master tonight. Swami-Ji will make the necessary introductions. Everyone else will be greeters, and after everyone has entered, we will lock the doors."

Bud and Sri Durga become the first line of greeters. Sri Durga hugs everyone who comes into the temple after Bud takes their money. The "donation" for the evening is suspiciously about a hundred times what it would cost to go to a dinner and dance club down the street.

Amrita posts Sara and me at the next line of greeting. My job is to make three horizontal stripes of ash on each man's forehead, while Sara affixes a sticker bindi (red dot) on the forehead of any woman who's not already wearing one.

Their reactions vary.

"Far-Out!" says one man, wearing a leather jacket with beaded fringes dangling from each sleeve.

"Can you make vertical lines like Vishnu?" one hippy asks.

"Thanks for the face paint," someone else says.

I also take to asking them where they're from and find out nearly everyone is from somewhere else: Israel, Australia, England, Germany, and there's even one guy from New York. There's not one Indian in the whole mix, except Raj, and Raj is busy playing music.

An older brunette woman in a low-cut top comes over to me and asks, "Can I get ash, for my inner Shiva?"

To which I answer, "Sure."

However, when I go to apply the ash, she dodges my fingers. "Actually," she says, "I just wanted to flirt with you a bit." She winks and walks away.

Throughout the night, she keeps coming around and running her fingers across my body, telling me how sexy I am right in front of Sara, who smiles with amusement instead of saving me.

Once everyone's arrived, Swami-ji opens by chanting a Sanskrit invocation into the microphone. Amrita sits in unwavering meditation while Prabhu stands to her right, relaxed, but ready for anything. Swami-ji projects:

"Intention is that which makes the difference between a Chakra Puja and an orgy, and our intention tonight is the transcendental. The beaches of Goa are known across the world for their hedonism, so we're here to balance the sexual with the spiritual.

"I am honored to introduce the teachings of our Master Das, as taught by the blessed Amrita Devi. Amrita's role tonight is that of an orchestra conductor. She will see to it that the group vibration is in concert. Some people may feel pushed and challenged to new levels of openness, while others may have to restrain some of their more carnal habits.

"Everyone is to eat and drink only what we provide for you; no dipping into your personal stash tonight. The kundalini rising must be concurrent. If someone becomes sloppy or questionable in the sacredness of their behavior, we'll give a little warning, and it will feel like Amrita's foot in your behind. Don't take it personally; it's for the highest good of the group. If you don't clean it up, Prabhu, Salvador, or Armani will see you out. Now let's form the opening circle," he says, instructing all the women to sit to the left of the men. He then hands the microphone to Amrita.

"Thank you, Swami-ji. Now with the ground rules out of the way, we will create a vortex of juicy, loving energy that will

transform each and every one of you. Start facing your partner. No talking, no touching, simply sit and gaze into your beloved's eyes."

Sara and I practice together as we move through partnered breathing, stretching, and dancing. We're instructed to expand the body into more pleasure. Every movement is seeking more pleasure. Amrita uses Prabhu to demonstrate each exercise. They look like lovers, which strikes me as strange, since I've never heard them say so much as two words to each other before tonight.

After the room is sufficiently warm and littered with discarded articles of excess clothing, Amrita guides everyone through what she calls *"the art of Tantric kissing."* This is the point where Sara leaves me to help the other women distribute food. At first, I feel awkward sitting alone while everyone else is making out, but when I look around and see lips, bodies, and breasts coming together, everywhere I turn, I can't help but become aroused.

Sara moves swiftly and purposely around the room, distributing packets wrapped in banana leaves to each couple. When she returns to me, she is topless.

Amrita delivers detailed instructions on how to experience the Tantric feast: *"Place the meat into your beloved's mouth. Savor it. Lift the wine goblet to your partner's lips, and then kiss their lips, sharing the taste of wine."*

She sensually spells out exactly what to share: grains, more wine, fish, more wine, sprouts, more wine, followed by mango slices. The sacred feast is topped off with a potent hash brownie. I suddenly see why the flyer promises an unforgettable journey that includes the cost of a meal and medicine.

Dinner is cleared. A ritualized disrobing begins. This is where men visualize ourselves as gods, and our partners as goddesses. With Sara, this is not hard for me to do. We undress the human costume to reveal the sky-clad divinity within each being.

"Now, Shiva should touch only Shakti's right side, while Shakti touches only Shiva's left side, from head to toe, like so." She runs her fingers lightly over Prabhu's side while dancing to a seductive drumbeat. As the lead couple, they put themselves in the center but keep a keen eye on all the other couples to make sure nobody strays into habit.

Amrita uses Prabhu's long, thin lingam to demonstrate the Tantric art of touch. She uses her fingers, palm, lips and tongue. For the women, she demonstrates where to press on the men's perineum, at the peak of his arousal, to hold back his ejaculation. She explains that at first, the sensation of orgasm will be mild, like the fluttering I felt today, but promises that with practice and awareness, this will expand into a full powerful orgasmic sensation. We practice PC pumping so the men can learn the precise muscle control that will help them suspend their release.

I'm in wide-eyed wonder at the visual feast of naked bodies, who, at first, seemed a little reserved, and are now warming to the pleasure, or maybe I'm warming because Sara is massaging my lingam. I marvel at the variety of women's body shapes and sizes. The range in nipple color alone is staggering. I see brown, crimson, cherry, peach, pink, even vermilion.

Amrita is in full participation with Prabhu as she speaks. *"Oral pleasuring and genital worship should be slow and delicious. Use your tongue as an instrument for massage, and use your intuitive creativity to explore different styles of stimulating sensations."*

From her back, Amrita instructs us to drink of the goddess yoni and sip her divine nectar. Immense moaning fills the room. My arousal drains into distraction and overwhelm. Sara reminds me to pretend that we're the only couple in the room, but I'm too interested by what everyone else is doing, including Amrita who's taken to dancing around the room, monitoring everyone's progress.

If a man starts penetrating a woman too soon, Amrita slaps him on the back of the head or playfully kicks him on the buttocks. Apparently, this is to prevent couples from breaking the ritual and straying into ordinary sex, but as certain couples continue to digress, Amrita does not seem concerned. She encourages everyone to pleasure each other without bringing about a climax. We take turns pleasuring each other in order to expand our awareness of the subtle arousal in the moment, without being distracted by the need to give back to our partner. Amrita instructs us to stay vigilant.

"We prolong the lovemaking by stopping to breath or by changing positions before climax, not by diverting the mind to other things. Don't just hold back. Your orgasm is healing; it's only the actual ejaculation that is depleting."

As the night goes on, the room spirals into total abandon, becoming an uninhibited feast of flesh and moans. Although Amrita continues calling out instructions, they become increasingly abstract and esoteric. To the untrained eye, like myself, it would seem that there's a whole lot of fucking going on.

As the hour approaches 3:00 a.m., many sleeping bodies crowd the corners of the room. I get the sense that partners may or may not stay loyal to each other. Amrita brings the evening to a close. She gives everyone a fifteen-minute warning so that if they're working toward yet another orgasmic wave, they can complete that cycle.

Amrita finally instructs us to lay in total stillness. *"Embrace your beloved. Hold their essence. Breathe together. Nothing to do, nowhere to go; just be and breathe."* Prabhu plays a Tibetan bowl, and we close the evening with a chant.

After escorting the last participant to the door, Mr.

Armani exuberantly hugs and thanks everyone for their help. "This is a dream come true. This room will be forever changed."

I wonder if his excitement is because he's carrying the torch for his teacher, Osho, or because of the fat wad of cash in his back pocket. He falls to the floor and prostrates to Amrita's feet three full times.

"We've met well in this time and space. We've put these bodies to good use, and now it's time to rest," Amrita says.

After Mr. Armani leaves, Prabhu and Bud push all the pillows and cushions to the center of the room. Swami-ji accommodates Amrita's vertical body in the middle of the pile and invites everyone to put their hands on or around Amrita's body-vessel.

The closer I get to Amrita, the more mysteriously drowsy I feel. Sara strokes Amrita's shoulders and chest. Others are drawn to different areas of her body. Pretty soon, Amrita is completely covered in devotee's hands of all shapes and sizes. It looks like a commercial from the united colors of Benetton. Soon I feel warmed with waves of comfort pulling me into oceanic unconsciousness.

25 Pushing Buttons

I wake to the sound of a bell, entangled in a puppy pile of mostly naked devotees. The sun has barely risen, but since the shutters are closed, I can't tell whose limbs are whose.

I locate Sara's body, still within reach, and wonder what I missed last night. There's a weird feeling in the air, like maybe there was an orgy. Of course, there was the Chakra Puja sex fest, but it feels like there was another more energetic orgy, which I was somehow involved in during my sleep.

Amrita is no longer amongst us. She is sitting in lotus at the altar, and Prabhu is by her side ringing the ting-shaw and singing, "Om Namo Shivaya, sunrise satsang."

Amrita appoints Sara to lead us in kundalini yoga movements to stimulate the blood flow before satsang. Sara guides us through a self-chi massage on our own bodies, including our own genitals.

I manage to power nap through both meditation and singing, and then wake up during an intriguing dialog about last night.

When Amrita asks us what lessons we gleaned from the Chakra Puja, we dance around details, such as the quality of the sound system, the inconsistent size of the food chunks, what people were wearing....

"*Enough!*" Amrita shouts, cutting everyone off. "*The purpose of this discussion is not to leak energy but to accelerate your growth. Ask yourself what one issue confronted you most during the Chakra Puja? Now meditate on that.*"

After twenty minutes of meditation, during which I

completely forget my contemplation, Raj blurts, "The evening ran too long. I only had enough music planned until midnight, and then I had to improvise. This was very challenging, but ultimately it kept me engrossed in the moment, and I realized all of life is like this ... unpredictable."

Without emotion Amrita says, *"Thank you."* She then calls on Jivana.

"There is so much that challenged me, but one thing was your request that we serve the food topless."

"Thank you," she says, in the same non judgmental tone. Jivana starts sobbing quietly into her hands, and everyone acts as if that's perfectly normal.

Amrita looks to Bud. "Actually, I felt everything up until we took our clothes off was rather unnecessary."

"Thank you," Amrita says again.

Prabhu speaks, saying, "The nudity didn't bother me but I felt it inauthentic and a bit hypocritical that we did not participate more fully in the journey. How can we hold a safe space if we are holding back energetically?"

"Thank you," Amrita says.

Sri Durga, who is next in the circle, says, "I was most challenged by the cost of the evening. I know it is not my business, but because of the high door price, I felt we were attracting participants who value drugs and sex over the spiritual teachings."

"Thank you," Amrita says.

"Is that all you're going to say? Thank you?" Jivana blurts out, obviously fuming.

"Do you have more you'd like to add?" Amrita asks calmly.

"Yes, I do actually. Nobody told me there was marijuana in the brownies. It was not right to put me in charge of the feast without telling me there were illegal drugs involved."

"Is there more?" Amrita prods.

"Just that I felt responsible all evening, like if someone freaked out or if something went wrong, I'd be the one to blame."

"I got that. Anything else?" Amrita asks.

"That's all," Jivana says, letting out a big sigh.

I sigh with her. Amrita looks in my direction, so I speak up, "I think she has a point. The pot brownies are a little beyond me. I'm not comfortable with doing drugs here; so next time, none for me."

"Thank you. And Saraswati?" Amrita prompts.

Sara begins, "I feel the general public is unprepared for this type of deep spiritual work. Many people got distracted by the sex and drugs and missed the whole point."

This comment lands like a slap in the face. She is referring to me. I know it, and it hurts.

Bud jumps in, "We just had a room full of people who have no training in Tantra demonstrate an awesome ability to let go of their egos and sexual issues and dive in. I think overall it was a pretty good show."

"What are you talking about? They were here for the sex and the drugs, and nothing was achieved or overcome," Sri Durga argues.

Amrita raises her voice and uses the singsong tone that I got so used to hearing last night. *"Now if everyone feels essentially expressed I want to bring your attention to the essential objective of the Chakra Puja. You're work is to worship the divine in whatever form she presents herself to you. Vajrayana Tantra is the practice of seeing God in every sentient being. A true master takes her worship even deeper. To the extent that it is possible, she makes love to every sentient being. That may be a sister, friend, mother, wife, lover, stranger. God comes in all different shapes and flavors.*

"I hope by now you can see the divinity of everyone in

this room. Can you imagine making love to them? This is your Sangha. These are your beloveds. I want you to contemplate an environment wherein you'd feel safe enough to abandon your limitations and inhibitions. In order to give your physical body for the play and pleasure of God, ask yourself how you can become more naked: emotionally, spiritually, and physically."

"As far back most people remember there is a sense of: I like this; I don't like that. I resonate with this person; I don't want to be around that person. It gives humans a sense of identity and control, but in the process of deciding what they like and don't like, they create attachments and aversions, which cut them off from the true flow of life.

"When we close ourselves off to new experience, we shut off from Truth. We go into automatic pilot: habits, memories, and past associations take over. This drastically limits our full expression, especially in lovemaking.

"Humans often decide that certain people are desirable and others are not. Specific acts are allowed, but others are not even attempted. How can you be in the moment if you are busy judging it?" She laughs from deep in her belly. *"This is very difficult for people to grasp, because they are attached to their attachments.*

"I am reminded of a story about the Dali Lama. One spiritual aspirant asked him, 'Is it true that Tantric masters sometimes eat their own excrement?' The Dali Lama smiled and said, 'The practices of enlightened ones cannot be understood from the position of ego.'

"To an enlightened master, there is no difference between a chunk of coal and a gold nugget; and yet, if a little bit of urine is placed in the mouths of many of my followers, they will not like it.

"Tantric sex is not about desire. It's about devotion. We do not make love because we want to scratch an itch or even because it's pleasurable. We make love to unite with the

divine, to experience our oneness with all that is. We make love to drink of our true nature. As such, our next process will be to look at how we can let go of our aversions in order to create an ecstatic Chakra Puja amongst evolved practitioners.

"Now, ask yourself what attachments you'd need to overcome in order to give yourself entirely to the beloveds in the room."

Bud's arm shoots up, and he says, "So you're asking us to meditate on what it would take for us to have an enlightened orgy, right here, with everyone in the room?"

"Precisely," Amrita says and sits back.

"Well, if we can have some medicinal brownies, I don't think I'd have any aversions to sleeping with any of you," Bud says.

"Is that not just an attachment to a mind-altering substance?" Prabhu provokes.

I argue, "Aversion, attachment, call it whatever you want. I'm not ingesting any mind-altering substance offered by a spiritual sect in the name of reuniting with God. To that, I'll admit I'm attached." My mind flashes on a field with nine hundred dead and bloated bodies scattered around a big tin tub of cyanide punch at Jonestown.

"But it's part of the ritual," Bud defends.

Swami-ji jumps in like a referee. "The ancient texts do prescribe meat, fish, wine, grains, and herbs, but they don't specify what kind of herbs. When it's available, hash becomes a popular interpretation, but it's not necessary."

"Okay," Sara says, "I have no problem doing everything required by the ritual, including drugs. I just can't bring myself to eat flesh. I'm a vegetarian, and that's my bottom line."

Bud leaps in. "That is such an attachment. Listen to how you call it flesh as opposed to food. You're attached to the philosophy of non-violence to animals. You're stuck at the level of judgment: vegetarianism, good; meat eaters, bad."

Don't Drink the Punch

Sara argues, "I don't even think my stomach has the enzymes to process it, and throwing up during Puja would be pretty un-sexy."

"Maybe the throwing up could be part of the teaching for you," Bud jokes. At least I think he's joking.

"Flesh, food, drugs, this is all inconsequential!" Amrita calls out. *"Look beyond the ritual, and ask yourself what's stopping you from opening your heart and soul and offering your body to your beloveds."*

Jivana speaks, "Well, I, for one, am married. I took sacred vows to my husband, and I will not partake in extramarital affairs."

"Ah, but how does your husband feel?" Amrita asks.

After a pregnant moment, Raj speaks, "I don't see any harm in it. My commitment to my guru is every bit as sacred as a wedding vow. If my master feels this is what needs to be done for my evolution, then this is what must be done."

"Thank you." Amrita asks, *"Do we have consent from everyone except our young bride?"*

Amrita continues in her teaching voice. *"You can't hide from this, dear one; you're going to have to face this teaching. Marriage is a simple construct. It's an agreement of mind and culture. It is not Truth. We cannot own another human being. We can't even reserve our body's attraction for one person. It's an illusion. You can't harden a part of your heart and not deprive your husband from all of you. Think about this: to the degree that you shut off a part of your heart to the Sangha that is the exact degree to which you cut off love from your husband. Your partner is one with the Sangha. He belongs to the universe, as do you. When you get that ... when you truly get that, your love becomes universal. You become liberated."*

The room is silent.

Jivana looks up, "It's too much to ask," she says, with tears streaking down her face. "Look what you're doing to my marriage," and then buries her head in her hands.

"*Resistance is natural,*" Amrita offers. "*The body-mind becomes very stimulated by the subject of sex. When it comes to pushing buttons, sex is the biggest button pusher,*" she continues with force and clarity, "*but the fact that you have such a charge is an indication that you have a healing opportunity.*"

Jivana continues sobbing into her robe. "I don't see how it makes us any more evolved to sleep with people we're not attracted to."

Amrita shows no compassion, "*Don't close your eyes now! A Tantrika doesn't check out when the lesson becomes difficult.*" Amrita's voice rises, "*This is the time to deepen your practice.*" After a pause where she struggles to calm herself down, she says. "Now, would you consider sharing your man with someone you love and trust? What if we appointed Saraswati to offer her body for Raj's pleasure and your healing?"

I feel a deep flicker of anger and try to stay calm as I ask, "Excuse me. But would that be with or without my involvement?"

"Without, especially if it pushes you against your growth edge," Amrita snaps.

"Well, I have to admit, I'm not very interested in whatever learning might come from seeing Sara sleep with Raj."

"Ah, so it's a perfect opportunity for you to examine your conditioned possessiveness," Amrita says so intensely she almost sounds desperate.

"Look at it like a laboratory, man; just observing human behavior," Bud says to me, trying to soften the edge.

"But we're not test rats, and I'm not so sure about the safety of this laboratory. You know lots of these kinds of experiments have failed in the past. Ever heard of Jonestown or

Heaven's Gate?"

Sri Durga stops me. "I think the master means for us to consider it, discuss it and digest it, but not actually do it yet."

Amrita roars, "No! This is not a mental exercise. This is a live Tantric offering." Now standing, Amrita screams "C'mon humans! What more do you want!?" She throws her body onto the floor and pounds at the floor with her fists, "Oh, Master, don't leave. Please don't leave."

Swami-ji rushes over and struggles to hold Amrita.

"Leave me alone, I want my Master." Amrita shouts in panic.

Swami-ji solicits Prabhu's help and the two men struggle to pin her down. "Just breathe, Amrita. It's okay."

"Master Das!" Amrita resists and screams with flailing fists. "Why now? Why do you have to go?"

"It's okay, Amrita. Let the master go," Swami-ji says, patting her paternally.

Amrita pleads, "Why?" sobbing into Prabhu's arms.

"Amrita, what are you attached to?" Swami-ji persists.

"I want to give myself to him. I want to make love with him inside me. His force feels so beautiful in my body. He moves my arms and hips with such rapture, such reverence," she convulses in a total tantrum. "Why won't he let me make love to him?"

Curling up into a fetal position she cries, "I'm sorry, so sorry. Please, come back to me."

The rest of us sit silently and stare. The magnitude of her grief is awesome. I dread the day that Sara and I must part. As she cries, I feel a comparable sense of loss.

Swami-ji finally addresses the group. "The path of left hand Tantra is a very tricky path. Do you recall when Master Das said that desire is like a labyrinth and people often get stuck creating more and more karma with their desire? Well, I'm afraid this is what's become of us. We've been fascinated by sex, and we've fallen from our path.

It's not Amrita's fault, she's giving us an important lesson. The master could come through you at any moment, in the form of truth, love, even poetry, but when he has completed his teaching, you must detach, let him go.

"Your ego will try to tell you that you are somehow special, or that you are deserving of his grace. Rest assured that is your ego, and it will drive him away. For Amrita, you can see that her frustration is like clenching a fistful of water: the more she tries to hold on, the further Master Das slips through her fingers.

"Amrita, please let him go so you can appreciate his teachings as they come through someone else."

26 Looking for a Lost Guru

We leave the smell of hash and hippy body order behind as we drive out of Goa. Amrita is curled up and sobbing in the back seat of the Magic Bus. Swami-ji hands her a pillow, instructing her to cry into it. "Get it all out, every last drop. Empty yourself."

Ganapathi asks Swami-ji permission to listen to a new Bollywood movie sound track he bought from a street vender with his meager driving stipend. The high-energy rhythm penetrates into spaces in my body I didn't even know existed.

We drive, and drive, and drive, aimlessly lost without the guidance of our master. Amrita is still crying. Perhaps she's emptying out for everyone's sake.

Sunset meditation happens in a vacant parking lot behind a restaurant. I'm distracted by the thought, "What if it all falls apart?" Any minute, this whole pilgrimage could spiral out into chaos. I can't help but think this is what happens when a bunch of disciples travel together with no single leader to follow.

My fantasy mind kicks into high gear. With the impending possibility that the pilgrimage might soon end, I'm obsessed with the possibility of taking Sara back to the States with me. I entertain ongoing scenes about introducing her to Mother. The script looks something like this: I buy Sara a bright new sundress and take her to the country club, where Mother either falls instantly in love with her or, after only a few months of seeing how happy I am, Mother invites us to tea

Don't Drink the Punch

and declares she's gotten over the fact that Sara's not from a wealthy Jewish family.

Sitting in supposed meditation, I now see myself walking the Venice Beach boardwalk with her or eating together on the promenade. I even imagine what an amazing mother she'll be. We could raise our redhead kids with a freedom and the parental attention I never had.

After an uninspiring chanting session, I let go of my distractions long enough to listen to Swami-ji.

"Channeling is not a new phenomenon. In the broadest sense, everything on the material plane first existed in the un-manifest and has been brought to us by the use of some physical channel. Great masters, throughout history, brought amazing creations to society through this process. Regardless of whether you call it inspired, gifted, guided, or simply tapped in, these artists are connecting with a higher source. Musicians such as Mozart, Bach, and The Beatles all channeled music, while artists such as DaVinci, Van Gogh, and Picasso channeled images. Sculptors channel form, mathematicians channel formulas, and inventors channel new ideas. It is a natural, creative process to be cultivated, not to be feared.

"Channeling is a transmission of truth from a broader perspective. There is so much that we cannot know from our perspective on the physical plane where we are limited to the five senses. Of course, this is why we have to be forgiving of whoever is channeling our master. Even though Master Das may no longer be constrained by a human body, we are. At times, the message is colored by the limits of the channeler. That is something we have to accept. We cannot expect a devotee to be more than half-human, but do not doubt that these teachings come from a higher source.

"That's why it's of paramount importance for you to set yourself aside, as much as possible. Be pure, and allow the teachings to move through you. This is why satsang is compulsory. Every sunrise and every sunset, we're purifying our bodies for the master to come through.

"Each of you is a channel for the master's work. Of this, I have no doubt. You would not be here if you weren't an appropriate vessel for his teachings. Trust your own voice. Don't fight the rising energy, or you will go mad. Learn to set your ego aside and listen to what the higher vibration has to say.

"That's the key. The master brings a higher vibration. Don't open yourself to anything less. I recognize him, because he is my master; he's lived inside me. You will recognize him, because he is the teacher of Truth, and when he moves through you, Truth is all you'll know. This is why you must look upon me as your peer, and when he comes through you, I am your student."

After about a week of aimless driving, I give up trying to figure out the tangled mess we've been navigating. My new meditation is watching the road without caring where the hell we're going. My gaze lingers over every dusty detail: the painted horns on the oxen pulling the bullock carts, the hungry look in the eyes of the horses on the side of the road, and the asymmetry of the dung-constructed shacks.

I've become immune to the violent swerving from near-miss collisions. My stomach no longer leaps to my throat. I am simply the witness. I sit by the window and watch without reacting and without numbing. I even embrace the smell of diesel that fills my nostrils and lungs without triggering my vomit reflexes.

I'm also becoming accustomed to the taste of chai. I'm distinguishing subtle differences in the recipes. Some chai venders favor cardamom, others cinnamon. There's a distinct flavor of palm sugar in some. The one commonality: they are all boiling hot and must be sipped with caution.

I'm hungry by the time we pull into to a busy, air-conditioned restaurant, in a small, hot city at the foot of a steep, green mount. The place is crawling with pilgrims and rickshaw traffic.

We disembark at the restaurant steps. Waiting to be seated, we stand among loitering beggars and hungry sadhus. A cute street urchin, about seven years old, approaches us and tries to eavesdrop, without understanding. Then he speaks like a little recording, "Hello. How are you? My name is Sanjeet. What is your name?"

"I'm Saraswati. This is Salvador."

"Where do you come from?" he asks in a monotone voice, like a little cyborg.

After we tell him, he stares at us, with no frame of reference for either USA or Brazil.

"I live here. I am from Tiruvannamalai." He recites a nursery rhyme while clapping his hands: "Arunachala, Akshara, Mana Malai."

Saraswati claps and sings along with him for several rounds before he puts his hand out, asking for money. I reach into my pocket, but Sri Durga stops me. "If you pay him now, you will seal his fate as a beggar for the rest of his life."

Saraswati shows him a new clapping game. He learns it, and continues to beg, but she tickles, teases, and plays with him until we're called into the upper-class restaurant and are shown to our seats.

Swami-ji orders "eat-all-you-can" meals for everyone, and during the flavorful feast, he tells us that this town is famous as a home of a saint named Ramana Maharshi. At the ripe age of sixteen, Ramana abandoned his family and his studies and was called to the sacred mountain of Arunachala. He bowed down to the guru within the stones and never left it again, staying for over forty years. He possessed only a loincloth and a walking stick.

Raj asks if we can hike up the mountain. Swami-ji bobbles his head. "Perhaps it will help us reconnect with our master. Then we'll be guided as to where we'll go next." He resumes slurping, and sipping flavorful food from his fingers.

Nailed to the wall behind the cashier counter is a line-up of all the usual suspects: Ganesha, Lakshmi, and Saraswati, framed in glass, draped with garlands and smeared with sandalwood paste and cum-cum on their heads and feet. Above them, there's a huge framed picture of Ramana Maharshi. He looks leathery, unshaven and emaciated, but his eyes pierce me with compassion. I turn away and his eyes follow me, like old pictures in a haunted house.

We are an absolute spectacle, eight well-fed, bright-eyed Westerners, dressed in white, walking our full bellies down the narrow streets to the nearby entrance of the massive temple of Arunachaleswarn. We're told the main temple is closed for the bathing and dressing of the deities, so we get comfortable on the temple steps for sunset satsang.

During meditation, little gray monkeys descend upon us from tall trees and overhead power lines. Swami-ji declares he has received confirmation that Master Das is, in fact, here, and we will raise our vibration enough to break through to him.

A mother monkey, carrying her baby on her back, scoots in close to Swami-ji. "This means all of nature is listening. The monkey is very auspicious in India. All animals are seen as vehicles to the divine. The swan carries Saraswati, an elephant for Lakshmi, and a rat for Ganesha. Nandi, the sacred cow, is never far from Shiva. These animals are all worshipped as divine servants to their masters, but the monkey is special.

"In the Ramayana, we learn about Hanuman, the Monkey God who represents the ultimate type of selfless service. See, Lord Ram represents the perfect lover, pure and divine in every way. Sita is his one true love while he is here on Earth, and during a dark battle, a fierce demon warrior by the name of Ravana steals Sita away from Ram and takes her to the island of Sri Lanka. That's when Ram calls upon Hanuman, the courageous king of the monkey army. Hanuman takes a flying leap over the ocean and onto the island. He then uses his tail to set fire to the demons, saving the beloved Sita and returning her safely to his Lord Ram.

"When Ram says, 'How can I repay you?'"

"Hanuman says, 'No need.'"

"Sita says, 'But, we want to thank you.'"

"And Hanuman says, 'You are my Divine Mother and Father. My service to you is my payment.'"

"Sita says, 'How can that be?'"

"Hanuman says, 'I've got you here in my heart,' and he tears his chest open to reveal that inside his heart there's a little Sita and a little Lord Ram.

"That's how devoted we should be. Fix your heart on serving the divine at all times. That is the ultimate reward. True service is ego-less. The real Self strives only to serve the divine in every moment.

"It's why I practice channeling ... to give my master my body and voice; that is my ultimate reward. Now, let's find a hotel for the evening," Swami-ji concludes.

After taking a bucket shower at a local guesthouse, Sara climbs into bed while I duct-tape the mosquito net to the bare walls around her. I cuddle up under the covers, and fall into strange slippery dreams ... something to do with flying monkeys. They look like those freaky little creatures that fly around the wicked witch in the classic film I saw so often as a boy, *The Wizard of Oz*.

27 Who Am I?

At sunrise, we sit on the rooftop of a large guesthouse with a gorgeous view of the sacred mount. During meditation, an immense, peaceful light sweeps over me. It feels like it's sweeping over everyone. I slowly lift my eyelids and find the sun has not yet risen. I glance at Sara, and by the half smile on her serene face, I suspect she's experiencing it too. My eyelids melt back down, and I turn inward again to find the glow is still there. It's real and soothing.

During chanting, I sit with closed eyes and bask in it. The devotional music outside amplifies the profound peace I feel within.

Raj is talking. Despite his thick Indian accent, his words land deep inside me. *"There is one question that rises out of awakened consciousness. It is the same question you were born asking yourself. It penetrates beyond words into pure experience. The most direct path toward Self-realization: simply ask yourself, 'Who am I?' It's not like an intellectual question to which there is an intellectual answer. No, it's much deeper. 'Who am I?'*

"It is the only important question. All other questions are peripheral. Who am I? It has a magical power to it, like a mantra or an incantation. This question opens you directly to the energy of the divine eternal Self, the part of you that is God. In Sanskrit, it's called Jiva or Atma. It's the part of you that has always been with you, and will always be with you.

"In the West, it's called the soul, but the concept is not as clear. People have fear-based notions that if they really

contemplate this question, they'll become selfish or self-centered. You see, in the West, there's a huge emphasis on individuality. People seek be different and stand out. Instead of pursuing oneness, Westerners often pursue unique expression. They over-identify with their possessions: the car and house and clothes that make them different. You can get stuck on who you think you are or how others see you, but this is not your eternal nature.

"*Asking this one question takes you beyond your self-concept and allows all those mental trappings to fall away. Who are you beyond your clothes, name, and ethnicity? Who are you beyond your gender and even beyond your chakras? What is your true nature? Dive whole-heartedly into this question and you will find a doorway, directly to the divine, to the part of you that is absolute and real.*

"*The key to this doorway is in the present moment. You must start with what you are aware of, right here and now. If you are sitting right now and your back aches, bring awareness to that experience, because it is present. The mind exists in the past or in the future, and you must enter reality, as it is now.*

"*Don't infatuate yourself with being someone who wants things in the future. Start with the self exactly as you are, not who you've been or who you want to become. There's no need to become more flexible or more comfortable to experience your Self. That is just the mind distracting you. You don't need to shave your head to become Self-realized. Do you understand this?*"

"*So today, self-enquiry begins. We will go to Arunachala to contemplate the Self. Arunachala is the navel of the earth, the origin of the universe, and self-enquiry is the basis of jnana yoga, the yoga of knowledge.*"

Raj uses his hands to indicate his Solar Plexus as he says, "*This is the source of knowledge. In Japan it is known as the hara; in Sanskrit the Muladhara. Whatever you call it, it's the seat power, the center of Self."*

After breakfast in the guesthouse, Raj leads us toward the legendary mountain. I stop before an overweight lady, who is sitting on the earth and stringing flowers onto a thread. I buy Sara a strand for five rupees.

After clipping the fragrant blooms into her tangled red hair, Sara thanks me with a scandalous public peck on the lips.

Glancing around to see if anyone saw us, I notice the fat flower lady is sitting in the shade of a massive wooden wheel, about nine feet in diameter. Overhead, there is a three-story wooden sculpture, with deity piled on top of deity, temple style.

"It's a festival float for special holidays," Swami-ji says, pointing to the third floor. "That's where the priest gets on."

The massive temple on wheels is parked up against the third story of a building, with a balcony for the priest to board.

Swami-ji tells us, "Oxen pull these floats through the streets on special holidays. Horns and drums are played, and noisy crowds surround them, making a big ruckus. It's a sight to behold. On non-holidays, it just sits here, and business happens all around."

On the temple steps, Raj explains, *"Hundreds of pilgrims come here daily to circumambulate the sacred mount, tens of thousands come on the full moon."*

We leave our shoes at the entrance of the temple and set out on a rocky path with dry grass and shrubs around. We walk silently, contemplating: "Who am I?"

It seems like a funny thing to be asking oneself at the age of forty. You'd think I'd already have figured it out by now.

I remember once, as an undergrad, a psychology professor asked everyone to evaluate his or her identity on a

3x5 card. We were told to list ten answers to the prompt: I am...

I am a student.

I am single.

I am an American.

I am a son.

I am Jewish.

I don't remember what else I put, but the professor made a big deal out of how all the women put, 'I'm a woman,' where very few men noted their gender, and almost no white students wrote white, whereas every minority in the room stated their ethnicity. That about covers the extent of my contemplation of who I am that has occurred before today.

Now our master, dressed in Raj's body, is asking us to look beyond identities, beyond the stats written on my California State ID.

Sex: M

Hair: Brn

Eyes: Blu

Ht: 6-01

Wt: 175

I wonder how much I weigh now. I must've lost at least ten pounds during that whole malaria ordeal. I haven't seen a gym in nearly four months; and though the vegetarian food is filling, I'm craving a Whopper. I remember getting through college on cheeseburgers and OJ.

Okay, who am I? Well, right now I'm a man on a pilgrimage. I'm sweating in my white cotton shirt, walking barefoot behind my lover, over increasingly-jagged pebbles, trying to meditate while walking around the foot of a mountain in a loud and chaotic Indian city.

For the most part, I've tuned out the honking rickshaws and the bells and bugle sounds from the temple, but I can't concentrate with the excited squeals and laughter of school kids gathering grass a few yards up the mountain. The patty-cake beggar kid from yesterday drops what he is doing and runs over to Saraswati.

"Sanjeet!" Sara exclaims, holding up her hand for a high five. He doesn't know what to do, so he tries to shake it. While still walking, Sara shows him how to slap her hand, and he is enthralled by the invention of this new greeting. He runs ahead, trying to high five everyone in our single file line. Soon, finding that we are mostly in meditation, he falls back beside Saraswati, swinging his arms like a little monkey. It's a funny contrast to see Sara's playful sidekick when we're supposed to be pondering this immensely profound question. So far, there's nothing terribly deep about it.

Who am I? I am skeptical and amused by this practice.

Who am I? I am confused about the purpose of this walk.

Who am I? I am the one who's thirsty and relieved to see Swami-ji ordering chai from a tall sadhu with a crooked spine. I watch the crippled Swami limp over to bring us halved coconut shells full of a strange brewed tea with flecks of flora in it. I drink while I walk.

Who am I? I'm the one who'd prefer a cold beer, but you know what they say: "When in Rome…." I slurp the last drops out of the shell and discard it in a pile on the side of the path.

I hear a deep voice say, "I'll take historical Self-realization gimmicks for 800, Alex." I then hear the famed Jeopardy game show music playing in my head: "Do-do, Do-do, do-do, Do."

"And the question is ... who am I?" The studio audience applause sign lights up. The crowd in my head goes wild, cheers and whistles, just as we complete our 14 KM trek.

Shortly after lunch, we begin our climb up Mount Arunachala. My raw and bruised feet are happy to reunite with their sandals, but they don't spare me from the dry heat and thorny shrubbery on the way up. I'm especially grateful to have fresh coconut juice offered to us, along with more chai. We pass through a wooded area, and a grey monkey family swings its way across our path.

When passing a natural granite cave, a naked ascetic emerges with his eyes rolled back as though he is in supreme bliss, and he pauses to urinate right in front of me before sitting back down to meditate.

After each of these distractions, I drop my contemplation and it takes awhile to pick it back up.

Who is it that is approaching the top? It's me, the one who's been hiking since sunrise. Who is it that hears chanting? I do. But doesn't everyone? What separates me from all the others who hear the same thing? Who am I?

At the top of the mount, we sit under a shade structure for meditation, during which all I hear is, "Who am I?" on the inhale and, "Who am I?" on the exhale. Once set in motion, it seems to repeat itself of its own accord. "Who am I? Who am I?" I hear rhythmically with every breath.

Raj reprimands me for enquiring without contemplating. To be fair, he doesn't reprimand me specifically, but during satsang he says, *"Several of you are asking yourselves: 'Who am I? Who am I? Who am I?' as though it were a mantra, not allowing space for insight, revelation, and breakthrough to occur. Mere repetition is not the objective of this practice.*

"The purpose is to attain direct experience of the Truth of your being. This question, when asked with a sincere heart, will guide your awareness toward that which is eternal in this moment. There is a Truth beyond illusion, and it is absolute. Enough talking about it already, let's do the practice. Who wants to volunteer?"

No one leaps forward.

"We'll begin with our new bride."

Jivana's face flushes. "Me?" she asks, looking at Swami-ji, who is not about to save her.

"Yes," Raj says, and Jivana steps forward and bows at her master's feet.

"What are you conscious of in this moment?"

"What am I thinking? If my mother knew what was going on here, she'd be outraged," Jivana asserts. "You mean like that?"

"Yes, thank you. So if I'm sitting in satsang, and the thought occurs to me that my mother would be outraged, then I take that opportunity to ask myself, 'Who is it that is thinking about her mother?' and then I stay open to whatever arises. Can you do that for me?"

"You mean now?" she asks.

He nods.

"Yes, Raj. I mean Guru-ji," she closes her eyes.

After a pause, Raj asks, *"And what occurs to you?"*

"Pardon me?" Jivana says.

"Tell me who you experience yourself to be, in this moment?"

"I am a very loyal wife, too loyal."

"Thank you. Can you take it deeper? Who is experiencing herself as a loyal wife?"

"I'm sorry," Jivana shakes her head.

Raj expresses compassion. *"Are you anxious because I asked you to be my example in front of the Sangha?"*

"Yes," Jivana admits.

"Good. Who is it that is feeling anxious?" he persists.

"I don't like this little game. I don't know what you want from me. Please call on someone else," Jivana pleads.

"It's okay if you don't know how to practice self-enquiry. That's precisely why I've called you up here, to instruct you. So ask yourself, 'Who am I?' and notice what

comes up for you. Can you do that for me?"

"Yes." Pause. Jivana continues, "I don't know what I'm doing here. I don't even know what Tantra is. I'm totally lost."

"Thank you. You are speaking your truth, right now, and that is exactly what you need to do, but be sure to focus on the question 'Who am I?' not any other question such as 'Why am I here?' or 'What does it all mean?' Otherwise, you'll go into stories, reasons, excuses, and that's the mind. Enquire deeply, with constant perseverance, who is it that feels lost? Ready to try again?"

"I am trying," she says defensively.

"Relax and stay open." Raj smiles. *"Now you can sit back down."*

She bows at her master's feet and returns to her original position.

"As you can see, the enquiry is organic, and alive; the object of your contemplation changes in the moment, because each moment is always different. We began with self as the loyal daughter, and then observed the sense of self shift into uncertain beginner. You must investigate and clear through each object of identification that arises. Every identity and distraction is a doorway to deepen the enquiry.

"That's enough for now. More will be revealed, as you are ready. Do not let go of your contemplation on your journey down the mountain."

We stand and stretch, and I find myself asking, "Whose feet hurt? Whose knees ache? Who's appreciating the gorgeous view of a windy city with dilapidated rooftops?"

28 Contemplation Camp

After packing up, we follow Sri Durga across the hotel parking lot to a separate structure behind the main hotel entrance. It's a large freestanding hall with outdoor showers and communal bunk beds. Raj is meditating at the end of the room on a woolen carpet with his back toward the window. There are enough beds for everyone to sleep in a bottom bunk. Although there's no privacy, we each find a place to arrange our own little stack of possessions before sitting down together for lecture.

Raj says, *"Ah, so you've had your share of the outdoors today. Sri Durga has made arrangements for us to stay in this guesthouse for the next several days. It will be our temple. Thousands of Truth-seekers before us have done similar practices, usually out in the desert or in caves, but you are fortunate; this is more comfortable.*

"Your bunk will serve as a little cave. You can meditate inside your cave or on the floor, as you like. We're going to be meditating in more frequent repetition and for longer intervals. The single focus of this practice is to realize your true essential nature.

"During this process, I will not be dispensing spiritual teachings or expressing Truth as I know it. It's important for you to see me as your master, following all the instructions I set forth, and coming to me if you have questions; but I am not your source for Truth. That is within you, and you have to find it for yourself.

"In the next few days, only expect the unexpected. You

will be confronted with resistance of every kind. You will be intrigued, bored, nauseous, humored, or whatever else comes up. It is all part of the clearing, which is necessary to reach the underlying truth. Use every challenge as an opportunity to deepen your contemplation.

"Who is it that is confronted? Who is it that is disappointed? Who is it that is excited, afraid, tired? Observe whatever you are experiencing in the moment. Ask yourself that very question as you fall asleep. Contemplate upon waking and contemplate while eating the meals that will be provided for you in the adjoining room. At times, you will contemplate while stretching your legs in the parking lot. You must even contemplate while you are listening to my lectures on how to deepen our contemplation. Got it?"

Throughout the first day, Bud has a goofy grin, Prabhu's brow furrows deeply, but what Jivana suffers is the most disturbing. She goes completely cross-eyed for hours. It's as though she's trying to find herself by staring at her nose.

During the first lecture, Sara slumps silently into a blank stare. The master asks Sara how she's doing, and she says that nothing is coming up.

"Good, this is good." He turns toward the Sangha and says, "If you ask who am I and what arises is: I am a yoga teacher ... I am a lover ... or even I am an entity existing beneath my senses ... these answers are all born in thought. If you observe them as they arise, without attaching to them, they will eventually fall away. All answers arise from the mind. Ultimately, our destination is beyond simply answering the question from the mind. Now Sara, tell me what you are conscious of."

"When I ask myself who it is that feels empty, nothing comes up. When I ask myself, 'Who is it that feels full?' still nothing arises."

"You are making progress. Continue your contemplation," Raj urges.

"But what if nothing is beyond the mind?" Sara asks.

The master takes a long pause, during which he stares at Sara, his eyes unmoving. I can tell he is not thinking, but knowing, when he simply says, *"Stay open."*

"Namaste." She bows.

Dinner is bland and simple. There's jasmine rice, dhal, and a tangy red juice with dried hibiscus flowers floating in it. Sri Durga sobs into her rice. She's muttering something about how grateful she is to have a bowl of rice. While eating the same rice, I detect a rich, full, unbelievable flavor in each little grain, like there's some kind of subtle perfume in the food. Something about the contemplation of Self seems to amplify my sense of taste. In fact, all of my senses are heightened. I notice the texture and the way the food moves through my mouth. My tongue masterfully moves to position each flavorful spoonful onto my teeth to be chewed. It feels like the first time I have ever eaten. I wash it down with a tangy-sweet sip of hibiscus juice and find myself enquiring: who is preparing the food, and what are they putting in the punch?

Occasionally, Raj checks in with individuals on their progress. There are times when the room becomes loud and restless with people breaking down or acting out. Like popcorn in a fire, you never know who's going to shudder, laugh, or cry out next. Everyone's excited except Sara who is still totally stoic. It seems she has either found the answer or perhaps has given up the question altogether.

Raj asks me how I'm doing.

"I'm concerned about others. In particular, I'm concerned about Sara."

"Who is it that is concerned about others?"

"I'm the one who cares about others. I've always been

the one who wants to help people, especially people I love. That's just who I am, so of course, I am distracted when they act out or don't act out."

"So you're experiencing yourself as distracted. Stay with that. Who is it that is distracted? Take your time. Stay open and really contemplate."

He nods to see if I understand, and I nod back. Suddenly, Amrita bursts into a weird pranayama episode. At first, I think she is exaggerating, but then she begins shaking and trembling like a volcano about to blow. Heavy breathing turns into wheezing. Her beet-red face grows even redder. Big veins in her neck bulge and little capillaries in her face are filling.

"Do not fight against it," Raj instructs.

To which she lets out a deep growling moan, still undulating, she cries out, "Oh, God. Oh, God." She seems scared and out of control.

"Surrender!" Raj yells.

My heart is hammering in my chest. My hands sweat from just watching. I'm afraid she's going to burst a blood vessel and create permanent structural damage. When she does explode, it's with screams, "Take me! Take me! Oh, God, take me!"

I'm riveted, witnessing an orgasmic release through every pore of her body. Her face shape-shifts into several different people, none of them recognizable. It's like she's moving through past lives or something. She gradually de-escalates from moaning to panting to heavy breathing. Her body relaxes deeply in its frame. The room is silent. Everyone is looking at her, but no one dares speak.

After a moment, Raj instructs us to continue our contemplation.

I resume with, 'Who is it that is distracted? Who is it that is triggered? Who is it that is afraid? What am I afraid of?'

I'm afraid that even if this really is the path to

enlightenment, I might lose my mind, and nothing will look the same anymore. I never wanted this. I mean, I didn't ever set out to be enlightened. On the other hand, I'm afraid everyone will become enlightened except me. Since I don't even know who I am right now, I guess I don't have much to lose. Maybe I do know who I am, but I just don't know that I do, or I'm brainwashed into thinking that there's more to who I am than this.

This whole mind trip seems to be pulling me farther and farther from the truth. I mean, I used to think I knew who I was. What the hell is really going on here? That's it! I'm out of here. I turn to Raj and say, "This is bullshit! I don't buy into this indoctrination. This whole thing is a big brainwashing scheme!"

"Thank you, Salvador. I've heard your honest feelings. Now tell me who you are?" he says, without missing a beat.

"I'm serious! I'm going to leave."

"Not just yet, Salvador. This process is like a moving vehicle; it's not safe to disembark until we come to a full stop. A point is coming when we will hit a critical mass of consciousness or clearing."

"But I can't handle another minute," I say desperately.

"Don't underestimate yourself. Just ask yourself who is it that is afraid. Who is it that wants to run? If you truly contemplate this, you will soon see your fears and dramas are constructs of the mind. They are not direct experiences of Truth. Once you see this, you will be liberated from them. Now tell me who you are."

"I'm fucking pissed!"

"Good, who is it that is urinated off?" he says, with a subtle hint of a smile. *"Ask yourself, and keep asking, even if you don't like what you're feeling or finding. Who is it that wants to defy his master? Who is it that wants to quit the pilgrimage?"*

By this time, I'm so confused that I don't know what to do except resume the contemplation. Instead of wanting to know who I am, I want to know what is really going on here. Who is it that thinks this whole process is unhealthy, that it's not grounded or sound? It seems every answer I can possibly conceive of is, of course, of the mind. Everything is mind.

Who am I beyond this fucking mind? I am no one, and this question is going to make me go mad. Only crazy people are supposed to be out of their mind. Why would an intelligent group of individuals intentionally want to go out of their minds? Are they conspiring to make us insane? Is Sara in on this? I'm serious. What are they putting in the food?

I awake in my bunk bright and energetic; and since no one imploded overnight, I decide to give self-enquiry another crack.

"Who am I?" I contemplate. Well, I'm the one who's moved off my bed to sit cross-legged on this chipped and broken tile. I'm experiencing an ache in my left knee; it's like a dull and constant twinge, but that's not me. It's my body. I know I've heard that before, everyone has, but right now it seems true and obvious that this spine that holds me erect, this head that contains my eye sockets, nose, and mouth, is not me. It's just a watery sack of bones, flesh, and skin, and it's moving on its own. It hurts when it feels like hurting and falls sick when it's run down.

Who is experiencing the pain and the pleasure of this body? I am, or at least I think I am, because my nervous system sends messages through my brain, which sends messages all over my body. This I learned in anatomy class; but who is it that feels the twinge of discomfort in this knee? I do, but only if I choose to focus on my knee.

I can also focus on the breath. I note the methodic rhythm of air moving in and out of my nostrils. My belly rises and falls. Who is it that is watching my breath? I'm the one who's distracted by what my body is doing. It breathes. I don't breath, my body does. Or do I? I stop breathing for a moment. It's uncomfortable. I decide to take another breath. Relief. Ah, I get that sometimes my body breathes, sometimes I breathe. But I am not my breath. I can watch my breath, and that means it's not me. If I can observe it, then it can't be me.

Okay, that's weird. My skin just puckered, and there are these freaky contractions in my mid-back. Who is it that's freaking out? I contemplate. Who is thinking? Who is the one asking the question, "Who am I?"

I am me. Aren't I? Clearly, my body is having a strange reaction, and it's very distracting to my enquiry. Who is it that's talking to himself? It's me. No wait, it's not me; it's my mind. My mind doesn't like the idea of me asking myself who is thinking. My mind doesn't want me to realize that I am not my mind.

Oh. My body is relaxing now. Evidently, I am not my thoughts, because I can observe them, though I can't control them. They seem to do their own thing, like the body. So if I'm not my thoughts, who is it that is thinking this right now? I am. No my mind is. Maybe it's like breath. Sometimes I am thinking, and sometimes my mind is. Right now, I am the one thinking. Who is it that is thinking? I don't know. This is exhausting. Who is aware of his enquiry?

Maybe that's it. Maybe I'm awareness. Who is experiencing himself as awareness? I pause. Silence. Space. I'm no longer thinking. I'm observing. Everything seems to float in and out of my consciousness. My knee, my breath, the voice in my head… it all happens on its own accord, and I am just a conscious witness.

That seems too simple. Who is it that doesn't believe he is awareness? Now I'm back to my mind. My judgment. Who am I? Who am I? Who am I? Who am I? Now I'm back to the mantra, but that doesn't lead anywhere. I rediscover the space between the thoughts and nothing happens. Who is it that is impatient? I contemplate this. Then I amend the enquiry: who is it that is observing his impatience? I am. I am the observer.

Who is the observer? Now I stay open. That's when it happens. The heavens crack open and I hear angels singing, harps playing....

29 Heart Broken Open

So maybe the heavens don't really crack open, but it sounds like it, because of the melodious words I hear falling from Sara's angelic lips. She has her arms outstretched and her head thrown back toward the sky as she cries out in total bliss.

"I'm the Truth that I seek. I am the God that I pray to." When she lowers her chin, I see her bright face with huge wet, glowing eyes like a feline in the full moon.

"I'm the Buddha that I bow to. I'm the one that I thank when I'm grateful. I'm the grace that descends before every meal, every breath, and every time I make love."

Raj throws his body down on the floor before her feet. His hands fly back and forth from her feet to his eyes. Sri Durga follows. Next, I step before her, lay my belly to the earth, touch my hands to Sara's toes, and I feel electricity through my arms.

Everyone prostrates in turn at Sara's feet except Jivana. Raj turns in her direction, "Offer your prostrations to the Goddess."

"Must I?" she asks, looking defiant. Firmly in her place, she screams, "But she's clearly gone mad!"

"Jivana Devi! Do not defy the master!" Raj strains to say through a tight jaw.

Sara speaks again in her heavenly voice, *"It's okay, dear one. I should be bowing to you."* My heart wells at the sound of her voice. *"I should bow to each one of you. You possess so much divinity. More than you even know."*

Swami-ji continues, "Saraswati is in perfect vibration to

channel Master Das now, but her body is a fresh vessel. It takes a tremendous amount of energy to sustain that vibration. We prostrate to help Saraswati ground. By touching her feet, we are drawing the teachings down, grounding her nervous system so she can handle more energy. She's like a lightening rod, and we want the master's charge to come to earth and illuminate us all."

Jivana reluctantly unfolds from her meditative pose and slowly bows at Sara's toes.

Swami-ji walks Sara over to the throne where Raj has been sitting. Raj takes his place on the floor before the chair.

Swami-ji says to Sara, "Master, let us hear you speak."

Saraswati says, *"Thank you. Let us meditate. Sit tall and stay present to what arises in the heart. Surrender to the full experience of being."*

This is our sunset sitting. The energy in the room is so great that various members of the Sangha emote freely with tears or fits of laughter. Saraswati finally opens her eyes. They are deep and dizzying to look at.

She begins, *"Spontaneous tears, shuddering, and laughter are evidence of the true Self overflowing in the human body, which is generally not able to contain the full glory of the Jiva (the Self). We are consciousness, bliss absolute, and when we experience identities, emotions, and phenomena, it is just a fraction of this absolute.*

"When we experience an emotion, any single emotion, it is only a partial experience of the whole. Today, you will be initiated into yoga of the deep heart. In its potential form, love is the totality of all emotions. It is the entire spectrum before it passes through the human heart, which is a prism that separates feelings like colors. Love is pure white light. From it, all emotions are born.

"Imagine each emotion represented by a single color. Take red, for example. You can liken it to anger. It is only one

aspect of the human experience. You could mix it with yellow, which we liken with happiness, and it becomes an excited orange. Mix in another primary color, like blue as sadness, and you might create a whole range of secondary emotions, such as jealousy, hope, disappointment, they are like secondary colors.

"But those are only isolated aspects of the whole, which is Love. The source of all colors is pure white light. It's analogous to pure devotion for the divine. It comes through different beings in varying wavelengths.

"Unconditional love is not simply a feeling or the need or an experience of love; it is an energy unto itself. It's absolute. Love lives in the heart of man, every poet, priest, politician, saint, sinner, and of course every lover. Love is the animating force within this body and within all sentient beings; yet it's not that complicated. Love simply is. It's the profundity and the simplicity that you see in a lover's eyes. Just as they are. Just as everything is, right now, and eternally will be. Let us purify our hearts to experience true light."

We close satsang by passing a ghee lamp and drawing its sacred flame into our heart. I am purified.

Saraswati instructs us to prepare for bed. Swami-ji puts a paternal hand on my shoulder and asks me to step outside. In the parking lot, under an annoying fluorescent streetlight, we situate ourselves on the curb.

He pulls his legs into lotus under his robe and he asks me, "Do you remember the story of the Ramayana?"

"The one with the monkey king?" I ask.

"Yes, the part in which Hanuman reconnects Sita and Ram and expects nothing of them. What do you think this story has to do with you?"

Oh shit. This is a test. "I don't know. Is Sara like Sita?"

"Yes," says Swami-ji.

"And I'm like Ram, except she's enlightened, and I'm not," I guess.

"That's not exactly it."

"She's not enlightened?"

"No, you're not Ram. In this incarnation, you're more like Hanuman, a warrior, a protector, and a very powerful servant to the divine."

"Then who's Ram?"

"The point is that it is an honor to serve the God and Goddess from the bottom of your heart, without expectations or conditions. I want you to be prepared, because it may be difficult to see her as our master. Now she is no longer just your partner, she belongs to the universe. It's important for you to see her as the divine being that she is, for the benefit of the Sangha. If you treat her like the Divine Mother, she too will be able to see herself that way. Got it?"

"Got it," I say, Namaste-ing.

In my bunk bed, I review the conversation in my head. I know Swami-ji is imparting important wisdom, but I feel angered that Swami-ji sees me as a mere monkey-man. How exactly is one supposed to treat the Divine Mother? These are cultural rules I somehow missed in school. Am I supposed to stop longing for her touch? Am I allowed to fantasize about the day we fucked in the banana fields? Am I even allowed to hold her hand? I must've been absent the day they taught that one.

My body stiffens with the stark suspicion that this is all part of their brainwashing scheme. In the darkness, I stare at the box spring grid above my head and wonder, "What if she's having a psychotic episode? How is she going to function in the world if she goes around thinking that she's the Divine Mother? Are we just buying into her delusional fantasy?" I don't want to be an accomplice to her demise. My tripped-up heart keeps me up late into the shortened night.

There's a sharp and sudden knock at the door. Some of the men from the hotel staff are barking something in Hindi from the other side of the door. It's some kind of bust. Sri Durga is out of bed and outside trying to calm everybody down before Swami-ji even wakes with a growl and a few coughs. Eventually he joins the negotiation and the muffled shouts get even more heated.

Swami-ji wakes Raj; and after an undetermined amount of time, the two men tear Jivana from her bed. They muffle her protests as they guide her out. Swami-ji returns, and instructs everyone to stay calm and quiet. We're told to get dressed quickly and pack everything. None of the other devotees ask any questions, so I keep my mouth shut. Flashlights are passed around, and Sri Durga sees to it that Saraswati is swiftly packed up and comfortably seated in the Magic Bus beside Jivana.

I offer our bag to Prabhu and Ganesha who are working quickly to secure stuff to the roof. I catch a glimpse of the cop cars crowding the front office of the main hotel. Prabhu tells me to "get in and shut up" as we slip out the back entrance, unseen by the police who appear to be questioning the hotel owner, and investigating the main house.

We drive through the remainder of the night, without comment. Who is the one running from the law? I am angered. I am irritated. I am entitled to know how we got involved with the cops. I expect it's because of the pot party in Goa. We could conceivably be charged as drug dealers, or accomplices to Mr. Armani's crack house. I'm horrified by the unsanitary images of Indian jail conditions that keep flashing across my mind.

I resort to mantra and breathing practices to distract myself from these disturbing pictures. I'm surprised by the sudden effectiveness of these simple techniques.

During the pre-dawn hours, we pull into an overgrown, empty lot to clear our minds for sunrise satsang. After a short yet deep meditation, Saraswati speaks. It is clearly Sara, and yet it is not Sara. "Who is it speaking?" I jokingly ask myself; but all questions and concerns dissolve into a new contemplation: How much love can my heart contain?

"Shakti is the manifest force of nature and chaos, beautiful, yet unpredictable. The world falls into disarray and demise if Shakti is not balanced by Shiva. Yet pure consciousness is not complete unto itself. It is the merging of these two that gives life. Father must come down, Mother must rise up; and in the center, there is a dynamic, awe-inspiring interplay.

"Where do these two meet? In the human heart. The divine entry point where spirit meets form. Ancient Rishis sat by the river Ganges and divined a perfect symbol to illustrate the meeting point of the divine lovers. The heart chakra is expressed as a six-pointed star, one triangle pointing downward, earthbound, while the other pointed toward the heavens, Mother Earth making love to Father Sky."

A familiar image forms in the middle of my mind. At first, a golden glint, and then it crystallizes into the diamond-encrusted Star of David that Mother has always worn fast around her neck. She's worn it for as long as I can remember. She tells the story of how, before I was born, my parents were remodeling their beachfront studio when a burglar broke in and ransacked the place, stealing her jewelry box from inside her dresser. The Star of David was sitting right on top, but because it had a few specks of paint on it, the burglar mistook it for a fake and left it alone. She had said it was a miracle, more important to her than the oil burning for eight days on Hanukkah.

Other than that story, the six-pointed star never had much meaning to me. I always associated it with the holocaust, probably from all the movies and museums I was forced to see as a child. I always assumed the Christians had the cross ... where they crucified Jesus, and we had our star ... under which millions of Jews were marched into ovens. That was my association ... until now.

"This is the intersection between not only feminine and masculine, but the light and dark, empty and full. This symbol contains all that is, but its true meaning can be grasped from a non-dual state. Let's meditate," Saraswati says.

I fall into the unexplored abyss in the middle of my chest, realizing that there is so much more space there than I ever noticed before. It is vast and soft and bottomless. Somehow, my purpose on this pilgrimage makes sense. If all this work is to realize the meaning of this one symbol, it all seems worth it.

In closing satsang, Saraswati announces that our next destination will be the arms of the Divine Mother Amma Chi. We will experience devotion at the feet of a living saint. Whatever love you didn't receive as a child, this woman will give you with her hug.

We pile back into the Magic Bus. I surrender to the road, tired but hopeful.

Crossing from Tamil Nadu into the lush, clean, southern state of Kerala reminds me of crossing from the border of Tijuana back to beautiful San Diego. There's a palpable difference in cleanliness and poverty, perhaps accentuated by the beauty of the setting sun.

We check into a luxury hotel, at least luxury by local standards, which might be comparable to a Best Western, complete with color television. Saraswati is assigned to sleep with Sri Durga, while I bunk with Prabhu. Though I'm bummed to not sleep with my beloved, I'm happy to be out of the dorms.

By the bedside, there's a visitors pamphlet that reads, "Welcome to Kerala: facts for travelers." It goes on to boast that Kerala has a 90% literacy rate, the highest in all of India. It's interesting to hear the political structure is proudly Communist. And then it seems to go off the deep end, suggesting the water is so clean that you can drink out of the tap, though I'm not about to bet my life to find out if it's true.

Finally, it cautions travelers against public affection such as hugging, holding hands or kissing in the streets. I read this again. Are they serious? I know it's a cultural taboo, but I assumed it was an unspoken rule. I didn't expect it to be an enforceable state law, written on pamphlets for out of town visitors.

I push the biggest button on the simple clicker and the television comes on, bombarding me with spunky scenes in which scores of skinny women in colorful saris gyrate their hips and swoon over a man on a motorcycle with a black leather jacket, who sweeps the heroine away. The overt sexuality is surreal; I can't help but laugh.

Prabhu stomps over and turns off the television. "Sorry, it was habit," I say, sitting back and looking around the stark room.

After meditation and an elevating kirtan, I find the sunrise view of the distant backwaters from the hotel rooftop breathtaking. Saraswati pierces me with a brief gaze.

"I sense there is a question in your heart, creating confusion that clouds your practice. It is natural for every devotee to ask if they can trust their master, especially when one feels they have not realized the Self. They wonder how they can trust themselves, let alone the Sangha. And is the guru really speaking Truth? This is an important crossroad on the path. The devotee must walk the line between defying the teachings altogether, or surrendering too completely to a teacher, trusting a power higher than they perceive themselves. It is a path only you can take. You must walk alone. A living guru can be a powerful guide, but they can also lead you

astray.

"Humans have, at their core, a desire to connect and plug back into their divine source. Dedicating yourself to such a teacher of light, a dispeller of darkness, is exactly that, a plug into God. The danger is that it is not necessarily the most direct line. The disciple often becomes lazy, letting the guru to do all the work, especially when they see their master as enlightened and themselves as a mere student.

"In Tantra, there is no middleman. You must experience Shakti or Shiva in yourself, and thus be capable of unlimited access to source. Gurus can be great guides, as living proof that divinity is possible in the human body. They can create openings for you to experience more of yourself. However, they must not be substituted for the experience of Truth.

"A karma yogi may realize themselves in the service of their guru, but karma yoga is different than a Tantra. You are to follow a guru only if they lead you toward your beloved."

At this, Jivana throws herself at Saraswati's feet. Crying and muttering. "I'm sorry I've forsaken you. I'm so sorry."

Saraswati says, *"Jivana, is there something you'd like to share with the Sangha?"*

Sobbing, she picks herself up. "Yes, my lord," now bowing at Raj's feet. Raj lifts her head compassionately. "I didn't know what was happening. I was mistrusting of you. Out of fear I called my mother. I told her you had gone mad and that Swami-ji had kidnapped us. I gave her directions to where we stayed, and then she called the police. But I know now, I was the one who was mad. I'm sorry I put you all in danger."

She bows again, "Master, you are my guru. Please forgive me." She continues prostrating at Raj's feet. "Oh, husband, you are my lord."

30 Goddess Worship

We circle the streets of a polluted South Indian city in search of a location that falls directly in the crease of our torn map. Neither Raj, Swami-ji, nor Ganesha know how to read or speak Malayalam, the native tongue of Kerala, so obtaining directions to this holy event proves no easy task.

Every overhead phone pole and palm tree is plastered with a poster of a dark, round woman, with a sweet smile and glowing halo. In some images, she's even walking on water. She is known across the planet as the "Hugging Saint." The local posters read: "Mata Amritanada Maya Math." Her disciples call her "Amma."

On the recommendation of a local fruit vendor, we follow another road as far out as it will go and hit the beach. It's a concrete and polluted-looking shore. I watch an old man defecate on the beach wall, while Swami-ji asks for directions from a rickshaw driver who speaks in sketchy English. After a few more U-turns, we finally arrive.

A huge overhead welcome banner stretches across a brick alley that is crowded with hawkers of devotional artifacts on either side ... posters, pins, mala beads, books, and cards. It's a regular festival with rich and thick smells of incense and food. There are huge lines of waiting people that wrap around the entire complex. The height and styles of people in the crowd indicate that they came from all over India.

After adjusting to the overwhelming assault on the senses, we discover a small shrine to Ganesha at the entrance and sit to center ourselves. While meditating, I witness a variety of pilgrims practicing their familiar antics, crossing their hands on opposite ears, bouncing up and down on one-leg, even slapping their own faces.

An older German man in white robes, similar to ours, descends on us and offers to take Saraswati and all the Western disciples to a short line for foreigners. Swami-ji stays behind with Indian born Raj and Jivana, with the agreement that we will all meet at Ganesha's feet at sunset.

I hear amazing sitar music echoing through the main hall when we are ushered into a special line that cuts in front of thousands of people. We buy flowers and leis to offer to the Divine Mother, and then are prodded along. As soon as we take our place in this small line on the far right side of the hall, the door beside us opens, and a dozen white pajama-clad disciples come out and part the red sea of people, creating an aisle toward the stage.

Enter Amma. She is wearing a white sari and a tall tin crown. I'm hypnotized by her little brown feet adorned with dazzling jewelry. Rose petals and marigolds shower down from gathering disciples, some down on their knees washing and anointing her feet with essential oils.

My breath catches in my throat. It's as though I'm standing before a superhero from another dimension. She leaves this striking image in our minds while she continues walking on through the crowd to take a seat at the onstage throne. Darshan is about to resume.

There are cameras projecting the overhead images of Amma hugging and blessing whole families at a time. People are chanting, crying out, and fainting all around. The line for foreigners is moving quickly. As the line shortens, my heart pounds harder.

I widen my scope to try to see what the hell I'm supposed to do when it's my turn. Everyone appears to be giving offerings, getting a hug, and moving on. Easy enough.

Why am I so nervous? I take a few more steps forward, and then I'm swept off my feet.

The white pajamas have a hold of me. I'm pushed and positioned into a large, warm lap that is magnetic and smothering. My ear is smooshed against her thigh. Where did my lei go? She smells like rosewater.

She's chanting, *"Manamanamanamanamana,"* and I'm wondering if I am supposed to chant too? When she runs out of breath, she lets me go. I'm light as a feather, floating out of her lap, and out of this atmosphere. Saraswati is now in her arms; it is a beautiful fading vision. Amma recognizes her, doesn't let Saraswati go, but the disciples rip her out of the arms of her mother. In English, Amma shouts, "Come, be with me," but we are pushed back out amongst the masses.

Sri Durga, Amrita, and Prabhu disperse to meditate, chant, mill around, or go shop.

A little light-headed, I stick by Saraswati, who is grabbed by a white-clad Amma-disciple saying, "There you are! I've been looking for you. Amma wants you to come on stage."

Saraswati takes my hand and we're ushered through a long line of white pajamas and seated directly behind Amma. This is like being selected for the live studio audience for an Oprah show. Wide-eyed, I look around the stage. It's a white sea of Western disciples in sweaty states of doting stupor.

Amma sits cross-legged at the edge of the stage on a substantial floor pillow made of natural fiber and built-in back support. To her right, a woman feverishly removes people's grasping hands. Her job is to protect Amma by unhooking fingers from her robe. The audience's focus is 100% on the Divine Mother, so her helpers serve more like unseen angels than security guards.

To Amma's left, two more angels take leis, apples, cards, gifts, and offerings, while giving Amma a handful of ash and candy to dispense to each person she hugs. I'm boggled by the lightning speed of this exchange. How does she manage to embrace, hold, and kiss so many people, and still make everyone feel special? They're crying, singing, and shaking with gratitude. In the distance of the crowd, I catch a glimpse of a scoreboard, keeping count of how many people she's hugged. It proudly reads 11,000, and it's not even noon.

I look closer at the saint's smiling baby face. I notice a few beads of sweat on her forehead, her blotchy skin, and the peach fuzz around her ears. I'm struck by her humanness. No matter how incredibly enlightened she is, she still inhabits a body, and she's still susceptible to physical illness and death.

I close my eyes, and for the first time since I was a kid, I find myself praying.

Dear God, please watch over the wellness of this woman's body and give her energy to do your work. Amen.

At sunset, we gather in front of Ganesha. Our Indian friends have been given numbers, but still have not been called up for their hug.

Saraswati declares, *"Continue expanding your heart in the presence of the Divine Mother, until we've all received darshan, and in the meantime, don't be seduced into believing the Divine Mother is blessed with anything more than is dormant, latent, or potential within you."*

During sunrise satsang and after several days of participating in this mad and massive display of guru worship, I screw up the courage to ask what Amma has to do with Tantra.

"Good question!" Saraswati responds gleefully, laughing as though she were waiting for someone to ask. *"First and foremost, Tantra is Goddess worship. Of course, without God, there can be no Amma, but without Goddess, there can be no Tantra. Secondly, in these dark times, Tantra is sexual healing. It's creating alignment where the kundalini is stuck.*

"Amma comes from a culture wherein women are not respected and hugging is not allowed. So what does she do? She commands respect and hugs everyone. That is Tantra. Further, she uses Tantric Ritual. Many Vedic scholars would debate this, but in reality, the foot washing and the flower bathing are ancient Tantric traditions.

"Tonight, we will experience a Tantra Puja in the most traditional sense. The moon is ready and my body is ripe for a powerful communion with the living Goddess."

After fasting all day and picking fresh flowers from the empty lot beside the hotel, the Muslim manager of the night shift, who seems to have a crush on Sri Durga, agrees to lend us the hotel banquet room for our special worship.

First, we purify our minds with meditation, then Sri Durga opens a back door and chants an invocation before Saraswati enters, carrying a staff and wearing only a sarong.

We bow as she walks to the front of the room, and after several prostrations to the altar, Saraswati positions herself on an ornate pedestal, which is apparently designed for the purpose of this type of Puja, because it has a moat around it to catch the overflow of offerings. She drapes her right hand over the head of her cane and Sri Durga leads us in chanting the 108 names of the Goddess.

Saraswati releases her coverings and stands naked, except for a yellow marigold garland, a belly chain, and silver anklets around each ankle. The chanting grows louder as we throw flower petals at her feet. Sri Durga takes a few steps up a small ladder beside the pedestal. Swami-ji hands her a pitcher of warm hibiscus juice. The chanting intensifies while the sweet red punch is poured reverently over Saraswati's soft white skin. Her nipples pucker. In fact, all of her skin responds, but she is in deep trance. Sri Durga bows and steps aside to let Swami-ji shower her delicate body with warm milk.

Saraswati exudes bliss as layer upon layer of each offering drips down her delicious skin. Each devotee takes their turn, contributing offerings such as thick crème, herbs, and powdered sugar. When it's Prabhu's turn, I notice the rapture in his movement. Pouring honey over her body is his meditation. He spoons the last drops from the pot and watches them drip onto her body. The honey works like glue, causing flower petals to stick to her body. It's more mesmerizing than a lava lamp.

Garlands are stacked so high around Saraswati's neck that they cover her chin. Swami-ji breaks the garland strings open, and lovingly tosses each flower at body. I watch as they stick or cascade to her feet. When all the offering containers are empty, we continue offering our empty hands, smearing the offerings on her now messy body. The sensation is intoxicating between my fingers. Everyone moves with pure love and protection toward her.

Through the duration of the ritual, I stop seeing my Sara. She is no longer mine. There is nothing special about my touch. In fact, she is in such a trance that she has no idea who is touching her. At first, I see the beauty of this unconditional and impersonal love, but I can't help but notice a tight discomfort in my gut. I decide to sit back in meditation, but start feeling separate and alone. I may understand it all in my head, but in my heart, I'm lost and a little needy. I try to remind myself that I just met her. The fantasy of her being the mother of my children does not entitle me to her.

I long to hug her and hold her and have her hug me back. At first, I feel as though I want the other guys in the room to say, 'Wow, you are so lucky to have her. She is so amazing,' but then, I realize they don't see me as lucky, because they don't see her as mine, and they're right. She does belong to the universe.

As the chanting continues, I see her face morph. She

is every woman, mother, sister, auntie, grandmother, and girl. With milk and powder coloring her hair, she even turns into white-haired crone.

The small Sara is long gone and the Divine Mother is standing before us in her full glory. Something stirs deep inside my chest. My insecurities melt into tears. In the fervor of devotion, no one cares. Nobody notices, except me, and I see I'm not the only one in tears. Amrita is wailing and rocking. Sri Durga has melted into a prolonged prostration at the base of the mote. I let go of my grasp. My fingers uncurl toward the sky. I sit on my heels, with my hands turned upward, and continue to sob.

The singing, offerings, and ecstasy of this ritual continue late into the night. I keep thinking we're going to conclude, but we don't. I'm exhausted by the unending devotion. I struggle to maintain a hold of reality. I'm slipping into short fits of unconsciousness. There's so much beauty around me, not only in Saraswati's body, but also in the faces and movements of other devotees. The beauty anesthetizes me, lulls me in her lap. Like an opium trip, I see colors and sensations swirl around, but there are gaps in time, as I wake up to buzzing sounds that don't seem to be coming from anyone in particular, but through people.

Once, the sound of my own chanting wakes me. I struggle to understand the words I sing, but ultimately, I'm swept under.

Sri Durga caresses my shoulder, which draws me into awareness of the room. The colors and smells are still strong, though the pace has mellowed. The ceremony closes as Divine Mother Saraswati is rinsed with pure water, fresh and cleansing ... holy water. She bows to the water bearer on either side of her and steps down.

The room becomes silent. Head buzzing, ears ringing, I watch while she reaches between her legs and draws a drop of menstrual blood from her yoni with her ring finger and smears it on Swami-ji's third eye. He bows to her. She moves on to Raj, then Prabhu, Sri Durga ... until she touches my forehead. In that moment, I close my eyes, and am supercharged with a light that reminds me that somewhere inaccessible to my consciousness I do know who I am. I don't know whether it's true transmission or my expectation, but either way, it's enough.

Saraswati takes my hand and leads me into the honeymoon suite adjoining the banquet where weddings are held. The room is womb-like, with a round bed, red velvet walls, and maroon carpet.

Saraswati still harbors pockets of milk and powder in her hair. Her body is cold to the touch on the surface but hot underneath. Her warm lips press against mine to share her steamy breath. I'm drawn into another unconscious space, so deep I grow dizzy. She steadies me with her embrace. I'm in awe of the tremendous overwhelming gorgeousness of the Goddess before me. I feel honored to touch her and be touched by her.

Wordlessly, she encourages me to take off my pants, and when she reaches down to hold my lingam, my body shudders. I am already fulfilled. As such, my lingam does not grow. I have no desire for anything other than this blessed moment, with this blessed woman. She holds it in both hands and honors it as if it were a sacred object from an ancient altar. Waves of devotion flood my being. My body softens. Each pregnant moment rolls forward offering fullness, richness and ecstatic bliss. Is this a whole body orgasm? My cells buzz in the realization of my climax.

With strength returning to my system, I gently lay her on the bed and slowly spread her legs. I sink down between them and warm her lips with my breath. I scoop dabs of cream and honey from her nearby scarf, and use them to massage and decorate her yoni. She is in deep ecstasy. I reach my first two fingers into her carefully and massage her outer lips with my thumbs. I'm listening to her every move and it's as though I'm wordlessly guided on how to touch her. It's a slow, sensual dance of flesh and feeling.

She takes my other hand up to her heart, and I feel a powerful circuit. The heart is open and her yoni is opening as I explore the space from which all life comes. This is the ultimate connection to source. She flushes with emotion.

When she is ready, like a lotus in full bloom, I massage her lips with my soft lingam. Her depth invites me in. Upon entering her, a glowing light emanates from her pelvis to mine. It expands with breath and engulfs us both. Bodies fall away, and we become one person.

Floating back down from her crest, it becomes clear to me that sex is meant to be an act of worship. It's not for getting off or even for procreation. Making love is not about desire. It's about devotion.

At the height of this vivid, real, and powerful realization, she thanks me and I think, "But serving you is my pleasure." I understand how the Monkey God felt toward his Goddess Sita.

31 Sound of Spirit

Swami-ji knocks on our door to rouse us for satsang. I'm surprised Prabhu didn't ring his bell and wake us like usual. During sunrise meditation, Sri Durga shows up wearing her orange robe, walks to the front of the rooftop, and sits before us. Astonished, I look at Saraswati, who's sitting beside me, wearing her plain white robe. I wonder how she knew what to wear today. Is it because we made love last night? Did she give up channeling the master in order to be with me?

An earthquake like memory of Saraswati's light body overwhelms me. I'm still absorbing the evening's indescribable experience and it's opening me to new possibilities.

Chanting reactivates a flow of devotion in my body. Judging by the blissful glances in Saraswati's direction, others seem to be feeling it too. Sara acknowledges them with a knowing nod.

Sri Durga says that the entire Sangha is still high from last night's Puja. She continues, *"The greatest dilemma for rational beings is how to integrate what's in their heart with what's in their head. There are entire civilizations that have over-rationalized their existence, and living from the head only creates struggle and war. In contrast, there are also ancient Goddess cultures that placed so much emphasis on feeling from the heart that they didn't make necessary preparations for survival. Many of the sacred teachings of Goddess cultures have consequently been lost.*

"In order to be fully balanced in your realization, you must equally honor these two aspects of being. We do this by

activating and purifying the throat center. This is the bridge between the head and the heart." Sri Durga places her hand on her throat and says, *"This is where father thought and mother feeling come together.*

"It is easy for energy to dam up in the throat either when people don't understand what they are feeling or when they don't feel what they are thinking. The two are equally problematic. If you are not able to articulate what is in your heart, you become blocked. Physically, the throat is smaller in circumference than other areas along the spine, so energy tends to dam up here very easily.

"An open throat center helps make life meaningful, for it is with the throat that we communicate, sing, laugh, cry, and express. In order to keep this channel open, it is essential to have a continual flow of prayer, mantra, and clear communication. Small talk won't do it. No, that's not the kind of communication we're talking about. Idle talking is a dangerous distraction on your path. You must contain the energy and stay focused on what's alive in you. Speak only of those things of consequence that add meaning to your existence."

As Sri Durga talks, I tune into Sara's breath. Out of the corner of my eye, I watch the rise and fall of her chest and notice that my breath is moving in the same rhythm as hers. It must be a subconscious connection because Sara seems completely enraptured by Sri Durga's speech. I wonder if I'm somehow vicariously absorbing the teachings through Sara's interest in the lecture, because I can't seem to concentrate on my throat chakra or anything the master's saying, right now.

The energetic link between Sara and myself feels so strong that I can almost see it. I know it sounds strange to be thinking about energy in tangible terms, but it's as if there were tendrils extending from my chest to hers. At times, the stringy energy filaments are everywhere between our bodies, but they seem to be concentrated in the heart region.

"Salvador, you look so blissful. Would you like to share what you're conscious of with the Sangha?" Sri Durga asks.

Jumping at the sound of my name, I say, "I'm sorry. I'm distracted."

"Apparently. What is the nature of your distraction?"

"With all due respect, it's sort of private," I say, embarrassed by how obvious my post-coital glow must be.

"Come talk with me afterward."

"Thank you," I bow.

"I will continue offering darshan until noon, and then you will rest today so you can absorb and integrate last night's teachings. Use this time to exercise your voice and be in your truth, whether that's in the form of speech, poetry, or song. This is a practice that keeps you aligned with the moment. If you are not in your truth, then you are not in the moment. To withhold is an act of violence, it cuts you off from your life force; whereas speaking your truth brings spiritual alignment."

After our final chant, I scoot up and ask, "You wanted to talk to me?"

"Yes, and Saraswati, too. I'll speak with the both of you," says Sri Durga.

Sara bows deeply to Sri Durga's feet, and I follow suit.

"Salvador, what is on your mind?" Sri durga probes.

I shrug, "Last night's Puja went pretty deep."

"I agree, but in order to continue to deepen, you must not be distracted by fantasy. You must continue to align with Truth. Can you do that?"

"What does that mean?" I ask.

"Lover," Sara interrupts, taking my hand, "can you speak what's really in your heart?"

I'm silent for a moment, feeling surrounded by two powerful women who are ganging up on me. Cornered, I close my eyes and reach inside. "Well, I'm curious to know who I was making love with last night."

"You'd like to know if I was there?" Sri Durga asks, with a demure smile.

"Not you, but the master, which is you, so I ... yeah, I guess that's what I want to know," I say.

"Who did you intend to make love to?" Sri Durga tests.

"Well, I'd like to think I was making love to my beloved, Saraswati."

"And was Saraswati pleased with the offering of your body?" Sri Durga asks.

"I believe she was," I say, smiling and feeling relieved to see Sara nodding.

"Then it appears the intended offering was received. What else concerns you?" Sri Durga says, staring into my soul.

"That's it," I say.

"My child, as long as there's something in your heart that you're not able to clear with speech or otherwise, it will distract you from meditation, satsang, and all other sincere spiritual pursuits."

"Right." I take my time, trying to formulate a question, and then finally say, "So, I want to know if we'll make love like that again."

"If you truly made love to the Goddess Saraswati last night, then the answer is no. You will never make love exactly like that again. The same experience can never be repeated. Divine energy is spontaneous and creative and only happens in the moment. It requires a total departure from routine or habit. However, if you want to cultivate a similarly spectacular, sacred sexual experience, there are a few things I can share. Would you like that?"

"Please!" I resound.

"You must be able to see the Goddess that you know is there."

"That's easy," I say, feeling Sara's hand melt in mine.

"And do not be a victim to your assumptions or pictures

from the past. Always approach her as though for the first time."

I bow a simple "Namaste."

"Most important right now is that you continue to speak from your heart, even when it's difficult. It is that connection to Truth that will keep the path of the kundalini clear. If you let the doubts and deceptions cloud you, you cannot tap into what is real, right now, which is a necessary ingredient to transcendental lovemaking."

As an afterthought, after bowing and thanking the master, I ask, "Where's Prabhu this morning?"

Sri Durga narrows her eyes, as though she is trying to "feel" for the right answer, and says, "I don't know."

"Oh." We leave it at that and walk out.

I rip off my shirt and collapse on the hotel bed. Tired from the late night and early morning, Sara curls her head onto my chest. I am silent, still, grateful.

"So, would you like to talk?" she asks.

"Not really," I sigh. "I think I'd rather stay unconscious. I hear it drives the girls wild in bed." She digs a hard thumb between my ribs. "Ouch!" I say, trying to tickle her while she squirms away from me. "What do you want to talk about?"

"What did you think of today's teachings?"

"I'm embarrassed. The master caught me fantasizing."

"I thought it was sweet," she says, unhinging her bra.

"Yeah, but Sri Durga probably thinks I'm being resistant to working on my throat, because I was not paying attention today."

"Well, are you resistant?" Sara asks.

"I was thinking about it during lecture, and I guess I think a lot without talking about it to anyone. Speaking one's truth is kind of a foreign concept in my family."

Sara comforts me by saying, "I think that's how it is in

most families. That's how it was with Nana. She would cover her ears and say, 'Não me diga isso!' if it was bad news or something she didn't want to hear. That's why it's so important to have a Sangha and a teacher you can really trust."

"And then," I also have to admit, "I wasn't one hundred percent comfortable talking to Sri Durga about our sex life."

"But that's not Sri Durga. That's a Tantric master and it's an absolute privilege to receive advice from someone of his status."

"My truth is that it's always been a little uncomfortable for me to really be myself in front of the master."

"Wow, Salvador, that's huge," Sara marvels.

"Is it?"

"It's awesome that you admit that. That's a serious block. Now that you notice it, you can offer it up for healing," she excitedly beams.

I observe her expand and feel myself shrink. This is the one area that I have a hard time talking to her about. I consider what it would sound like if I actually spoke my truth: "Hey, I love you, more than I knew humanly possible, and I'm afraid you love God more than me. Actually, I think I could handle that. The big scary truth is that I'm afraid you love this cult more than me." But of course, I don't have the balls to say that.

She directs a piercing gaze into my eyes. "What are you thinking?"

"It's pretty rare for me to really speak my truth," I say.

"Yeah, I can relate. I always thought I was pretty expressive, being a teacher and all, but I discovered a whole new level of expression when I was channeling," Sara says.

"What was that like?" I ask.

"I simply felt peaceful, and Truth would come through me," she replies. "It feels so natural, as though the thoughts originate in me. I didn't have to think. There was a clear knowing of what needed to be heard. It was that simple. Yet, in the back of my head, I'd wonder, 'Did I just say that?' What a high!"

Sara continues, "I've been practicing yoga and meditation for most of my adult life, always trying to experience something more; and now it's as though I finally, actually understand the reason for it all. This is the real thing. It's like the dress rehearsal is over, and this is for real. I can see farther down the path than I could before. The master has created an opening inside of me, and everything feels possible. I'm committed to sustaining the master's transmissions. I'm going to keep expanding to accommodate even more love. There is no end to his infinite love.

"I wish you could experience what it's like to be inside my body." She hugs me tight. "That's the purpose of making love. It's the closest thing we humans have to being in each other's body. It's like a direct door to the non-dual."

"I like the sound of that," I say, firmly squeezing her bottom with both hands.

"What was it like for you to be with me as a channel?" she asks, stripping the top covers down off the bed.

"It was strange, at first. When you were talking, I didn't have much to say. Normally I'm stimulated by your conversation, but there were moments while you were channeling when I felt total peace, like there was nothing more that needed to be said. It didn't even matter what you were saying, so much; it was more the way you were saying it. I didn't want it to stop, except of course, it was hard not to make love to you ... until last night."

"Why did you wait?" she asks, straight face with blinking eyelashes.

"Because I didn't know what was appropriate, you know, with your being the master and everything."

"You can always, in every circumstance, just be yourself."

"Right, but what if I'm not exactly sure who that is? When the master was talking through you, my mind would go blank. Like back in school, when I really liked a girl and wanted to ask her out, I'd go up to her and totally forget what I was going to say. It's like you'd put me under a spell, and I go all quiet inside. But at least with you, I don't get sweaty palms or butterflies in my stomach."

Smiling, Sara says, "Thank goodness, I hate clammy hands."

"You're fired," I exclaim. "I'm speaking my truth here, and you're cracking jokes."

Sara takes both my hands in hers and looks into my eyes. "What I hear you saying is that, when the beloved is talking, there is truly only one of us here, and since they are speaking Truth, there's nothing more to say."

"Exactly," I say, without adding anything or taking anything away.

"Yes. Silence can be profound and intimate," she says seductively peeling off her robe. "But Silence is so comfortable. We assume too much. The growth edge is for us to use our voice and speak our truth, even when it's uncomfortable, and I, for one, am going to choose the growth edge."

"So what do you suggest we do?" I ask, caressing her neck.

"There's only one thing to do," she says, stripping off my robe. "Let's make love and be really noisy!"

32 Kirtan in Kerala

Sara sounds into my lingam as though it were a flute. It sends an amazing vibration through the base of my penis and my balls. It induces an excited paralysis. I don't know how much time passes, but eventually she slows down, takes a few breaths, and says, "Now your turn."

Though insecure about what I'm doing, I'm honored to give back to her. As soon as I position myself between her legs and hum on my exhalation, she grows wet and wiggly. I'm vibrating tones through my lips to the inside of hers. She undulates and quivers her entire body. Soon, she's convulsing and thrashing around in the throws of an awesome orgasm; I feel it on my lips, my cheeks, and deep in my jaw.

I ask if I can enter her and she cries, "Yes! Please, but don't stop humming."

So I rise above her spread legs and slowly position myself inside her, missionary style. On the first thrust, I hum a little joke, "Mmmmmmmmm, soup is good food."

She gasps, "I'm serious."

Finding my rhythm, I ask, "What do you mean? What do you want me to do?"

"Hum with me." She's chanting "Om" so I sound out the "Mmm" part with her.

"Louder."

"This is weird," I say, trying to brush it off.

"But, why?" she asks in a naturally-seductive voice.

"I feel like it's what the woman's supposed to do."

Sara flirts, "Oh, baby, am I going to have to beg for it?"

"Beg for what?" I ask.

"To hear your voice. Let me hear you moan, just a little." I breathe loud and sound a little on each thrust.

"Ah. Ah. Ah. Ah." I concentrate on my rhythm and after a while, it becomes like pranayama. It's putting us both into a trance.

"That's right," she whispers. "Moan not from your throat but from your whole body." I moan deeper, and I feel blood rush to my erection.

"I feel it vibrating in your lingam. It's like a lightning bolt."

She moans from that same deep place, with a rising sense of electricity. I feel her muscles vibrate as she sounds. Despite a few passing concerns about the hotel neighbors, I concentrate on letting go, and she responds with even more surrender. In a few moments, there is a sense of abandon, and I'm experiencing a new high. My Sara feels different to me. Or am I different? Regardless, I'm making love to that newness.

After almost a week, Prabhu's still missing and Sri Durga's still giving teachings on mantra, sounding, kirtan, and channeling. Though I appreciate the general premise of her teachings, my concentration seems to be slipping. There's a distinct feeling that we're hanging around in Kerala to see if Prabhu will come back.

At the end of satsang, Sri Durga announces that we've been invited to attend a very exceptional kirtan taking place at a private home this evening in honor of some guru's birthday. She reminds us that devotional singing is one of the most direct ways to purify the throat chakra. She closes the satsang, just as she does every day, by chanting: "Om Mani Padme Hum, may all beings be free from the cause of suffering." After which she adds, "May Prabhu be free from the cause of suffering."

We add our sandals to the stacks of shoes around the large columns at the entrance of a beautiful mansion overlooking the backwaters of Kerala. Beyond the foyer, there is a main hall with high ceilings and a platform set up for the musicians. We position ourselves around the stage to meditate while the band tunes their instruments. Eyes closed, I sink into the depths of my tiredness.

An Indian man with long black hair is testing the microphone and strumming his sitar. A young, long-haired studly guy in a loose paisley shirt arranges a whole family of Indian drums. A plump Indian woman passes around a big basket of small percussion instruments, such as tambourines and shakers. Sara selects the finger cymbals, and the musical journey begins.

I notice that the cool drummer dude sends flirty glances in Sara's direction each time she chimes. I feel a funny pang of jealousy. I always wanted to learn the drums, but Mother made me stick to piano lessons. It's so bourgeoisie. You can't exactly lug around such a beastly instrument while traveling in a third world country.

I let the music fall into me. It feels like liquid lead through my heavy veins. Twice I pull myself out of a swift and unintentional sleep nod. I look around to see who noticed, and I realize everyone is absorbed in their own state. Harmony and rapture make people look pretty drugged up. There's a fair amount of swaying and twirling about the room, so I decide no one will notice if I slip out for some fresh air.

I make my way through the French doors to the viewing deck and take a seat in a mesh chair on the patio by the railing. After a few deep breaths of smoggy air, I reflect on the week's events or rather, non-events. Prabhu's brown eyes float into my mind. He's such a hard nut to crack, always so quiet. I'm never sure what he's thinking, but it seems as if he sits behind those dark eyes and judges people. It's creepy the way he left without saying good-bye to anyone, especially Saraswati. I know he is secretly in love with her. He seemed to disappear the same night she took me into the honeymoon suite. I'll bet he couldn't handle the jealousy.

I'm also a little relieved that he's gone. Deep down, I think I've been afraid to be the first person to leave the pilgrimage. Now that he's gone, it'll be easier for me. I'm surprised to see everyone sort of bless him on his path. I've been worried that I'd be excommunicated or made an example of. Isn't that what traditional cults are supposed to do?

I now have total permission to check out at anytime I want, and Sri Durga might even add a little prayer for me. I imagine Saraswati's lips chanting, "Om Mani Pad Me Hum. May Salvador be Free."

That's when she appears out of the darkness and takes a seat in the mesh chair beside me. Resting her hand on my arm, she asks, "What's going on?"

"I just came out for some fresh air," I say.

"Well, you sort of struck out, didn't you?"

"What do you mean?" I ask defensively.

"The smoke, I mean, it's not very fresh. I heard the family that owns this house also owns that logging company," she says, pointing across the water bank to a not-so-distant smokestack.

"So, that's what's making all this smoke," I say, and then become silent.

"What's on your mind?" I hear concern in her voice.

"I guess I don't feel like I fit in."

"Me neither," she says.

"Are you serious?" I ask.

"Yeah, we're Tantrikas, not Bhaktis," she reminds me.

"But you looked like you were having so much fun."

"I am, but in this moment, I'd rather be real with you than in bliss with them." Sara places her hand on my thigh, and asks, "What's really going on?"

"You really want to know?" I ask.

"No, I'd rather stay unconscious," she jabs at my ribs.

"I don't know what the hell I'm doing here."

"You mean at an upper-class estate in Kerala?" she asks.

"No, I mean on pilgrimage with you," I say.

"Oh."

I squeeze her arm and reassure her. "Being with you is obvious; I'm learning about devotion. That's why I've hung in so long, but I don't know if the rest of these teachings are for me anymore. Actually, I'm pretty sure they're not, and I can't even say exactly why. It's so far removed from my reality. I'm not sure what it all has to do with me or my real life."

"Well, it's not supposed to be easy. Tantra is a very steep path," she says, trying to hide her hurt.

"What's that supposed mean? Sara, do you stop and wonder what it's all about? I mean, we're a couple months into this, and I've been doing all the work, waking up early, meditating, putting up with all the inane, mindless chanting. I'm even preserving my ejaculation, or at least trying to, but I still don't know what the hell Tantra actually is."

"Are you still looking for answers? These are things that can't be explained. The more you learn, the more you realize you don't know shit and that there is no way of knowing everything," Sara explains in a condescending tone.

"Great. That's great," I snap "We're on a pilgrimage into the void."

She turns from me, and I put my arms on her shoulders. I continue, "I just don't know how safe we are. The cops might still be after us, Prabhu's turned up missing, and you have to admit some of these teachings are just downright bizarre."

"Tantra is not for everyone," she says, looking toward the dark swirling waters below. "Remember, in the beginning, we agreed you'd only stay on the path as long as it was right for you?"

"I know, and at some point I'm sure we'll have to say good-bye," I try to reason.

"Well, what do you want from me? My permission? My blessings? What?" she snaps.

I'm silent. Warmth and confusion fill the space between our bodies, and then it hits me. In a rush of truth, I turn her towards me and say, "I want you to come with me, back to Santa Monica. I've been afraid to ask, because I don't want to come between you and God, but I see now that the pilgrimage happens wherever we are. If we can practice in this mansion, we can practice in my beachfront condo in California.

"I'll take you to the Self Realization Lake Shrine. Malibu is not too far, and that is every bit as exotic as the places around here. In fact, Venice Beach is exactly like Goa. You'll meet lots of other yoga teachers, while I can start making a name for myself in the film industry. The only thing I want more than to make a contribution in this life is to do it with you." The air I breathe somehow feels clean again.

"It's beautiful to hear you speak your truth." She loves me with her hug.

"So what do you say?" I ask.

Into my ear, she whispers, "I'll meditate on it."

We embrace long enough for my insecurities to melt into hope, but not long enough to get ourselves kicked out of this house or the state of Kerala.

We return to the hall where the energy has elevated. My tiredness has been replaced with invigoration. The sitar player is chanting call-and-response style with more familiar and simple songs. "Sita Ram! Sita Ram!" His head is thrown back, and he continues calling to the divine lovers.

Usually, in Kirtan, when someone is deeply inspired, I think of them as singing to God, but in this case, he is both singing to God as well as from God. Like God is singing to himself. My body jerks and spasms to the music. Devotion pours through my throat as I call out to Sita and Ram. I hear a penetrating voice, deep and harmonious, flowing through as though this body were a flute. I wonder who is singing so beautifully.

People smile as they catch my eye, and there's a glint of love and acceptance. I glance at Amrita, tears streaming down her cheeks as she sings, and I think, "That's how I feel inside." My forehead crinkles, but no tears come. My tear ducts are dry and clogged. I guess this is what it means to be crying on the inside. I close my eyes and sing my heart out.

33 Back Water Boat Ride

An air-conditioned Ambassador cab drops me and Sara off at the boat rental office. It is a dilapidated wooden cottage, surrounded by overgrown grass, logs, and lazy, long-nosed dogs. The round woman at the counter barks orders at two leathery brown men. One is wearing a flannel dhoti, while the other dons a sheet wrapped around his waist like a big, puffy diaper. They poke around preparing the boat while we sign the poorly-translated paperwork and pay our $7 US rental fee.

The younger of the two men walks us out to the dock and helps us onto the majestic wooden barge. I understand immediately why everyone at Kirtan insisted we not leave Kerala without cruising the backwaters.

We spend almost the entire first hour in silent appreciation of nature's glory. The noontime sun reflecting off the water creates bright halos around the trees and branches that shoot up from the muddy water. The man with the puffy white dhoti stands at the tip of the barge, steering with one hand on a paddle and the other hand held across his brow, like a visor. The man in plaid runs the motor.

I try to ask the old man how long the boat is, and he responds by pointing at an egret and says, "Bird."

"Yes, bird," I say, guessing it's about 24 feet.

"I'm fantasizing that this boat is big enough to sail us home," I tell Sara.

"I am home," she says, lying on her belly on the shaded deck.

"Is that what you've decided?" I ask.

255

"I'm a yogi," she says. "I'm always at home in my body."

"But, have you thought more about my invitation?"

"Yes." She sits up.

"And?" I ask.

"I'm grateful that we're making this memory together, sailing the backwaters. Check out those clouds," she says, pointing at a spotted streak in the sky.

"So that's it? You're not coming back with me?"

"It's not my path," she says, softly stroking the back of my hand as if that's going to ease my disappointment.

"But how do you know?" I ask in a sullen whisper.

"Because I'm on it."

"Oh." I decide not to argue. There is nothing to dispute. It's not that she's being stubborn, just right. I wish I knew what it felt like to be on my path instead of lost, floating aimlessly down this river.

"You want my truth?" she offers.

"Always," I say with a forced laugh.

"I think you're running away. The closer you get to God, the more your rational mind is confronted and wants to stay in control. You're blocked in the throat chakra; you've always hated chanting. It's no coincidence that your ego is telling you to run. We're asked to speak our truth, and all a sudden you can't wait to go back to something safe, something familiar."

"It's not all of the sudden. I've been questioning these teachings since the beginning," I defend.

"And why haven't you said anything?"

"I didn't ... I just.... Look; I didn't want to you to think I was closed-minded. I was afraid you'd find out that this is not my truth, and that you'd say I wasn't spiritual enough to be your lover. But my truth is that I don't know what my truth is, but I know this is not it."

After a brief silence Sara speaks. "I have to admit, there's sadness in my heart around this not being your path; but Salvador, I'm even sadder to think that I would keep you here longer than is right for you, and you need to know how grateful I am to you. It's because of you I've taken my Tantra practice to a whole new level. I never could have touched these teachings alone. I've found a profound new teacher, and that is Relationship." She kisses me. "For that I thank you."

We return to silence. We watch several women washing saris on the shore, and this fascinates us until they pass out of view.

"This speaking the truth is funny stuff," I say. "I have this horrible habit of denying what I'm feeling, as if that's going to make it go away, and then I gag and choke over my biggest fear, until finally it comes out, and then somehow, it doesn't seem so big anymore. Why is that? It's as if speaking the truth breathes life into it, and then it grows organically into something else. I guess that is the work. I see you do it so easily. I'm touched by your commitment to what's real."

"Thank you. And what you see in me is just a reflection of you."

"I don't know about that," I say. "I see so much in you that I'll never be."

"Like what?" she asks.

"You have this insatiable lust for the divine."

"Yeah. I guess I do," Sara admits. "But you're the one who recognizes it. That explains why I love looking into your eyes. Your love has opened me to see new things about myself. I see my own devotion reflected back to me, and you have it too; you just don't see it yourself, but to me it's clear, almost Zen. You're so grounded, and romantic. I'm devastated by your having to leave. I'm going to miss you," she sobs, letting the floodgate open. "And I'll miss who I am when I'm with you."

"I'm sorry I've been so resistant. I know if I stay on,

there's a lot more work I could do," I offer.

"But you can't stay just for me," she says, wiping her face on my robe.

"But you're my Goddess, Saraswati, and I am every bit as committed to you as you are to your God. In that way, my journey isn't any less than yours."

"I love you," she says, still sobbing.

"Besides, if I leave now, I'll be running away from the only true love I've ever known." I hold her tight until her shallow sobs turn into deep and soft breaths. We kiss, fondle, moan and sigh for the remainder of the ride, not caring what the boatman in diapers may think.

34 Close Encounters of the Third Eye

Lying in deep sleep, my body is one with the hotel mattress. Too hot to cuddle, Sara's on the other side of the bed. I hear the soft rustle of her stirring. She lifts off the bed gracefully, as if levitating. I rub my eyes as she moves around in the bluish glow. She dresses in a dream-like trance, unlocks the door, and then walks out leaving the door ajar. I wait for her to return.

After a moment, I call after her. No response. I slip my robe on and peek out into the hall. No Sara. I walk down the stairwell to the hotel lobby, but there's no one at the front desk. I step outside and see someone turning the corner over a hundred yards away. I call out to Sara, but she's completely out of sight.

Anxious to know where she's going, I break into a run down the street, turn the corner, and find an empty intersection with a number of different directions she could have gone. I turn one corner, and then the next, passing locked shops and homeless, sleeping bodies. My heart sounds in my ears, I wake a sleeping rickshaw driver and ask him if he saw anyone. Squinting his eyes, he simply offers me a ride. I have him drive me down a number of streets, all looking the same, dark and empty.

More than half an hour later, I decide to go back to the hotel to tell Swami-ji and the others to start a search party. Not having money to pay the driver, I instruct him to wait outside while I retrieve my wallet.

The door to my room is still ajar. My heart sinks at the

Don't Drink the Punch

site of our empty bed, but I'm relieved to find my money belt still tucked under my pillow where I left it. After paying the driver, I notice the desk clerk has returned. I ask if he's seen Sara. He nods and points in the direction of the banquet hall. My hands fly instinctually to my heart in "Namaste" to thank him, but in truth, I'm thanking God.

I walk through the short passage, and when I open the door, I see the first of what will be two confronting sights that evening.

Prabhu is mostly naked, in a loincloth, collapsed into a chair on a small riser. His skin is completely smeared with white ash, and his matted hair is poking out from a saffron turban that covers most of his forehead. Sara is on her knees before him with her head resting on his lap.

"Ah, Salvador has arrived," he says in a scratchy voice, as I continue walking toward them.

Sara slowly rises, holding some type of poultice in one hand and gray bandages in the other. Apparently, she is performing first aid on his scratches and cuts.

"Did you get into some kind of fight?" I ask.

"Were you worried about me?" he says, cracking a smile.

"I was worried about Sara. You left without saying anything," I say, reaching out to her.

She looks at me apologetically. "I'm sorry. Our master needed me."

"Oh, I didn't know," I say, realizing Prabhu is the new channel. I bow before him and sit down on the floor by his feet. "How'd you get so scratched up?"

"I will complete my private darshan with Saraswati, and then I will talk with you," he says.

Confusion and doubt grow hot in my skin. I do not speak. I do not move.

"I know it's difficult for you to grasp right now, and

that's understandable, but this is an important teaching only Saraswati is ready for."

He rests his dirty hand on her red locks.

"Is that what you want, Sara?" I ask.

She nods somberly.

"Fine," I say, and I walk out the way I came in. Leaning against the wall on the other side of the door, I practice a few rounds of Rudhra breath to calm myself down. Despite the emotional upset, my concentration is surprisingly sharp, as it often is in the presence of the master.

Within a few minutes, I hear Sara gasp, and I instinctually rush back in to catch Prabhu, turban off, revealing a cracked-open forehead. A narrow beam of light pours toward Sara, who has the most blissful hint of a smile.

In a second, the vision is gone and Prabhu turns toward me with a few drops of blood between his eyes and says, *"I didn't realize you were so eager for these teachings. The moon is not ready. These grounds are not ripe; but when the time is right, you will know how to serve me. Go now, and bring me my saffron robe. Salvador, you are to tell the others we will meet here before sunrise for satsang."*

He reaches into his dirty carpetbag and hands me his ancient and worn bronze bell.

When I return from my rounds of waking everyone and preparing myself for satsang, I find the desk clerk in a heated discussion with Sri Durga, who is no longer wearing orange.

"Master," Sri Durga says, interrupting Prabhu's meditation, "the banquet hall is booked for a wedding rehearsal at 8am this morning. Perhaps we should return to the rooftop."

Prabhu dismisses her argument. *"Not a concern of ours. The bride has broken the arrangement to be with her lover. We will complete long before the room is needed."*

The attendant bobbles his head and reluctantly leaves

the room.

Prabhu draws the heavy curtains closed, and sunrise happens without our notice. He instructs us to concentrate on a single point in the middle of our minds. My meditation mixes with my adrenaline to produce an alert and charged mental state. The vision of Prabhu's open third eye flashes repeatedly in my mind.

After meditation, we chant only one song to Kali-Durga.

Prabhu says, *"Swami-ji will now tell you the story of how his master left the body and came to inhabit many bodies."*

Swami-ji, looking a bit unsettled, glances several times at Prabhu, whose face reveals only expectation for Swami-ji to comply with his instructions.

"It's not a story I'm accustomed to telling, because it's so easily misunderstood." Swami-ji clears his throat. "I was seventeen and despondent about my responsibilities at home and school. My father's guru felt a pilgrimage would cure me, so I set off to see the temples but had a secret agenda to end my life by flinging my body into the Mother Ganga.

"During the three-day walk to the river, I was crossing through the cemetery grounds at sunset and heard a deep, melodious voice chanting a Kali-Durga sloka. I followed the voice to find my master sitting at the base of a tree with yellow blossoms. He was covered with ash, in perfect stillness, a vision of perfect light. In that instant, I fell to my knees and begged for him to take me as his student, and from that day on, I devoted myself to his service.

"I don't know how many bodies he'd been in before the one I met, but after only three years of practicing with him, he gave me specific instructions on how to dismember and discard his body after he vacated it. Then his soul slipped out on the new moon.

"I suffered such a terrible grief when he left. I thought for sure I would die, but when I finally resumed practicing what he taught me, I realized he never left. He entered my body and continued to teach through me. Everything I've done is to serve him. He urged me to continue school, learn English, and work with Westerners; but above all, he insists that I continue the practices at sunrise and sunset. His final promise is that our practices will always evolve. New transmissions are imparted with each new student."

Prabhu spontaneously points to Raj, who scoots forward, bows to Prabhu, and asks Swami-ji, "Did our master ever teach you how to leave your body?"

"No. That was one of the many powers he had that we never discussed. Most of his teachings were silent. He initiated with shakti-pat (power of transmission). He touched my forehead and created an opening in me. That's how I was given the gift of opening others, like yourself, to his voice. I've watched many lives transform by his guidance."

Raj turns to Prabhu. "Forgive me Master, but this is such a remarkable power, I'm curious if it can be replicated or proven?"

Prabhu directs a deep stare into Raj whose body softens with some nonverbal teaching. After a few moments of tense silence, Prabhu speaks, *"Got it?"*

"Thank you," Raj says and bows.

Prabhu outstretches an arm to the window frame behind him and plucks the thin metal pull from the curtain rod. He snaps the plastic coating off the metal wire by swiftly flicking it against his knee. He then rests the miniature javelin across his lap. Prabhu closes his eyes and goes into a deep state of Pratyahara (withdrawal from the senses). After a moment, he inserts the wire poker into his own cheek, opens his jaw slightly, and pierces through to the other side. He then opens his eyelids revealing only eye whites. He parts his dry lips and clamps his teeth down on the metal wire twice, making a tinny chomping sound. He then lowers his pupils, looking out at the Sangha, before deftly withdrawing the skewer. There are visible holes, but no blood.

"The greatest attachment for most humans is the body. The greater the attachment, the more stuck they become in the illusion. Once you master the mind and are able to control the senses, only then can you perceive Reality.

"When a yogi advances to mastery on his path, there are many siddhis (supernatural powers) that may present themselves. This phenomena is greatly misunderstood and misused, especially among Tantrikas, as they naturally become very powerful, but don't always use that power wisely."

Bud chimes in from the back, "What kind of powers?"

"We're talking about the basic power of reality over illusion. It can look like manipulating non-linear time, being in two places at once, levitating, shape-shifting, or moving through space instantaneously.

"For some avatars (living incarnations of God), it's the power of manifestation, like Sai Baba, who is known to produce endless sacred ash and Rolexes from his empty palm. This I have yet to experience firsthand; but, of course, it begs the question: 'What is the point?' Tell me, what use is it for this yogi to self-anesthetize and pierce a wire through his own flesh?" Prabhu provokes.

Swami-ji answers, "You show us your power, Master, to help us believe. You are pointing to what's possible...."

Prabhu cracks a half smile and continues. *"If one practices taming the mind and opening the third eye regularly, siddhis are bound to come, and then a new temptation is born for there are many town folk that will pay a hefty fee to have someone cast a love spell or end a legal battle. This is what we call black Tantra, and it can go as far as killing people with mere thought."*

Swami-ji can't seem to contain his curiosity. "Master, I admit at times I would like the power to heal or to cultivate greater psychic wisdom, because they can be used to serve others. But these other siddhis that you speak of, those that are considered black Tantra, do they not create bad karma?"

"Swami-ji, do you not recognize that it is only your judgment that draws the line between what is good and bad karma?" Prabhu informs.

Swami-ji persists, "Then is it best to stay away from all forms of alchemy?"

"Ah, but if you are a true Tantrika, that is impossible. If we chose to withdraw from our bodies or the world, as do many Vedantic ascetics or Buddhist meditators, we might not have as much effect on the physical plane; but since the playground in Tantra is the manifest world, the consequence is invariably magic. Your awakened consciousness naturally transforms the manifest reality. That is inevitable."

Prabhu's attention turns on Amrita who is rhythmically swaying back and forth riding waves of visible bliss. "I get that you are cautioning us not to attach to these powers out of spiritual greed," she says.

"This is the teaching of Amrita's Chakra Puja. If you succumb entirely to your desires during sexual practices, you will most likely get lost in sensation and lose site of true union. However, if you deny your desires entirely, they will run you, and you will also miss out on enlightenment. If you become proficient in your sexuality, practicing presence during the act, you may realize ecstatic levels of being beyond body.

"So it is with yogic powers. If you focus all your energy on the attainment of these powers, you become attached and may never realize the ultimate liberation, but if you run away, you are equally trapped; your fears will run you. True realization occurs when you dance with what is, transcending the physical phenomena. Misuse of these powers will obstruct

your path to total realization.

"When you do gain these powers, come to understand them until they no longer fascinate you, and then nothing can distract you from ultimate Truth.

"With this in mind, I'm going to invite you to set aside your conditioning about black or white, wrong or right, and introduce you to profound practices around the nature of death and destruction.

"How are you to live in light if you are afraid of the dark? It's through death that we find the doorway to eternal Truths, and these cannot be accessed in fear and denial. Understandably, these practices will confront you, but it is a simple process of purification. Shed your resistances, and you will have greater discrimination, dispassion, and equanimity in all that is.

"To rise to this level of practice, you must increase your willingness. You must overcome your preferences and aversions. Many of the rituals we will be doing have been maintained by the lowest caste, whose job it is to watch over funeral pyres and outcasts. In Tantra, we do not recognize classes. As a Tantrika, you must be of every social status, age, and religion. You are Shiva and Shakti, and if you want to experience life and be truly alive, you must also delve into death.

"Tonight you'll be initiated with Kali Puja. It will be a dark moon this Tuesday, perfect to worship our mother liberator Kali. This is how we celebrate Mangala Mars, the planet of war and death. During the next few days, you are to drink only lemon water, as we are fasting. Pack your bags and gather a few offerings. For Kali we give: red-flesh, death, limes, neem, chili, and other spices or symbols considered inauspicious. We will then go into the graveyard for a ceremony that is foreign to you, a profound and important ritual. Don't be afraid. These are ancient rituals for the healing

of the world."

Sri Durga closes the circle with a Tibetan prayer.

Immediately after the chant, the front desk manager spills into the room, places a lei of flowers around Prabhu's neck and bows at his feet. Swami-ji interprets his enthusiastic cries: "Oh venerable Master, forgive me for doubting you. I am forever your student. The wedding was scheduled for today, and now it's cancelled. Just as you have predicted, the bride ran away with her lover, bringing great shame on the family. Your powers of prediction are so perfect. Will you please do a Puja to ensure the bride's family will still pay for the room rental?"

35 Naked in the Cemetery

We drive for hours along a winding, unpaved road, not far from the coast of Tamil Nadu. Parking under a twisted acacia, we leave our sandals in the Magic Bus and walk barefoot on the warm earth. The compacted dirt path narrows into the brush. Once the headlights on the Magic Bus are turned off, I see only two remote lights in the far off horizon and hear the creepy hiss of the nearby ocean. Feeling the warm earth under my feet bewilders me. It's as though I'm stepping into another dimension. The moonless sky and ocean mist cloud the visibility.

Sara is behind Swami-ji. I am behind Sara. Bud is behind me, and the nocturnal sounds harmonize around us. I sense that many naked sadhus have walked this path before us. The farther we walk, the more the city lights fade from the faraway ridge.

We enter into a large, powdery clearing, with silvery ash covering the ground. There are bone piles, and other evidence of people's Pujas. In fact, several of those people are still wandering around like ghosts. They do not seem to notice us. Each dark corner of this cemetery plot hosts a naked sadhu sitting in a trance beating a two-sided hand drum.

Prabhu and Swami-ji disrobe, so we follow, hanging our robes from the thick brush, sparing them from the ash-covered ground. Sara helps steady me while I slip out of my costume. Her skin glows in the starlight; the white robes look like ghosts stretched out in a row behind the two orange leaders.

We all sit before Pabhu who instructs us on how to open

the third eye. As we listen, Swami-ji prepares a pyre for Agni. I orient my sense of self amongst the humans that are no longer. Bones are stacked in little structures scattered about.

When the fire is lit, I make out an order to the mounds of bones, ash, and dirt around us. Prabhu sits near a pile of skulls, which is clearly an altar. He explains that the mounds represent Shiva's sacred lingam. A chill creeps up my spine. I try to stay calm by focusing on my mantra between each inhale, exhale, inhale, exhale, inhale, exhale….

After Swami-ji offers a few opening prayers, Prabhu demonstrates how to protect and prepare our bodies for ritual by smearing ash on our skin.

"Your body is your greatest attachment. Think of death while you rub this ash on each square inch of your skin. One day, your flesh will turn to ash. That is all that will remain. You think of yourself as man, but really you are the consciousness within the matter."

It's a slow, meditative, even sensual process. Massaging the chalky powder onto our skin is supposed to offer psychic protection. It is also supposed to keep us warm, so that we don't need clothes, but as the night wears on, the chill creeps in.

We become substantially warmer as we fling our offerings, herbs, limes, and even bloody meat into the fire. The smell of burning flesh is supposed to attract wrathful Gods and spirits. Prabhu adds medicine called "dusty men," which reportedly lets off an irresistible aroma to the Gods, helping tame their wrath. Prabhu then launches into a tale that's more horrifying than any ghost story I've ever heard at Camp Hess Kramer.

"The world was under a terrible spell of disrepair and war. Our Mother Durga was at battle with a fierce demon called Rakta-bija. She had ten arms with a deadly weapon in each, but after many attempts to slay this demon,

Durga realized that she had only made matters worse. From every drop of blood that Rakta-bija spilled on the earth, one thousand identical demons would spring forth. Whenever she wounded the beast, she would suddenly find herself swimming in a sea of enemies. Thus, Durga meditated, and upon opening her third eye, she produced a black-skinned, bloodthirsty Dakini, with gnashing teeth and a lolling tongue. That's how Goddess Kali was born.

"*Kali licked up every drop of blood shed during the battle. She then found the original Rakta-bija and sucked him dry, draining him of life and winning the war.*"

We chant and dance around the fire, offering our ashen bodies to Kali and the ten wisdom Goddesses. Prabhu then initiates us into aspects of the Poa ceremony. We practice the act of ejecting our consciousness out of the body by using the mantra, "Phat!"

Stomping the left foot and crying out, "Phat!"

Eyes roll back into people's heads, "Phat!"

Bodies slump over. Screams and shakes abound as the mantra pops from devotees like dried corn in the pyre. Amrita is uninhibited in her naked performance. She is loud and free, fondling and gyrating her private parts without a shred of shame.

As the night matures, I see several people spreading their robes or clearing beds in the ash to sleep on. Since I feel my immune system is still recovering from the malaria, I decide to hike back to sleep in the Magic Bus. Despite the goose bumps on Sara's white skin, she refuses to come with me. I crawl in through the front and curl up in my seat, trying not to wake Ganapthi who is sleeping in the back.

The pre-dawn sky is cyanide blue. I awake and realize I am a little late for satsang. Rushing back to the clearing, I find everyone sitting silently, au natural. I struggle through a very distracted, cold, and contracted meditation in which I find myself asking, "What the hell are we doing here?"

Prabhu begins beating a damaru (two-sided hand drum) while Swami-ji plays a trumpet made of a human thighbone. In a booming voice, Prabhu cries:

"Kali is mother.

"Kali is protector.

"Kali is transformation.

"Dispeller of illusion.

"Kali cuts through ego.

"Kali cuts through time and all distractions.

"Kali is the blue-black Dakini that drinks blood in order to give life.

"Kali is ever present.

"Kali come to us.

"Come to us, Kali Ma!

"Kali stands behind you now. Don't turn your head. She is strong and thirsty. Can you feel her breath on the back of your neck? She stands barefoot in the belly of a cold and stiff corpse, its entrails entangled between her toes. She wears snakes around each ankle and dances in a skirt made of human arms. These are the hands of time dangling around her full round hips. Her skin is blue-black and naked, her breasts dripping with life-giving milk. In her right hand, she holds a hook knife, and in her left hand, she holds a skull cup. She has come to liberate you from who you think you are.

"Kali I feel you here.

"Kali I invite you in.

"Kali free me from this flesh!

"Drink of my resistance, my aversions, and preferences all.

"Kali take my arms as your girdle, let my scull adorn your necklace, O Mother of many forms, bring down your sword and liberate me from my separation from you.

"The mantra 'Phat' will project your soul out of your body, which is a mere vessel, that you may give yourself back to your source. Only through divorcing yourself from your greatest attachment, the body, can you liberate your soul."

We spend the entire day learning the elaborate and subtle details of visualization of the ancient Chod ritual. Through lecture, transmission, and dance, we practice cutting ourselves from greed, anger, ignorance, arrogance, and doubt. To the best of our abilities, we cut ourselves away from our thoughts, and even our own personalities.

At sunset, Raj offers Jivana's body as our altar. She lays face down in the earth. Prabhu uses the charred end of a burnt stick to draw a yantra onto Jivana's upper back. The yantra is three triangles, one inside the other, placed inside of a concentric circles enclosed within a square with four doorways. Prabhu concludes by piercing Jivana's skin, drawing blood in the center of her back to make a bindu (focal point for meditation) in the yantra. Jivana does not flinch.

We continue our practices above and around her, while she lays face down, knees bent, legs spread, for hour upon hour. From time to time, I find myself worrying that she is not getting enough oxygen. Or that she's suffocating from breathing too much ash.

As I dance, I also ponder, "Who are the other ash-covered Sadhus? Where do they go during the daytime? What are the herbs being put in the lemon water that we are offered for breakfast, lunch, and dinner?"

Shortly after Swami-ji's Agni is burning bright, the blue-black Dakini returns. This time, I not only feel her warm breath on my neck, but it smells like rotting flesh. My hairs stand on end. My skin crawls. I cry out, "Phat!"

Ejecting my soul up and out of my body, it doesn't quite make it into the third eye of the Dakini, but she sniffs it in through her nose, and I can feel my breasts grow round, my hips widen and fill, and my feet ground firmly against the earth. I raise the hook knife in my right hand and slash straight through the ego. In front of me, my old body slumps to the ground like a heap of lifeless flesh. I am without a forehead. The body that used to be Sal is severed precisely above the eyebrows. Blood drains out and beads up in the ash against the earth.

    Sal's shoulders look surprisingly small and sunken. His skin looks lighter than usual. I turn to find my hand full of hair, a scalp filled with fleshy bits and sticky brown shag. I kneel down on one knee and use the hook knife to scoop the skin and hair off the scull cap, which I set on a tripod above the sacred fire. The scull cap grows into a huge disc as I disassemble the remains of the body. I sink my curved knife through my joints, which brings an unexpected relaxation to my blue-black knees and hips and ankles. I'm hacking at the body's lower limbs, crunching and pulverizing not only the bone but the marrow, as well. Looking at all my own features, scars and birthmarks, I am no longer attached. I pluck the stringy tendons and sinew from the bone, as if I am pulling pork flesh off a swine.

    I deposit the entire body-mass into the large scull cup and watch the now unrecognizable flesh bubble and burn. I dance, erratic, liberating, and unpredictable. I do not tire. I cannot stop. I move, and the world moves with me.

    The rhythm of the drum calls me to move my blue-black body. *"Om Ah Hung, Om Ah Hung, Om Ah Hung..."* The sadhus chant into the airwaves. Tonight the white moon hides as its red counterpart hangs low in the sky. I dance, and the stars dance around me. I breathe, and the wind blows through me, and when finally I thirst, my brew is ready. The steam of the nectar rises up to mingle with the moon. I lick my lips at the rich aroma of this body slush stuff that has become a wish-fulfilling ambrosia. I drink and everything dissolves. I'm nourished into deep nirvana. My form retreats into the vast space of existence. There is no end to my being. There is no beginning. There is just a starry sky, without the stars or the sky.

I am expansion beyond word and form. Lost in the cosmic void, I am existence absolute. I have only tasted such liberation in total unconsciousness, in deep dreamless sleep.

Without a body or a sense of self, I am lost in vast space. From the infinite distance, I hear the faint resonating sound of a conch shell growing louder. It is the call of Dharma. From primordial sound, words form, and then meaning.

What pulled me out? I don't remember. It was nothing dramatic, maybe an itch or a dream. Maybe it was fear that I would never come back, but I regret it, whatever it was that pulled me back. I curse it. At sunrise meditation on the third day, I find myself thinking fondly of those lost moments, which feel so close, yet a painful world away.

After satsang, Sara and Amrita create a huge labyrinth with bones and debris and different colored ash. Swami-ji and Bud disappear with the Magic Bus, having been sent on a secret mission by Prabhu. The rest of us spend the day in practice, walking the labyrinth, visualizing, and meditating. Around noon, I am unable to keep my eyes open. I curl up at the base of a tree in the corner of the cemetery and fall asleep.

I awake with a horrible foreboding. I'm drowning in every moment. I can't breathe. I feel that my top has become my bottom, and the confusion is too great. The repercussions of this practice are profound and irreparable. I fear not only my own death but also that of everyone involved.

Before sunset Swami-ji and Bud return with a body. It is a young woman who died from some type of consumption or lung disease. She is little, about the same size as Jivana. Swami-ji guesses she's from a lower caste family who couldn't afford to bury her. Unmarried women of this age are so uncommon that she could easily have been a prostitute. Swami-ji follows Prabhu's instructions, carefully arranging her body where Jivana had been the night before, face down, legs spread, knees bent like a frog. I try not to look at her face.

While turning my final loop in the labyrinth, I am consciously placing one bare foot in front of the other, and step into a peaceful clarity around my need to leave. It's sudden but it's sure.

During lecture, Prabhu explains how profound it is to actually prepare a body for cremation. The act of physically cutting the flesh off a dead body, into specific small pieces, will supposedly help us overcome our attachment to our own physical form.

Help! I feel we need psychological help. He turns to me and asks if I'd like to share. To which I say, "It's time for me to leave."

"Ah, that's the ego." Prabhu diagnoses.

"No, this is my truth."

"Let me tell you something, Salvador. If you leave now, you'll be incomplete for a long time. It's like stepping off the operating table before the surgery is finished. You will have no means of reconciliation, no integration, no healing. You will go on starting relationships and not finishing them. You will not progress easily through karmic cycles. However, if you make peace with Mother Kali, you will have peace with all women. If you stick it through, the rewards will be unimaginable, beyond belief. You and Sara will experience new levels of bliss unknown to you before."

I clench my jaw, and bow a Namaste. I know we've been warned us about the paranoia that characterizes the stage before a breakthrough, but if this is some kind of test, I'm willing to flunk. I can't bear it anymore. As soon as the formal satsang completes, while others are stretching and moving their bodies, I pull Sara under the tree where I napped.

"How are you doing?" I ask, trying to read her eyes.

"I'm well," she says, avoiding eye contact. She kisses me square on the mouth. "You feel good," she says.

"Actually, I don't. I'm pretty uncomfortable with these practices."

"They are uncomfortable practices."

"This isn't resistance. This is genuine concern for our safety. Remember when I got malaria, Sara? The master didn't intervene then. I could've died. We were dealing drugs in Goa, we were chased out of Tiruvannamalai by the cops, and could've gotten thrown into jail. In fact, for all we know, there's still a warrant out for our arrest. Now we've acquired a dead prostitute from God knows where, and Prabhu's about to teach us the fine art of cutting up dead bodies. Sara, how far do you want to go?"

"All the way ... if we have to. Didn't last night's experience mean anything to you? That was a taste of what total realization could be," she says.

"How do you know what I experienced?"

"I am compassion, Salvador. There is nothing you feel that I don't." A strand of hair wisps across her eyes.

"Then you know how trapped and desperate I am?" I say, delicately moving her hair behind her ear.

"Yes, and that's the ego. It's terrified because you're nearing enlightenment."

"Sara, doesn't it occur to you that there's a reason every human being is born with an ego? Isn't the ego's job to protect us? I'm not interested in annihilating the one thing that ensures my survival. That's why my gut tells me we've got to go."

"I'm sorry, Salvador, I'm going to complete this journey. It's for the healing of the planet," she says.

"But if you change your mind...," I start.

"There is no mind to change," she interrupts.

"I know this is not a rational practice, Sara, but I'd like

to keep my mind. That's why I'm getting out of here before anything else happens. Sara, if you come with me now, I'll be your devotee, your servant, your lover, your lord ... but we've got to move!"

"Now?" she asks.

"Right now," I say. "Otherwise, they'll make it difficult for you."

"Go then, if that's what you want. Ganapathi went back to the Magic Bus." She walks into the brush and plucks Prabhu's orange robe off the bushes. "Put this on and tell him to take you to the city. Just meditate during the whole ride, and then when you get into the city, you can take a cab to the airport."

"Sara, I love you more in every dazzling moment. You are my Goddess," I say.

"I am an empty reflection of you," she says.

"I'm going to write my address down and put it in your bag. I don't know how to contact the ashram. Please call me as soon as you can."

"Go now," she says.

"I'll be flying via Bangkok, if you want to meet me later."

"I'll be with you in spirit," she says, holding back her emotion.

I throw myself on the earth at her feet. After a few silent breaths, she bows Namaste, and walks away. I stay out of view of the Sangha as I slip on Prabhu's robes. Ganapthi is shifty and uncertain about taking my directions, but I transmute my nervousness into authority and follow Sara's instructions to the letter. Except, instead of meditating on the way, I write a five-page love letter in her sketchbook and include all the rupees and traveler's checks I have. It's at least enough to get to Bangkok, with a promise to pay for her trip to America when she's ready.

Act IV
Homecoming

36 The Wrath of Kali-Durga

As the aircraft taxies into Bangkok International Airport, I force my eyes shut and make believe I'm arriving for the first time after quitting my job in Chang Mai. I tell myself India never happened, but Saraswati did. The sharp ache in my chest proves it.

I go through the motions at customs. I make reservations at the airport's hotel for one night's stay before my sunrise flight home. Instead of leaving the airport right away, I'm drawn to the up escalator where I first saw Saraswati. It's a masochistic act, I know, but I can't keep myself from stepping on the moving stairway. At the top, I watch the metal steps being sucked back into the machine. My heart sears as though it's being sucked into the cracks at my feet and shredded by the steel teeth of the escalator.

I sit in the corner of the Blue Mountain coffee shop, a few tables away from an Asian businessman who occupies the very spot where I introduced myself to Saraswati. I stare at the place mat menu, not because I'm thirsty, but because the pain is so heavy I can't lift my head. If she were to change her mind and follow me out of Hades, this is where she'd come; it would be the only logical meeting place, that is, if all the logic hadn't been brainwashed out of her.

I consider ordering a cup of that half-coffee/half-tea concoction and staying awhile, but I can't bear another painful breath and get the hell out of there.

The airport hotel has crisp, white sheets, with hospital

corners, something I forgot existed. The room also features instant hot plumbing, two bottles of purified water, and a magnetic key swipe. After several hours of laying there, no sleep, no meditation, just total numbness, I look around for my bag, but remember I don't have one. All I have is an orange robe and my money belt. I decide I should probably buy something to change into before arriving in Los Angeles.

While hailing a taxi in the parking lot, I realize this is the same place where Saraswati and I bought fake papers from Miranda. "Pat Pong Road, please."

The small driver has the good sense not to try to talk to me during the 45-minute ride through the city.

I marvel at how clean and bright the streets seem. I wander through organized aisles of new products and think, "Is this really Pat Pong?"

My memory is that it was dark and seedy. I also notice Christmas hats and Santa beards floating through the crowds. Traveling in a mostly Hindu and Muslim country, I'd completely lost track of the season and feel unprepared for the holiday madness.

A homeless mother sleeps with a dirty child bundled under each arm in an ATM cove, and I think, compared to the naked sadhus in India, they're living in luxury. They're each wearing flannel pajamas. They've got a cardboard bed, a number of dirty blankets, and a big bag of stuff they carry around.

A few sex clubs scream out as I walk by. They used to elicit excitement and temptation, but now they seem distasteful and showy. Several girls in short red skirts and Santa hats offer to, "Sucky, fucky," as men go by. Still, I feel no temptation, no curiosity, and no judgment either.

I trace backwards the same path that Saraswati and I walked, with virtually no thought. When I arrive at the scarf stand across from McDonalds, I wonder if I'll ever see her again. I want to buy her that purple scarf she never got. It takes all the energy I have to haggle with the saleswoman over the price of the scarf. When I go into my money belt, I realize I only have enough cash for my cab rides and airport tax. I guess I'm not supposed to buy the scarf. I give up shopping and figure I'll make do with my orange robe for now.

My company paid for my twice-transferred first-class seat to the USA. After take-off, I recline and sink into the ridiculously posh leather seat. The guy in the aisle seat next to me is reading the paper and mutters something about feeling sick about the tragedy in Phuket, but the last thing I want is company, so I don't ask what the hell he's talking about. I ask the flight attendant to anesthetize me with Kahlua and milk.

As expected, the shuttle driver at the LA airport shoots me a funny look when he picks me up. Since I have no bags and I'm paying for a private ride, he offers for me to sit up front where he's busy listening to talk radio.

After a few minutes he asks, "Where you coming from, brother?"

"Thailand," I answer.

"Were you hit by the tsunami?"

"What tsunami?"

"Oh man! You haven't heard? It's all over the news. This huge wave wiped out all the resorts in Phuket."

"When was that?" I ask in disbelief.

"Yesterday. They say it started with an earthquake in Sumatra or something. I don't even know where that is. Anyway, it caused a huge tidal wave and nearly sank Sri Lanka."

"Sri Lanka's off the coast of where I was in India," I explain.

"Yeah, it got India too."

"Where? Do you know where? Were people killed?" I

ask.

"I don't think they know how many yet. The reports are still coming in, but the death toll is estimated in the hundreds of thousands. Listen to this." He turns up the radio, and I hear a feature story with graphic details about the Sri Lankan coast from a reporter who was vacationing there. The driver reaches one arm behind his seat and produces an *LA Times*. The cover displays miles of devastated coastline. I skim the article while listening to the harrowing details in stereo.

I set down the paper and ask the guy if I can turn off the radio, and I close my eyes. Everything goes black. I see Saraswati's beaming at me from behind the void. Her bright green eyes gleam in full lucid detail. I feel incredible peace. Instead of loss, I get a strange sort of comfort in my core.

My house looks like it belongs to someone else from some other time. The front yard obviously has not been tended in months. The mailbox is stuffed with junk mail and yellow cards requesting I go to the post office to pick up the overflow. Dead and shriveled plants line the walk to my front door, which is littered with old papers. Thank God I don't have any pets.

Inside, there's a distinct smell of stale air, but it seems strangely cleaner than I remember leaving it. I run the bath, boot up my laptop, and hit play on the answering machine. After the third concerned message from Mother, I turn it off. I come across a multi-colored map on the web that confirms the tsunami's path. Sri Lanka was swamped first, and then the wave hit the entire southeast coast of India, as far up as Madurai, where my plane departed from, and wrapped all the way around to Kerala, where the Divine Mother Amma Chi resides. The cemetery grounds were in Tamil Nadu, which was hit the hardest, unknown numbers killed.

I Google tsunami in Tamil Nadu and am sickened by the reports of dead fishermen and homeless families. Black dread fills my chest, and I can't go on. I shut the machine down and then submerge my body in the filling tub. Not normally a bath-taker, I fantasize that I'm in the Ganges River, melting into the arms of the Divine Mother. Saraswati's eyes are there again, looking back at me with love.

The next afternoon, while Mother is at her weekly bridge game at the country club, I call and leave a message on her home phone telling her I've arrived home safely. "I'm going to take a few days to recover from jet lag, and we can celebrate Hanukkah together sometime after the weekend."

Fighting a sore throat and itchy eyes, I go into my closet and am confused by all the options. I throw on a pair of Levi's jeans and find that the only tee shirts I own are brand name. I feel constricted and pretentious. Funny, I thought I would want to burn this robe when I got home from India, but after considering the alternatives, I'd rather burn everything else in my closet.

I pull designer clothes off hangers and make a pile for Goodwill. That's when I discover a large oil painting wrapped in a sheet against my closet wall. I vaguely remember buying this painting on impulse at a garage sale some years ago. I unwrap it and lay it on my bed in absolute awe.

My whole story is right there in modern abstract. There's a dirty brown background with eerie tan stains that look like faces. Off center, a gorgeous green-eyed angel heralds the end of the world, which looks like a huge blue wave surging below her knees. In the corner, diminishing with perspective, there are rust-colored robes hanging on a clothesline. Wispy lines float around the angel, reminding me of whole families of lost souls making their way back to the light. In the center, there is a large void, a blaring hole that the artist decided to dedicate to emptiness.

In a tender rush, I re-experience my forehead at Sara's

feet and my belly against the cool cemetery earth. Was that the last time I'll ever bow to my beloved? I wince and sob. How could I leave? My fists fill with bedspread, knuckles gripping tight as I throw my body to the floor, the painting slips to the foot of the bed, and I curl up on the carpet. What have I done? Clenching my teeth, I grunt out my pain.

After an indeterminable duration of thrashing and emoting, there's a strange awareness of the one who's acting out. It's the body that needs to release and let go. The body is doing. That's what it does, but my spirit is untouched. My heart may ache, but my soul is somewhere out there soaring with Saraswati.

In the overcast afternoon, I manage to walk down to the corner market with the intention of buying some basic staples. Overwhelmed by the variety and options of packaged food, I instead wander into the nearest coffee shop. I order my first Starbucks chai, and I'm surprised how good it tastes. It's nothing like the chai in India. The frothy syrup melts on my tongue and amplifies my thirst for the rich, deep connection that Saraswati was for me. I hold the "grande to-go" cup close to my chest and walk barefoot on the grey beach, listening to squawking gulls. I walk until I tire and fall asleep in the sand.

Several days go on like this. Letters and calls come in from people both concerned and relieved. Everybody's asking to hear about my trip. Finally, my independent filmmaking buddy, Dean, stops in to take me to a New Year's Eve party in Beverly Hills.

"I'm too tired and sick," I tell him with a raspy voice while lying on the couch.

"I can see that, but this is a once in a lifetime event. Everybody who's anybody is going to be there, and the only way that I got in was by telling Carmen Electra that you were making an independent film about the tsunami, using footage from your first-hand experience. C'mon, man. You've got to go; you're my ticket in."

"You've got to be kidding," I say. "I didn't even have my camera in India."

"She doesn't need to know that," he pleads, and he even selects a suit from the disaster pile near my bed.

37 The Cosmic Car Alarm

The Spanish-style mansion is crawling with plastic people in dazzling dresses and suits. All the freshly-perfumed wanna-be celebs are mingling with the has-been hits in the living room over an ambient jazz band. Outside, there's a huge lap pool and lavish ice sculpture, and joints are passed shamelessly from face to face. The cocaine is more discreetly snorted in the bathrooms.

I lose Dean to a giggly blonde by the pool. I find myself sinking into a stiff leather couch in the less-crowded sun room. I drop back into my breath, trying to drown out some woman's tirade about her dress tailor's incompetence.

A thin, black guy with a beret lifts his chin at me. "You the one that just got back from India?"

"Yes, I'm the one," I hear myself say.

"Man. How was it?" he asks, sitting down beside me.

"There are no words for what I went through," I say.

"Don't leave a brother hanging," he says, curious.

"I'm still in shock," I answer.

Some eavesdropper with spiked hair chimes in, "Have you seen the aerial photos of the tsunami yet? They stitched together a bunch of satellite shots to show the damage."

The girl in the Donna Karan designer dress adds, "Oh, yeah. My accountant forwarded me that link yesterday!"

The conversation digresses into where everyone was were when they first heard the news, what a tragedy it is, and how much money they're donating. I grow quiet again.

"Do you know anyone that was hit?" the black cat

289

persists.

"There was a woman I was traveling with," I say.

"Is she okay?" he asks with sincere interest.

"Don't know," I shrug, while staring at the floor, unsuccessfully trying not to care.

"At least you got out, right?" he says.

"Yeah, but I'm the only one. I was traveling with an ashram of a half dozen people from all over. They were beautiful people, and I was the only one that left."

"You think they were wiped out?"

"We were right there, in Tamil Nadu," I say, unconsciously shrugging again.

The punk kid with spiky hair leans in and says, "Major bummer, man. That's worse than having your hard drive crash and losing everything."

"Yeah, major bummer," the Donna Karan woman adds.

I want to stop, but my mouth keeps moving. "The thing is I loved this woman. I wasn't done loving her. I don't think I'll ever be."

"Why'd you leave?" someone inquires.

"I just knew I had to come back. It's like I got this calling. We were with this cult, and the teachings got too intense for me. I lost touch with reality, or perhaps got a glimpse of reality. Anyway, it scared the shit out of me, so I left. I asked her to come with me, but she couldn't. She had some kind of pact with God, and as hard as I tried, there was no changing that."

"You want some tequila?" An arm reaches around the couch and puts a bottle in my face.

"No, I think it's time to go home," I say.

Before I stand up, an expensive dress lands in my lap, "You want some company?" The sweet blonde looks into me with drunken longing.

"Maybe next time," I say, and I split before anyone

catches me crying.

Gripping at the steering wheel of my parked Acura, across the street from the mansion's huge, circular driveway, I feel as though there's a fissure running down the center of my heart, making it difficult to breath. I slide my seat back, pull my legs up in a half lotus and pray for Kali to come take me from my suffering.

Mantra sweeps me into another realm, where all thoughts disappear into nothing. The void swallows my pain. It swallows my relief as well. The void keeps on swallowing until there is nothing left. I am suspended in space, beyond time. Suddenly, Crash! Beep-beep! Whooo-whooo! Buzz-Buzz!

I'm showered with stark clarity. I am the one hearing the sound of a distant car alarm, and the sound, which reaches my ears, is me. I am the listener and all that is being heard. This is direct knowing. I open my eyes and see the steering wheel and windshield without veils or filters. I tilt the rear view mirror into my field of vision and see my reflection. I'm seeing as I've always seen but never noticed before. I am both, the reflection and the one looking into this plastic oval mirror frame. I'm looking into Buddha's knowing eyes.

It's not possible to explain it in logical terms. It's not like being stupid or crazy. My mind still works, it's just not compulsively filtering everything I experience anymore.

I feel my feet as they slowly untangle from their cramped position. I fascinate on the fleshy channel through which awareness flows. I recline the seat and lengthen my legs, stretching slowly. Yummy. There is a warm rush, not only in my legs, but up my spine to my face. It's an exhilarating phenomena, this tingling, but I don't fixate on it, as it is just the body.

I focus only on the present, necessary moment as I maneuver my vehicle home, where I can deepen my reunion with the absolute.

In the comfort of my own bed, I fall into the loving eyes of the beloved Saraswati and experience myself as her lover, right here, in reality, where we are one.

38 Tea with Divine Mother

Mother shows up in the morning. She lets herself in, and I wake up to her sitting silently at the foot of my bed. One look at her familiar, concerned face and my chest caves in, my forehead crumples, and my arms become useless. Mother automatically takes me in her arms. She's holding me and crying to herself without saying a word. I don't know why she's crying, and I doubt she knows why I'm crying, but neither of us seems to care.

Eventually I stop, but she's still crying. I reposition my body behind her. I'm still in my boxers and half tangled under the sheets, but my arms are around her, and it's like I'm holding the Divine Mother, except she's my real mother.

"I was so worried," she says through her sobs. "Your employer told me you left your job, and then I got that strange e-mail from India asking when you were born. I didn't know what to think. Of course, when I saw the news, I thought I'd lost my only son." She finally pulls herself together.

"Oh, Mother, it's so good to see you," I say.

"Are you okay?"

"I'm fine. I mean, I'm not fine. I lost Saraswati. I lost the one woman I've ever loved."

"Except me, of course." She slaps my shoulder playfully.

"You know what I mean."

"Is that why you stayed so long? For a girl?" she asks.

"Yes, she took me on a pilgrimage."

"A what?" Mother asks in disbelief.

Don't Drink the Punch

"A spiritual pilgrimage in India," I say, hearing how surreal it sounds out loud.

"Get dressed," she says, getting up. "I'll make tea. I want to hear all about it."

I throw on last night's suit pants and splash water on my face. In the kitchen, Mother says, "I like what you've done with the place."

"Oh, stop it."

"I'm talking about the painting over the couch. Where did you get it?" she asks, pouring steamy water into two Hanukkah mugs.

"You hate that thing," I remind her.

"Never saw it before," she says.

"You did, too, a couple years ago. I bought it at a garage sale," I say, taking my tea over to the coffee table.

"But I never saw it up. It looks different, better; but still, there's something missing."

"That's exactly what draws me to it; nothing's missing." We both sit silently staring at the emptiness in the center of the frame for a moment.

"Thank God you made it back to me in one piece." She shakes her head and sets down her tea. "Now tell me about this girl."

"I always knew I had to say good-bye. When I left, I knew I might never see her again, and I left by my own free will. Now, there are thousands of people who lost their lives without any warning. At least I got to say good-bye. Many of these people lost their families, homes, schools, and their whole heritage." I wipe my eyes. "All I lost were my memories," I laugh, "and any illusions I had of permanence."

"What exactly did they teach you on this pilgrimage? You sound different."

"I am different. It's one of the few things we can count on: change, choice, and death. Everything eventually changes."

"After your father died, everything changed for me." Mother sits back and stares at me. "I thought I'd lost you too. Why didn't you call me?"

"We were in a different temple almost every day, and there were no cell phones, no e-mail."

"The girls in my Kabbalah study group are going to want to hear all about it," she says.

"I thought women weren't supposed to study the Kabbalah."

"I think that's part of the appeal. There are nearly a dozen girls in our group now," she brags.

"What does the Kabbalah have to say about Tantra? That's what I was studying in India," I offer.

"Isn't that the yoga Sting does?"

"I don't know. I never met Sting," I say.

"Did you learn to make love for five hours?"

"Mother."

"Well?" she persists.

"As a matter of fact," I smile, "I also learned meditation, mantra, and an excessive amount of mindless Kirtan, but Tantra is none of these things. It's not a technique or even a practice. Tantra is a way of being, beyond the doer and the action. It transcends the division between spirit and matter. Tantra is the non-dual experience of witnessing every moment at the same time that you're authoring it."

"Please say you'll come and talk to the girls about it. They would love to hear this."

"I don't think I'm ready to talk to anyone yet."

"It's mid-afternoon, Sal, and you've just gotten out of bed. You're unemployed. Your house is a disaster. This is the stuff depression is made of. But look at you. Now that we're talking, you've come alive. We've got to get you out. Telling this story is important."

39 There's No Place Like Home

After the making of the *Wizard of Oz,* a great number of little people moved into houses throughout Hollywood. Several custom-built homes even featured dwarf doors. Mother's parking the car in front of one such house, currently owned by the widow, Mrs. Kriesberg, who lives alone, within walking distance of the landmark Hollywood sign.

The modern décor contrasts with Mrs. Kriesberg's beehive coiffure, which she's worn for nearly forty years.

"Welcome, Solomon. You are all grown up. Look at you in your orange robe," Mrs. Kriesberg says, kissing my cheek and taking the store-bought flowers from my hands.

Mother twirls around in a modern living room admiring the folding card chairs, candles, and fresh flowers around an altar, then exclaims, "You've outdone yourself, Edith, look at all the trouble you went to!"

"Oh, it was nothing," Mrs. Kriesberg boasts. Turning to me, she says, "If you have a picture of your guru, feel free to put it on the altar."

"Actually, my master doesn't have a body, but thank you," I say, looking at the two bright-eyed Indian men in frames. "The bodies of these two men will do fine for tonight."

"Your son has a sense of humor, Claire. You must be so proud. How does it feel to have mothered a holy man? A real renunciate?"

"Actually, I'm not a renunciate. I'm a Tantrika," I correct.

"Tell me more." Mrs. Kriesberg sits us down.

Don't Drink the Punch

I surprise myself with my own clarity, "A renunciate gives up the temptations of the material world in preference for the sacred, whereas my practices are designed to bring the awareness of spirit into the sensual, even the profane. See, traditional yoga is a path of transcendence, whereas Tantra is a path of descendance."

"Is that what you're going to teach us tonight?" she asks eagerly.

"I don't have anything prepared. I thought I'd listen a little, and then perhaps share," I admit.

"Oh, honey, we normally sit around jabbing about what we've read in books. You have firsthand experience. Your mother has given me a few astounding details about your adventure, and let me tell you, the little I've heard blows our agenda out of the water."

"Perhaps we can open it up to questions when people get here; otherwise I don't really know what...."

"Fine, fine, go ahead and meditate or do whatever it is that you do, while I welcome the girls and get them settled," she says, directing me to a more comfortable chair in the center of the room, then darting off to get the door. I close my eyes and pretend to meditate, while secretly plotting how to start. My meditation ends when Mrs. Kriesberg addresses about a dozen aging ladies who've filled in around me.

"You probably remember him as the one who was enrolled in USC's prestigious film program, then mysteriously disappeared. Nobody would've pegged him as the type of fellow to join a cult. To film an independent documentary about cult survivors, perhaps, but not to be swept away to another country, indoctrinated into dangerous sex rituals, then come back a totally different person, but I'll let him tell us all about it. It's my honor to introduce our guest speaker this evening: Sal Levine, and please Sal, don't spare any details just because your mother's in the room. We're all modern women and we want to hear it all." Mrs. Kriesberg winks at me, then sits down.

"Let's begin with a centering exercise," I say, closing my eyes and issuing directions for meditation. My voice softens and my jaw relaxes. After all the bustling distractions subside, the words come to me with an exhilarating tingle:

"I don't claim to understand that which I am about to share. It's as if the story of Sal happened, and I had nothing to do with it. Maybe the retelling will help me heal this terrible loss. As you know, my travels coincided with this horrific international crisis, and consequently, everything that had any meaning to me died in the disaster."

As I continue telling the simple truths of my experience, I see little dots of light overlaid onto my physical perception. It's like being in a pointillism painting. The faces of these beautiful, aging women morph into the face of the divine as they lean forward to take me in.

I hear myself say, *"I'm not really here to tell you a story. I'm here to connect deeper with what's alive inside of you. What's burning in your heart?"*

"Oh, dear," a lady from the back of the room blurts. "When you found out about the tsunami, did you feel that God spited you? Or do you feel like God spared you?"

"Neither...or both." I explain, *"I feel Mother Nature acted out. That's what she does, while Father simply witnesses. It's the dual nature of the divine. The physical, manifest world is the Goddess in motion. She is all of life's circumstances, whereas God is that infinite, steady space that is life itself, and then there's the illusion that there is even a separation between these two. This interplay exists in the microcosm, within each individual, and in the macrocosm of the universe, so even my separation from Sara is an illusion. She only exists within me."*

"Still, you must be devastated by your loss," Mrs. Kriesberg tries to comfort me.

"I am. Saraswati was my first spiritual teacher, and I loved her as deeply as any devotee loves their guru; but we are not separate, especially since she's transitioned. She is more available to me now than ever. All I have to do is close my eyes." That is what I do before I resume speaking.

"There's a wonderful story in the Ramayana. Lord Ram asks his loyal servant, Hanuman, the monkey king, who he is. Hanuman responds, 'When I forget who I am, then I serve you. When I remember who I am, then I am you.'"

Another woman in the back of the room says, "That's lovely. Now, is there a book you recommend if I want to learn more about Tantra?"

"The original Tantric texts were a recorded dialogue between Shakti and Lord Shiva, in which Shiva supposedly explained the secret practices, so the whole treatise is a dialogue between lovers. It's my experience, however, that it was actually the other way around: the Goddess Shakti initiated Shiva.

"And I'll let you in on a little secret. Tantra does not exist on the page. It doesn't even exist in your mind when you comprehend the words I speak. Ancient Tibetan scripture may have been fine for feudal Tibetan times, but it has no relevance to you and me in this moment, and neither does Hindu Goddess worship, nor someone else's experience in India. There is no Tantra outside of you. Tantra only exists in the moment."

A little white-haired woman points an index finger in the air and says, "I've only got so many years left, and it's hard on my sciatica to fly inter-continental, but I've always wanted to go to India before I die. Do you really think it's worth it?"

"Not necessarily. You don't have to put yourself through hell to get to experience heaven on the other side. In fact, you're each already on your own pilgrimage. That's why you come to this Kabbalah study group. Are you not already on a path toward the Truth? People like to call it a path, but

in truth, you can realize yourself wherever you are. If you're ever waiting, you're missing the point. There is never anything to wait for. Ask yourself, what is so exciting about the next moment that you can't enjoy in this one, right now? Is it that you think the answer is somewhere out there? Is it because the man speaking is some 20 years your junior? Judging, waiting, or expecting something other than what is, is why people don't realize the Truth. Let go of any attachment you may have about what a greater experience of spirit might look like, because it's already happening, if you allow it. Get out of its way. Get out of your own way.

"*Start with the things you know to be true such as ... you are breathing. There is inhale, and there is exhale ... always. These are not opposite actions. They are simply two parts of the same process. You breathe in, because you breathe out, and then, when you realize that, in every moment, this miracle is happening, you begin to accept the non-dual nature of reality.*

A sweet demure woman raises her hand and when I nod at her she says, "I've been practicing meditation for some time, always watching my breath, and I've been taught to observe the ego and to transcend the mind's desires. What is the Tantric position on desire?"

"*Everyone has desires. They are natural. Instead of struggling to free yourself from desire, why not accept your desires and expand into them? Some want to be rich, to be more accomplished, to fall in love; and yet, what most people forget to ask themselves is why they want these things. I'm a perfect example. I spent years wanting to go to USC, to become a famous filmmaker. It was a compulsive desire that ran me for so long that I never even questioned it. Desire is an illusion. We chase after the hope of something in the future that we want to make us happy, instead of realizing that happiness can only exist here, now.*

"I stayed in India in hopes that I would come away with a good story. I thought I'd turn my adventure into a blockbuster movie, but it took coming home to realize that it is all an illusion. When you go to see a movie, there is a flickering light projected onto a screen, and you find yourself laughing or crying or covering your eyes in horror, but is the drama real? No more than a dream. There is no lasting satisfaction in a picture show. The ultimate reality is that we are all a pure blank screen on which life is projected. The Tantric path is one of integration, where you enjoy the show, without losing yourself in it."

A number of women are crying, or beaming in the recognition of Truth.

I conclude with, *"Do not be attached to where your next teaching may come from. That is all for this evening."* Then I close with a chant bow Namaste.

Mrs. Kriesberg says, "Thank you, Sal. Will you be coming back?"

"I don't know," I say, and various women shower me with encouragement.

"Please. We'll bring more friends next time," Mrs. Katz implores.

Another offers, "There are so many other people who would love to hear your message, young people too. I'd like to bring my son."

"I'll meditate on it and let you know," I say.

Before leaving, one woman stops me in the hall and asks if I plan to write a book or make a movie.

"The doing is really arbitrary. The doing is what the body does. I'm giving myself over to the Divine and we'll witness what happens. If she wants me to pursue film, so be it. If she wants me to continue offering satsang, so be it. I only want to surrender to her."

Mrs. Katz follows us into the foyer and whispers, "I

have a friend who is looking to produce a film along these lines. I have a feeling you'd have a lot in common. I'd love to introduce you. Can I invite her to your next event?" she asks.

"Why not?" I ask.

In the car, Mother insists on driving, since I'm her new "guru." After some silence, she says, "Well, you sure impressed the pants off them."

"I didn't actually do any of it," I say.

"Oh, and you're humble too!" she jests.

"Actually Mother, I'm serious. That was the master. It was almost all channeled."

"When did you learn to channel?"

"Tonight. This was my first time." After a thoughtful pause I say, "I suppose Master Das has no one else to carry on his teachings."

"Hmm," is all she says for the remainder of the drive home.

I recline my seat, resting my hands in my lap and closing my lids. Saraswati's clear green eyes are here, through which I see myself. I am Master Das's last disciple. I am also the teachings that come through me. That's who I am. I'm the heir to untold secrets.

Resources
Recommended Readings

SACRED SEXUALITY:
Amara, Sexual Agreements (2006)

Charles & Caroline Muir, Tantra: The Art of Conscious Loving (1989)

Daniel Odier, Desire: The Tantric Path to Awakening (2001)

Dr. Deborah Taj. Anapol, Polyamory: The New Love Without Limits (1997)

Georg Feuerstein, Tantra: Path of Ecstasy (1998)

John Mumford, Chakra & Kundalini Workbook: Psycho-Spiritual Techniques for Health, Rejuvenation, Psychic Powers & Spiritual Realization (1994)

Kenneth Ray Stubbs, Women of the Light: The New Sacred Prostitute (1994)

Mantak Chia, Healing Love Through the Tao: Cultivating Female Sexual Energy (2005)

Mantak Chia & Douglas Abrams Avara, The Multi-Orgasmic Man: Sexual Secrets Every Man Should Know (1996); Chi Self-Massage: The Taoist Way of Rejuvenation (2006)

Mantak & Maneewan Chia, Healing Love Through the Tao: Cultivating Female Sexual Energy (1986)

Mantak Chia & Michael Winn, Taoist Secrets of Love: Cultivating Male Sexual Energy (1984)

Margo Anand, The Art of Sexual Ecstasy (1989); The Art of Sexual Magic (1996)

Mieke Wik & Stephan Wik, Beyond Tantra: Healing Through Taoist Sacred Sex (2005)

Nik Douglas & Penny Slinger, Sexual Secrets (1979)

Osho, Tantra Energy and Relaxation: Discourse on Tilopa's Song of Mahamudra (1975); From Sex to Super-Consciousness (1979)

Sir John Woodroffe aka Arthur Avalon, Mahanirvana Tantra: Tantra of the Great Liberation (1913); Sakti and Sakta: Essays and Addresses (1965); Principles of Tantra (1968); The Serpent Power (1972)

Sunyata Saraswati and Bodhi Avinasha, The Jewel in the Lotus (1987)

SEX MAGIC:

Donald Michael Kraig, Modern Sex Magick: Secrets of Erotic Spirituality (2002)

Frater U.D., Secrets of Sex Magic: A Practical Handbook for Men and Women (1995)

Secrets Of Western Sex Magic (2001)

Napoleon Hill, Think and Grow Rich (1937)

SHAMANISIM:
Carlos Castaneda, The Teachings of Don Juan (1968); A Separate Reality (1971); Journey to Ixtlan (1972); Tales of Power (1975); The Second Ring of Power (1977); The Eagle's Gift (1981); The Fire from Within (1984); The Power of Silence (1987); The Art of Dreaming (1993); Magical Passes (1998); The Active Side of Infinity (1999); The Wheel Of Time (2000); Dorothy Bryant, The Kin of Ata Are Waiting for You (1976)

Max Freedom Long, Secret Science at Work: The Huna Method as a Way of Life (1953)

Michael J. Harner, The Way of the Shaman (1990)

Mircea Eliade, Shamanism: Archaic Techniques of Ecstasy (1964); Sandra Ingerman, Soul Retrieval: Mending the Fragmented Self Through Shamanic Practice (1991)

Terrence McKenna, The Archaic Revival (1992)

SEXUALITY:
Barbara Keesling, Sexual Healing: The Complete Guide to Overcoming Common Sexual Problems (2006)

Betty Dodson, Liberating Masturbation: A Meditation on Self love (1974); Sex for One: The Joy of Selfloving (1996); Orgasm for Two: The Joy of Partnersex (2002)

Beverly Whipple, John D. Perry, & Alice Kahn Ladas, The G Spot: And Other Discoveries About Human Sexuality (1982)

Dossie Easton & Catherine A. Liszt, The Ethical Slut: A Guide to Infinite Sexual Possibilities (1997)

Eve Ensler, The Vagina Monologues (1996) Play

Godfrey Silas & Leila Swan, Liquid Love: The G-Spot Explosion (2006) DVD

Janet Irvine, Talk About Sex: The Battles Over Sex Education in the United States (2004)

Jo-Anne Baker & Rosie King, Self Sexual Healing: Finding Pleasure Within (2001)

Joseph Kramer, Evolutionary Masturbations (2004); Fire on the Mountain: Male Genital Massage (2007); Primal Man Nude Massage (2007) DVD.

Lynne D. Finney, Reach for the Rainbow: Advanced Healing for Survivors of Sex (1992)

Marshall Herskovitz, Dangerous Beauty (1998; film)

Nick Karras, Petals (2003)

Peter A. Levine, Sexual Healing: Transforming the Sacred Wound (2003)

Rachel Venning & Claire Cavana, Sex Toys 101: A Playfully Uninhibited Guide (2003)

Wendy Maltz & Carol Arian, Sexual Healing Journey: A Guide for Survivors of Sexual Abuse (1992)

Zaihong Shen and Gillian Emerson-Roberts, Sexual Healing Through Yin & Yang (2000)

SPIRITUAL/SELF HELP:

Barbara DeAngelis, Secrets About Men Every Woman Should Know (1990)

Beth Hedva, Betrayal, Trust, and Forgiveness: A Guide to Emotional Healing and Self Renewal (2001)

Ceanne DeRohan, Right Use of Will (1985); Original Cause I (1986); Original Cause II (1987); Earth Spell (1989); Heart Song (1992); Land of Pan (1995); Imprinting (1997); Indigo (1999)

Don Miguel Ruiz, The Four Agreements (2001); The Mastery of Love (2002)

Eckart Tolle, Power of Now (2005); A New Earth (2007)

John Sanford, The Invisible Partners (1979)

Julia Cameron, The Artist's Way: A Spiritual Path to Higher Creativity (1992)

Kelly Bryson, Don't Be Nice, Be Real (2002)

Lawrence Lanoff, The Drunken Monkey Speaks: A Course in Freedom (2007)

Robert A. Heinlein, Stranger in a Strange Land (1987)

Wayne Dyer, The Power of Intention: Learning to Co-Create Your World Your Way (2004)

ZENDOW PRESS

Order Additional Copies
To order additional copies of *Don't Drink the Punch* securely online, please visit http://www.kamaladevi.com/sacred-sex-books-polyamory-products. This book is available at special quantity discount for bulk purchases, retail sales, fund-raising, and educational needs.

Get Connected
Author Kamala Devi shares a wealth of material on Tantra, intimacy, and spirituality at KamalaDevi.com. Please visit KamalaDevi.com for information regarding:

- Tantra Playshops
- Free Newsletter
- Event Calendar
- Spiritual Humor
- Current and future titles by Kamala Devi

Bliss Coach
Kamala Devi is sought after as a Life Coach, Public Speaker and Tantra Instructor who leads individuals toward success and Self-realization. To inquire about Kamala Devi's availability and services, please e-mail: KaliDas@KamalaDevi.com or visit: KamalaDevi.com.

Made in the USA
Lexington, KY
28 June 2019